The Perfect Blend

**Center Point
Large Print**

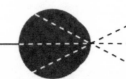

**This Large Print Book carries the
Seal of Approval of N.A.V.H.**

The Perfect Blend

TRISH PERRY

CENTER POINT PUBLISHING
THORNDIKE, MAINE

This Center Point Large Print edition
is published in the year 2011 by arrangement with
Harvest House Publishers.

The text of this Large Print edition is unabridged.
In other aspects, this book may vary
from the original edition.
Printed in the United States of America
on permanent paper.
Set in 16-point Times New Roman type.

ISBN: 978-1-61173-001-2

Library of Congress Cataloging-in-Publication Data

Perry, Trish, 1954–
The perfect blend / Trish Perry.
p. cm. — (Tea shop series ; 1)
ISBN 978-1-61173-001-2 (library binding : alk. paper)
1. Tearooms—Fiction. 2. Large type books. I. Title.
PS3616.E7947P47 2011
813′.6—dc22
2010046554

For my brothers, Chris and John Hawley,
two ends of a fascinating spectrum.
I love you both with all my heart.

Acknowledgments

What a pleasure it is to finish writing a novel and reflect on the people who helped it happen. I owe so much to:

The people of Middleburg, Virginia. I know I've replaced many of your fine establishments and people to create a fictional version of your lovely town, but I hope I've retained your friendly, fascinating charm. I encourage readers to visit. You'll love it.

Tamela Hancock Murray, for her unceasing, patient attention to my career and fretting.

Kim Moore, for her sweet way of making edits fun (for me, anyway).

The Harvest House family, for being an amazing, kind, and supportive group of people to work with! Are there *any* grouches there? I haven't met them.

My readers, for your awesome emails, reviews, encouragement, and support.

Melissa Hilty, for sharing her horse expertise with me. Go, Missi!

Chip Gruver, a real gentleman, of Gruver & Cooley (gruvercooley.com), for graciously sharing the Stone House with me. You added class to this project.

JoAnn Hazard and the Hidden Horse Tavern (hiddenhorsetavern.com) for a delightful, delicious taste of Middleburg.

American Christian Fiction Writers, Romance Writers of America (FHL), The Girliebeans, and Capital Christian Writers, for fantastic friendship, camaraderie, advice, and support, and for reminding me that plenty of us weird writers are out there.

Vie Herlocker, Mike Calkin, and Betsy Dill, my dear friends and critique partners. Thanks for opening those emails with "critique" in the subject line, over and over again.

Gwen Hancock, Barb Turnbaugh, and Wendy Driscoll, for your precious, constant friendship and prayers.

The Saturday Night Girls, The Open Book Club, and my Cornerstone Chapel friends, for injecting fun, laughs, and prayers into my life when I need them most.

Chuck, Lilian, John, Donna, and Chris Hawley, for love that will outlast everything else in life.

Tucker, Stevie, Doug, and Bronx, for making me laugh and cry so much this year, all for good reasons. I love you guys.

My sweet Lord, for inspiration, salvation, and so much more than I will ever deserve.

We love because he first loved us.
1 JOHN 4:19

ONE

S teph Vandergrift was jilted in a truly beautiful place.

She focused on her surroundings so she wouldn't break down and openly sob in front of people passing her on their way to work. Eyes blinking and chin quivering, she desperately sought distraction in the old stone buildings, lush spring greenery, and fragrant wisteria and lavender from the well-tended landscape nearby.

Rick told her she would love Middleburg, one of the most charming little towns in northern Virginia. When he proposed—

She breathed deeply against the urge to wail as if she were at an ancient European funeral.

When Rick proposed, he said she would even love his law firm's stately, historic building. This was where she sat now, her dark bangs in her eyes. Despite the warm spring air, she huddled outside on the front steps, certain her brain—or surely her heart—would burst if she didn't stop and collect herself.

A sudden leave of absence. That's what the receptionist told her. Rick had taken a sudden leave of absence. And Steph knew *she* was whom he had suddenly left.

She swallowed hard. She stood and dusted off her short flared skirt in an attempt to look nonchalant while she sized up her situation. Where was she going to go? Where? She wiped away a tear, but another one swiftly took its place. She needed to *not* do this here, in the middle of this quaint old town.

God, what do I do now? Please tell me.

Distraction. She needed another distraction right *now.*

Across the street a middle-aged woman stepped out the front door of a small building, the white-painted stone of which was gorgeously weathered. She bent to lift a watering can, and her loose blond curls fell forward. She tended to the flower boxes that hung, moss-laden, from green-shuttered front windows. Then she seemed to sense someone watching her. She turned around and smiled at Steph before calling out to her.

"Good morning, dear. Are you all right over there?"

Steph took a few steps away from Rick's building and tried to look purposeful. She managed to say, "Yes, I—" before her throat seized and then released a torrent of weeping and incoherent babbling.

So much for her stoic resolve.

Within seconds the woman was across the street and at Steph's side. She smelled like vanilla and strawberries.

"You poor girl. Whatever is the matter?"

Steph tried to speak between heaving sobs. ". . . were s'posed to elope . . . left *everything* . . . job, family, friends . . . he's not here . . . leave of absence . . . what . . . gonna do?" And then full-on wailing obliterated any further attempts at communication.

The woman enveloped Steph with her free arm, the other still holding the watering can, and steered her toward the little stone house across the street.

"You just come with me this instant. You mustn't stand out here all alone like this."

Yes. That was it. She was all alone. Rick had lured her away from everyone she loved. Everything she knew. She had left them all to marry him. It seemed like such a romantic notion, to elope after her parents had expressed their disapproval of Rick. And then what did the dirtbag do but desert her here?

The enticing smell of fresh-baked bread wafted all around them when they entered the little shop. Despite her anguish Steph sensed a rumble in her stomach. She thought she must be more beast than damsel to actually harbor hope for a pastry or two in the middle of this catastrophe.

"You have a seat right there." The woman coaxed her into a wicker chair at one of the lace-covered tables in the dining area. "What you need is a nice, soothing cup of chamomile. Just give me a moment." Before she went too far away, she

11

stepped back to the table and placed a box of tissues within Steph's reach.

Once Steph was alone again, reality descended. What was she going to do? Granted, she hadn't walked out on a stellar career. She could get another job selling men's suits in just about any department store, she supposed. But she didn't know anyone here in Middleburg. Should she hang her head and drag herself back home to Baltimore? Why had she made such a scene before leaving? She hadn't quietly sneaked away. No, she had to pull an all-out, in-your-face confrontation with her parents. A dramatic disconnect with her friends and roommates. And all of them had simply been trying to save her from exactly what just happened.

As she had always feared, her judgment was completely whacked. She had forgotten plans for any long-term career once she and Rick became serious. She thought she would spend the rest of her life married to an up-and-coming real estate attorney and raise their two perfect children and faithful dog in this adorable, classy town. Why had she believed that would happen simply because Rick said it would?

"Here we go, dear."

It finally dawned on Steph that the woman had a faint accent. British? That would fit with this cute little shop, with its delicately flowered wallpaper and elegant china cabinets. The small, framed

12

paintings hanging here and there looked like scenes of the British countryside.

The woman set a serving tray on the table and placed each item in front of Steph. A white porcelain china pot, painted with miniature violets, from which she poured tea into a delicate rose-covered cup and saucer. A plate with a couple of triangular biscuits on it. They smelled like butter and sweetness. And two dainty bowls: one holding strawberry preserves, and the other holding what looked like sour cream.

Steph realized she was able to stop crying as long as she stopped focusing on herself for a moment. She looked up and pressed a tissue against her nose. "Thank you so much. You didn't have to—"

"No need for that. Go on, now." The woman gestured at the food and tea and sat down across from Steph. Her gentle blue eyes reminded Steph of her mother during better times. "You'll feel better if you have a bit to eat and some nice, relaxing tea."

As soon as Steph lifted one of the biscuits, the woman said, "I'm Millicent Ashford Jewell. Everyone calls me Milly."

"Steph." She spoke around an absolutely delicious bite. She rubbed crumbs from her fingers and shook Milly's hand. "Steph Vandergrift. Thank you for being so kind."

Milly smiled and put a spoon of the cream on

Steph's plate for her. "Clotted cream. One of God's great gifts, in my opinion. Marvelous on the scones."

Clotted cream. Now that sounded downright nasty. But Steph was a self-admitted people pleaser, and she had never been one to ignore God's great gifts. So she put a little of the cream on her next bite of scone. And then nearly moaned, it was so fantastic.

"But that's just really thick whipped cream!"

Milly said, "I think you like it, right?"

"I love it."

Milly stood. "I have a few matters to tend to in the kitchen. Feel free to walk back and get me if you need me. We don't stand on ceremony around here."

The shop door opened as Steph swallowed a sip of tea. She followed Milly's delighted gaze toward the door and took another nibble of scone. Mmm. "Absolutely yummy."

A crooked smile spread across the face of the young man who walked through the door. He looked directly at Steph and acted as if her comment were all about him. With a lift of his eyebrows and a tilt of the head, he said, "Well, thank you very much."

Milly laughed and approached him. They hugged each other.

"Welcome back, stranger," Milly said. "How was vacation?"

Steph didn't pay much attention to their conversation after that. The man seemed to be in a hurry, which was fine by her. Otherwise she feared Milly might want to introduce them. She'd rather a man that attractive not look at her too closely right now.

Steph watched his warm brown eyes, which never seemed to lose their smile. She noticed he never once messed with his short, tousled blond hair or fussed with anything else about his looks. Yet, when he walked with Milly toward the kitchen, Steph saw how perfectly, yet casually, he was dressed and groomed.

Her heart was broken, thanks to Rick's wimpy, childish retreat from her life. But Milly's chamomile tea and warm scones made her feel a little better. And despite her circumstances and the many question marks in her immediate future, she was still able to appreciate a good-looking man. She leaned sideways to watch him at the kitchen door until he disappeared from view. He and Milly were out of earshot, so Steph surprised only herself when she whispered it again.

"Absolutely yummy."

TWO

The young man strolled back out of the kitchen too quickly for Steph to fuss with her own appearance. That was a hopeless cause, anyway. She hadn't looked in a mirror since falling apart on Main Street, or whatever it was called. But after her crying jag, she must resemble a character from Johnny Depp's version of *Sweeney Todd*.

Still, Milly's handsome friend smiled at her as he walked toward the door, pastry in hand, and tipped his imaginary hat. She raised her tea cup in response, like a doddering old aunt wearing a lace collar and orthopedic shoes.

What did it matter how she came across? She was an abandoned wannabe bride, and no man would ever look at her *that* way again. And right now that suited her just fine.

She was all ready to sink back into her self-pity when two young women strode in after the attractive guy walked out. The first woman was shorter and curvier than the other, and she called toward the back of the shop.

"Milly! Where are you, woman? We need provisions, stat!"

She glanced at Steph, her taller comrade silently strolling behind her. "How ya doing?"

But she really didn't want to know. She was just being friendly. Steph smiled and decided to try the strawberry preserves *and* the clotted cream on the next bite of scone. Maybe she'd never leave Milly's tea shop.

The women looked like sisters, but the boisterous one seemed the older and more assertive of the two. Both of them had long dark hair, and, when the younger one smiled at Steph, she revealed the same striking blue eyes as the other.

Milly smiled at them as she came out from the kitchen. Was there anyone she didn't smile at? "Shame on you, Christie. Yelling like that in my shop." She affected a schoolteacher's manner. "We use our tea shop voices in here, young lady." She tilted her head in Steph's direction. "Are you trying to disturb my other customers?"

Christie grimaced when she looked at Steph. "Sorry. I've never been very adept at the whole genteel thing." She mimicked holding a teacup, her pinky extended.

The second woman spoke, her voice softer but laced with similar humor. "Why do you think I bring her in here, Milly?" She turned to Steph. "She's in training. My own personal Eliza Doolittle."

Steph chuckled, but even she could hear how halfhearted she sounded. She appreciated Milly's stepping in, distracting the attention away from her.

"Will you lovely ladies be sitting for tea, then? I've just taken some scones from the oven, and I have some beautiful raspberries and cream. And a peppy English breakfast tea before you start your workday." She glanced at her watch. "I open late on Wednesdays, but for the beautiful Burnham sisters I'll make an exception."

As she had done for Steph. Really, such a nice woman.

"Can't stay now, Milly," Christie said. "I have a new horse boarding today, so I need to get to the stables before the client does. And Liz—"

"I'm opening the store today," Liz said. She reached her arms back and stretched as if she were readying for a workout. She did have a ballet-like build. "I'm supposed to get a delivery of protein powder and diet stuff I'll need to unpack right away. Will you let us take some scones to go? Pretty please?"

Milly sighed, but Steph saw a teasing twinkle in her eye. "This isn't a fast-food restaurant, you know, girls. What will I serve my sitting customers if I let you run off with all my wares?"

Christie put her hand on her hip. "I happen to know you provided Mr. Cutie Pants with a little pastry on the run right before we walked in here."

Liz nodded. "That's true. We passed him on the way in, and he'd already taken a big bite out of something that looked—"

"—and smelled—" Christie said.

"—awfully delicious," Liz said. "Are you playing favorites just because he's a hottie?"

Milly laughed. "I'm assuming you mean Kendall, and he's like a son to me, I'll have you know. I'm not playing favorites. He happens to need my baking services for one of his catering events. He's coming back today with a big order. So that was purely business. Goodwill."

"Uh-huh." Christie was laughing, and Steph couldn't help but smile as she watched the exchange between the three women. She suddenly missed her friends back home—friends she had probably lost over this mess with Rick.

Liz said, "Anyway, I'll be back later today for a real sit-down tea with a couple of reps from Sunshine Supplements. That ought to count for something now."

Milly had already turned toward the kitchen. "I'm defenseless against you girls." She glanced back at them. "Scones, then?"

"Please," Christie said. "Four of them." She looked at Steph for a second and gave her a mischievous smile, as if Steph had been in on the conversation. It was a gesture of camaraderie that lifted Steph's mood.

Milly returned quickly, a bag in hand. The women paid her and left, each tossing a friendly wave at Steph on her way out.

"I'll see you this afternoon, Milly. Thanks!" Liz closed the door as they left.

Milly came and sat with Steph.

"Two of my favorite people. Christie trains horses and riders. She's such a natural girl. Completely devoid of self-importance. Wonderful young woman. And Liz owns the local health food store. Simply lovely people."

Steph smiled. "They're sisters, right?"

"Yes. Both lifelong Middleburg residents." She cocked her head and regarded Steph, her features softening. "And how about you, dear? Obviously you're not from around here. Do you feel up to talking? Maybe about what happened this morning? I don't want to pry, but I'd be willing to help in any way I can." She placed her hands on either side of the teapot before she poured more tea into Steph's cup. "This is still hot, but you let me know if you'd like me to get you a fresh pot."

"Why are you being so nice to me?" Steph felt she could start crying all over again. She always found herself choking up when people were this kind to her.

Milly smiled. "How else would I behave? You've plainly had a rough morning."

Steph shrugged. "No one else out there seemed to notice." Okay, that sounded awfully pouty. She straightened her shoulders and decided to act like an adult.

Milly nodded. "Sometimes people are in such a rush they don't notice each other. I've been as guilty of that as anyone."

"Are you British, Milly? Is that a British accent?"

"Me? An accent?" She laughed. "Actually, I usually dispute having an accent. I've lived here most of my life, and when I visit back home—yes, in England—everyone there tells me I have an American accent. My mother was British. My father, American. They met during the war, and we moved to America when I was about ten."

"Wow, and you still sound kind of British after all these years."

Another laugh. "Lo, these many eons."

"Oh! I didn't mean to call you old." Steph felt her cheeks redden.

"I know you didn't. No, I think I would have lost all traces of England, but my first husband was British, and I moved back to England with him when I was twenty. When he died ten years later, I came back home to the States." She smiled. "I suppose I brought the accent with me."

"I'm so sorry."

"Having an accent's not all that bad."

"No, I mean I'm sorry you were widowed."

"Ah." Milly paused and straightened her apron across her lap. "Yes. Twice, actually."

Steph gasped softly. "You were widowed twice? In so short a lifetime."

"I turned fifty-five last month." Milly patted Steph's hand. "Thank you for the compliment. But yes, my second husband was several years my senior, and the Lord wanted him home a bit sooner than we expected. Marriage often turns out differently than we anticipate."

"I hear that." Steph sighed. "Sometimes it doesn't turn out at all." The moment she said it she considered how much more serious Milly's loss had been. "Not that my situation is anywhere nearly as bad as becoming a widow."

"Don't diminish your own experiences because of mine, Steph."

Steph shook her head. "I just appreciate how kind you've been. I . . . you probably figured out my situation from what I said earlier, across the street."

Milly smiled but said nothing.

"I babbled at you, right? I was supposed to get married today. My fiancé, Rick, was supposed to meet me across the street at his office. He's an attorney. We were eloping." She stared at the intricate lace of the tablecloth. "My parents weren't very happy about my plans, so eloping seemed the best thing to do."

"Mmm. But?"

Steph raised her head. "But when I got here, the receptionist at his office said he had taken a leave of absence. And either she didn't know or she was told not to tell me where he was."

"And you're sure the leave of absence wasn't so he could marry you and take some time off for a honeymoon?"

"I'm sure. When we planned this, he told me he couldn't take a honeymoon just yet because he was new to the firm. It's his dad's firm. Rick's first job. We met while he studied law in Maryland. That's where I live." She frowned. "Where I lived. Where I worked. I left it all to come meet him here. We were supposed to start a new life together. Here."

"And have you tried to reach him since you talked with the receptionist?"

"I called him right in front of her. I tried again while I waited for the elevator. And then in the building's lobby. He's not answering my calls. Or responding to my messages."

"Might he have left his phone somewhere? Or perhaps it's turned off."

"Rick's obsessed with his phone. If he could wear it in the shower, he would." She took a deep, resigned breath. "Milly, I've been dumped." Her voice shook on the last word, but she clenched her jaw and swallowed the lump forming in her throat. She took a long drink of warm tea.

"But surely you can't have been gone from your ties in Maryland that long. Your friends, your family, even your job—"

Steph's laugh was wry. "If you ever need advice on burning bridges, I'm your girl."

"How so?" Milly leaned back in her chair and rested her hands in her lap. She reminded Steph of her old college admissions advisor, one of the best listeners she knew.

She counted off on her fingers. "I quit my job. I was working in the men's suits department at Macy's. They have already replaced me. I fought with my parents over Rick. Really bad fighting. They have probably written me out of the will at this point. And my friends? None of them trusted Rick. And I *love* my friends."

Now she did cry a little, and Milly leaned forward to push the tissues closer. Steph tried to shake off the emotion, but she couldn't help remembering how angrily she had spoken to her roommates. "But instead of listening to their warnings, I just got mad at them. I pretty much severed ties there too."

The shop door opened and a group of women walked in. Milly stood from the table and checked her watch.

"Goodness, the morning always flies by."

"I should go." Steph lifted her purse from the floor.

"No, no, don't rush off."

"I've imposed—"

Milly put her hand on Steph's. "Not at all. These customers are old friends. And they know my assistant is off for a few weeks, so they'll be especially patient. You just relax, and we can talk a bit more if you like."

She turned and spoke gaily to the group, getting warm greetings in return. Still, Steph saw that Milly suddenly moved about far more briskly than she had before. She had spent time with Steph that she would have spent getting her tea shop ready for her customers.

Before she returned to the kitchen, Milly turned on a small CD player atop a short china cabinet. Soft, sprightly music—something classical Steph didn't recognize—added the finishing touch to the shop's atmosphere. At once Steph knew what she could do to feel more comfortable about taking up Milly's time. She gathered her dishes together and marched herself back toward the kitchen as if she had all the confidence in the world.

THREE

Steph walked into the kitchen more quietly than she first realized. As engrossed as an artist at a canvas, Milly didn't turn from her work to acknowledge her.

The bakery smells were even more heavenly in here, and Steph was impressed with how much food Milly had already prepared this morning. She must start before daybreak to accomplish so much.

While Milly wielded her spatula to move pastries from a large cookie sheet to several three-tiered serving trays, she muttered to herself. It sounded as if she were giving herself instructions about what to do next. She didn't look frazzled, exactly, but she was obviously more pressed for time than she had let on with Steph.

"I *thought* so," Steph said, and Milly jumped so abruptly she flipped a pastry across the room.

"Oh my stars!" She clapped her hand over her chest and laughed at herself. "You're very light on your feet, young lady!"

"Sorry, Milly. I meant to come help you, not make you throw food all over the kitchen." Steph set her dishes on a table and retrieved the pastry from the corner where it landed. It looked like a biscuit. Still warm, it had broken into a few pieces.

Milly waved away the comment, already composed again. "Don't worry. It's part of the process. Don't you watch reality TV? All the best chefs throw food about as they work. I appreciate your bringing your dishes in. If you wouldn't mind putting them in the sink—" She pointed her spatula toward the back of the kitchen, and then she nodded toward the pastry in Steph's hand. "You can toss that in the sink too. The side with the disposal."

"Sure." Steph took everything to the sink but returned to Milly's work space right away. "Actually, I had something else in mind."

"Mmm? Something else?" Milly had already refocused on the little biscuits, heaping little scoops of strawberries onto each one.

Shortcake! They were little individual straw- berry shortcakes for the ladies out front. Wow, what a way to start your morning. Certainly better than getting left at the altar.

"Let me help you today, Milly."

It took Milly a moment to react, to look away from the shortcakes. But when she did, Steph saw genuine interest in her eyes.

"Help me?"

"Yes, to thank you for rescuing me from a full- blown meltdown out there in front of Rick's office. It looks as though you could use some help, and I've waited tables before. As a matter of fact, when I was in high school I worked in a German *Konditorei*."

Milly tilted her head and smiled. "Did you? A real German pastry shop?"

"Yeah, at the mall. The pastries were different than these, and we didn't do pots of tea, just cups, you know, of coffee or hot water with tea bags. But if you tell me what to do, I'll fill in for your assistant. Or I can just stay back here and clean up cookie sheets and things after you're done with them."

"Well, aren't you lovely, Steph?"

Steph shrugged. "It's the least I can do. And it's not as if I have anywhere else to be. I don't want to go back to Maryland, not under these circumstances. And I don't want to go back to the inn and sit there alone. I'll probably spend the whole day *and* night crying if I do that."

"You're staying at the inn? Which one? The Fox and Hounds?"

"Yeah." She sighed. "Rick reserved it for a few nights. It was as close to a honeymoon as we were going to have for now."

She stopped short of her next comment: That empty hotel room was *still* as close to a honeymoon as she could expect. She studied her hands. They were cold, and the engagement ring Rick had given her felt loose enough to lose.

"I'd love to have your help today, Steph." Milly's voice was so gentle Steph thought she said something even kinder than she had.

They smiled at each other and both said the same thing at the same time. "Thanks."

Several hours later Steph glanced at her watch. The time had passed quickly, and before this moment she hadn't thought of Rick once. Milly and her tea shop were obviously God's answer to her brief prayer this morning. The distraction was a blessing.

But her feet were sore, thanks to her impractical heels. Waiting tables had been the furthest thing from her mind when she dressed this morning. As the last of the lunchtime customers walked out the door, she sank onto one of the chairs to rest for a moment.

The shop door opened, and in walked Mr. Distraction himself, the handsome blond from this morning. He was reading something in his hand as he entered, so he didn't immediately notice Steph. Like a flash she pictured what he would see when he looked up. She hadn't really repaired her appearance since this morning. Rather, she had rushed about, delivering trays of tea and food and doing dishes without a thought to her appearance. She hadn't even combed her hair. And because it was layered, she knew it could look pretty wild when she neglected it for too long.

She wiped under her eyes for the fiftieth time today, hoping to erase any mascara she might have cried off. Then she remembered doing that earlier and spreading raspberry preserves under one eye. Did she just do something similar? Yeesh, serving food and fussing with one's appearance really didn't mix. For hygienic reasons alone, she must have washed her hands and cheeks more times than an obsessive compulsive germaphobe since she saw this guy last.

His opinion about her appearance didn't matter, of course. Except . . . well, to be honest, it did. She got like this around stunning men, and she knew she'd act stupid if she didn't have a bit more confidence than she felt at the moment. He was striking enough when he looked down. She stood abruptly. She needed to make a quick dash to the bathroom to freshen up before he looked up at her with those dark eyes of his—

And that's just what he did. A smile of recognition lit his expression. "Weren't you here when I dropped by this morning?"

She panicked and blurted out her most recent thought. "I need to go to the bathroom."

His smile wavered for the briefest of moments.

Had she actually told him she—

His genuine smile came right back, all the way to his eyes. "And you've been waiting here for permission all this time?" He tsked and looked toward the kitchen, as if Milly were standing right there. "That Milly can be awfully proprietary about her facilities." He headed toward the kitchen and spoke over his shoulder just before he walked through the swinging door. "You hang in there. I'll put in a good word for you."

She stumbled over all kinds of thoughts, seeking something clever—or at least less humiliating—to say in response. But nothing came together fast enough for her to speak before he was gone.

She heaved a huge sigh. "I need to go to the *bathroom?*" She tried to find a silver lining, other than the fact that the guy obviously had a good sense of humor. She had to settle for this: Things could only look up from here.

FOUR

When Steph emerged from the ladies' room, slightly less disheveled, Milly and the man—what had Milly said his name was again?—sat together at one of the tea tables, conferring.

"I don't think you'll need more than five dozen of those tea sandwiches if your chef is making mini quiches," Milly said to him. She turned as Steph approached. "Ah, there you are, dear. Come have a seat. Kendall, this is my new friend, Steph . . ."

"Vandergrift." She looked at Milly, rather than Kendall, when she answered. She hated how shy she felt, and it seemed to be worse than usual after getting dumped by her fiancé. But she was a grown woman and needed to act like one. Despite the blush that heated her cheeks, she forced herself to look Kendall in the eye.

He was on his feet and probably had been from the moment Milly called her over to the table. His chivalry so impressed her, she almost said "gentleman" right out loud. What was it about this guy that made her want to voice every uncensored thought as if she were five years old?

"Hi, Steph." He enveloped her extended hand with both of his. No shake. Just a warm, confident mini embrace. "Kendall James." He stepped around the table to pull out a chair for her. "Join us. Milly is working her genius for a small event I'm having next week."

Despite having been surrounded all day by the delicious fragrances of buttery pastry and fresh-cut fruit, Steph caught a hint of other spices when she stepped closer to Kendall. She eased down into the chair.

"Thanks." She shot a look up at him, and the crooked smile he gave her hinted at their earlier exchange. She wasn't sure if his expression annoyed or flattered her, but she had to give him points for his manners.

And why was she giving him points anyway? The last thing she was interested in was another man.

Still, when she looked at Milly, she caught her sizing the two of them up, just for a moment, before she looked back down at the order form in her hands, her expression inscrutable.

Milly spoke as if she were reading from the form. "Kendall owns the Fox and Hounds Inn here in town." When she looked up, she wore an expression of sudden realization. "Didn't you say you were staying at the Fox and Hounds, Steph? Am I remembering that correctly?"

Steph had known Milly for less than a day, but she suspected her of pretending uncertainty. Was she the matchmaking type?

Kendall spoke up before Steph could. "That's good to hear. I'm sure we'll cross paths, then. I hope you're happy with your room?"

"Yes. I mean, I'm sure it's fine. I haven't really spent more than five minutes there. I just checked in this morning before I was supposed to meet my—" No, no, no. She didn't want to babble down that particular brook.

He said, "I'll make a point of having extra care taken with your room. Vandergrift, was it?"

"That's right, but the room is reserved in the name of Manfred because—"

There she was again, leaving her explanation unfinished.

In the abrupt silence that bloomed before them, Kendall lifted his eyebrows in expectation, patiently awaiting the rest of her sentence. She stared into his kind brown eyes and produced nothing more than an extremely loud swallow.

"Steph and I had a most serendipitous meeting this morning, didn't we, Steph?" Milly spoke as if the conversation had flowed without interruption. "I found myself in quite a fix without Jane being here to help. I thought I could handle the crowds just fine while she was out of town, but I don't know what I would have done without Steph's impromptu offer of assistance today."

"So you're here to fill in while Jane's visiting her parents? I think that's—"

"No, it was just for today. I won't be here for . . . that is, I don't expect to be staying . . ." Her words faded away as her thoughts interfered. Was that true? Was she going to leave today? Tomorrow? And where would she go?

Again Milly came to the rescue. "We're going to discuss all of that a bit more, Kendall. In the meantime, I think we're agreed on your order for next week, aren't we? Does this look all right to you?" She slid the form in front of him.

While he studied Milly's notes, Steph studied him. She truly wasn't looking for a replacement for Rick, but she'd be blind to ignore those dark eyelashes. How many blond men had eyelashes like those?

Although he angled his head toward the notes, he snapped his eyes up and caught her watching him. The smile he gave her suggested he had been thinking more about her than about his business with Milly. There was no way Steph could pretend she'd been doing anything other than staring at him.

"Kendall, stop flustering my friend. There's a good boy." Milly tapped the form, a subtle smile tugging at her lips. "Sign it, please, if you agree with it. My afternoon customers are coming in."

And that was true. Steph recognized Liz, the taller, health store-owning sister, from this morning. She had two women with her, both of whom carried cases wide enough to hold product samples and such. They must be the suppliers Liz mentioned bringing in.

Steph stood. "Let me get them, Milly." She was glad for a reason to walk away from this man's frustrating confidence. "You finish up with . . ." Seeing Liz had reminded her of the Mr. Cutie Pants comment from the morning. For the life of her she couldn't remember his real name.

He stood too. "Kendall." He looked disappointed she'd forgotten. She wasn't about to comfort him with an explanation.

"Yes. Kendall. I know." She put out her hand. "It was nice meeting you."

He took her hand. Again, no shake. Just that two-handed squeeze. "Pleasure." He had an amazing smile, and Steph found herself smiling back.

She waited until she turned away before uttering a quiet sigh.

Rick who?

"Well, hi!" Liz's face lit up after she looked at Steph for a moment. "You were here this morning, right? I didn't realize you were going to be working here."

"Just for today. I'm helping out a little. Milly will be free in a second, but I could bring you a pot of tea in the meantime."

Liz's eyes followed Kendall when Milly walked him to the front door. "Hmm." The appreciation in her expression made Steph wonder if she might be interested in him. They would be an attractive couple.

But Liz easily turned away from Kendall to respond to Steph. "Yeah, a pot of Earl Grey would be great." She looked at her guests. "Is that all right with you, ladies? We can decide on what we'd like to eat while we have tea. Milly does some beautiful little sandwiches and toasts, and her pastries are unbelievable."

"Sounds great," one of the women said. "I had a huge salad for lunch, but I'll indulge in a nibble or two. All work and no play, right?"

The other woman sat up straight and pursed her lips. "Tea is enough for me. I don't do gluten or sugar. Or meat or eggs. And no dairy. The tea is decaf, right?"

Steph made a deliberate effort to keep her expression passive. "Uh, I think Milly has decaf. I'll make sure."

"Excuse me, miss?"

Steph turned around to see Christie, the horse-training sister, standing behind her. She had pure mischief in her eyes as she addressed Steph. "I'm still waiting on my tofu-and-mung-bean rice crackers. And, really, how long does it take to whip up a whey-protein-and-rutabaga-greens shake? What *is* this place, a tea shop or something?"

Steph expected Liz to look horrified, but instead she merely smiled and gently rolled her eyes. She turned to her diet-rigid guest. "Ellie, I believe you know my sister, Christie."

Christie pulled a chair up to the table. "Don't mind me, Ellie."

"I never do," Ellie said, her air of disdain obviously only half serious. "We'll just see who's still around in sixty-five years."

Ellie's colleague chuckled.

"Sixty-five years?" Christie snorted. "I'll be well into my nineties. If the good Lord hasn't taken me by then, I may have to take up skydiving to give Him a head start."

Liz smiled and looked at Steph. "Sorry. That pot of tea would be great. Thanks."

"Sure."

Before Steph could step away, Liz stopped her again. "I don't think we were introduced this morning. I'm Liz. This is my sister, Christie. And Ellie and Barbara here are visiting from New Jersey."

Steph nodded at each woman in turn, but she didn't try to remember beyond "Liz" and "Christie." She touched her hand to her chest. "Steph. Nice to meet you." She walked away, glad to feel less dismissed than she had before Liz made introductions.

Liz and Christie stayed behind after Ellie and Barbara took their sample cases and left. Christie motioned for Steph to join them when she walked out of the kitchen. Before Steph sat down, Christie started talking.

"Milly tells us we should let you know we have a room for rent. You know something about that?"

"Oh. Maybe she said that because I'm staying at the Fox and Hounds right now."

Liz whistled softly. "That's going to run into some significant money if you plan to stick around Middleburg for more than a day or two."

"Do you plan to stick around?" Christie leaned back and gave Steph a smile friendly enough to make Steph want to stay. She could use some new friends, now that she had trashed her old friendships so decidedly.

Steph fidgeted in her chair. "I haven't decided what I'm going to do. My room is paid up for two more days. I assumed I'd leave then, but I wouldn't know where to go. I guess I do kind of need to start over. Somewhere."

"Just out of the slammer, are you?" Christie asked so casually that Steph thought she was serious.

"Stop it, Christie." Liz shook her head. "You don't have to tell us anything you don't want to, Steph. Milly knows enough to vouch for you, and that's good enough for us."

"Yeah. We'll get it out of Milly sooner or later anyway."

Steph laughed. She hadn't laughed all day. "I just don't know if it's a good idea for me to hang around Middleburg. My fiancé will probably return at some point."

"From where?" Liz asked.

"I really don't know. He . . . well, he stood me up at the altar this morning."

They looked like twins in their jaw-dropped, wide-eyed reaction.

"The *dog!*" Christie said.

"You know, it's probably my own fault for being so focused on the romance I didn't see anything else about him. He's too wrapped up in himself to be a husband. If I hadn't been so in love with the idea of being married, I would have seen that." Steph idly played with a couple of teaspoons on the table. "I'll get over this quicker if I accept it as a good life lesson." She gave them the bravest smile she could muster. "At least that's what I've been trying to tell myself all afternoon."

Christie crossed her arms and sighed. "And what's the name of this fine specimen of manliness? If he's from Middleburg, we might know him."

"Oh. I hadn't thought of that. Maybe I shouldn't be sharing this information so casually. This seems like a pretty small town."

Liz's innocent expression never wavered. "By all means, protect his reputation. We wouldn't want anyone else to miss out on such a good life lesson."

"Rick Manfred. His name is Rick Manfred. And he won't even take my phone calls."

Christie said, "You know how to get around that kind of rejection, don't you?"

"Stop calling him?"

"I knew you were a smart girl the minute I saw you." Christie smiled as if she had been through something similar—lots of understanding there.

"Do either of you know him? He's twenty-six, and I think he's lived here a long time."

They both shook their heads.

"No," Liz said. "That's just one year older than me, but he must have gone to one of the private schools when we were younger." She leaned forward. "Look, Steph, you should stick around. We'd love to offer you the spare room at our place. Milly speaks really well of you, and she's a good judge of character. And Middleburg is full of wonderful people. You just got tangled up with one of the few stinkers."

No one spoke for a moment. Steph considered their advice.

"It would buy me a little time to decide what to do. Where to go. But I don't have much money. I'd have to get a job pretty soon." She looked from Liz to Christie. "I wonder if Milly would be interested in hiring me while her employee is out of town."

Christie smiled and looked past Steph. "I have a pretty good idea what she'd say to that idea."

Steph looked over her shoulder.

Milly stood in the kitchen doorway, her smile

41

warm. The relief in her expression told Steph they could both benefit from Steph's working at the tea shop.

"Aren't you an answer to prayer, Steph. I thought you'd never ask!"

FIVE

When Steph walked into the cozy, gold-hued lobby of the Fox and Hounds, she had one thing in mind. The shoes were coming off, maybe even in the elevator. It had been hard enough to keep from walking barefoot through town.

She hadn't paid attention that morning to how far she walked from the inn to Rick's law office. She was so excited about eloping that the last thing on her mind was sensible shoes. Had she foreseen how the day would turn out—being on her feet all day at the tea shop rather than being whisked all over the romantic, lush Middleburg countryside in her new husband's BMW M3—she would have driven from the inn to Rick's office. Or worn shorter heels.

Of course, had she foreseen Rick's cowardly exit, she'd still be home in Maryland, thanking God she had listened to the wise counsel of her parents and friends.

She was diverted from slumping back into sadness when she saw Kendall near the elevator, talking and laughing with an elderly couple. If Milly hadn't told her Kendall owned the inn, and if the couple didn't have luggage with them, Steph would think this was a man and his grandparents. They all looked so fond of each other.

Kendall spoke to the couple loudly enough that she heard.

"If I had talked with you two before my trip, I would have stayed at one of the *pensiones* and soaked up more of Venice's local color than I did at the five-star. When I was a kid and we traveled as a family, I think my parents needed a break after putting up with my sister and me all day. They always opted for the more Westernized hotels. I feel like such a spoiled, clueless American."

So the vacation Milly had referred to had been a trip to Italy. He probably brought a very significant other with him. Probably some worldly, wealthy Middleburg socialite.

The older lady had a beautiful laugh, light as a wind chime. She made Steph smile.

"Not clueless at all," she said. "Or spoiled. We have wonderful memories of Italy, Kendall, but you know we've forgotten all of the discomforts and remembered only the charm. I'm sure you got plenty of local color and probably slept better than we did."

"Maybe, but—" Kendall locked eyes with Steph and stopped talking. He quit so abruptly the couple turned to see what he saw.

"Steph! Good! Come here, I want you to meet your neighbors."

Her neighbors?

She tried not to hobble as she approached them. This had better be quick or she just might scream. Was that a blister forming on the back of her heel?

"These are the Newcombs," Kendall said. "Laura and Jack Newcomb. They are in the Adams Suite, across the hall from yours." He turned his smile back on them. "Laura and Jack have celebrated quite a few wedding anniversaries here with us. This is, what? Your sixtieth?"

"Sixty-first," Jack said. He wrapped his arm around his wife's shoulders. "Our kids are treating us to this year's getaway."

"And this is Steph Vandergrift." Kendall spoke to them, but he met her eyes. "I had the pleasure of meeting her this afternoon, but I'm afraid that's all I know about her so far. She's a woman of mystery."

She felt as if she were supposed to fill in some blanks, but what could she tell these strangers? That she wouldn't be celebrating any anniversaries here? That she was floating around like a lost ship, without the slightest idea where to dock? She hoped her face didn't reflect the emotional or physical pain she wanted to hide.

"You make me sound a lot more glamorous than I am, believe me."

The elevator arrived, and Kendall opened the gate and old-fashioned door. He took the Newcombs' bags in hand. "Jimmy's helping another guest with her luggage. I'll ride up with you."

Steph followed Mrs. Newcomb and tried to casually rest against the wall of the elevator while the men boarded. "I love this old elevator," she said. "Feels like living in another era. The whole inn adds to that atmosphere."

Kendall nodded and looked around the elevator. "Yeah, this is a 1917 Otis. Used to be hand cranked. The workings are modern, but I want to keep the original car as long as I can. That's what I love about this place—the history."

Mrs. Newcomb got a twinkle in her eye. "Steph, you should spend some time with Kendall and let him tell you about this place. He's one of the reasons we fell in love with the Fox and Hounds."

Why that brought a blush to Steph's cheek, she wasn't sure. But when she shot a glance at Kendall, he smiled at her as if they both had reason to be embarrassed. Maybe Mrs. Newcomb was a notorious matchmaker in Kendall's life. Judging from his ring finger, she hadn't succeeded yet. Or, if he did have a girlfriend or fiancée—whomever he took to Italy—it was probably awkward having some stranger suggested as a possible date. It was one thing to be charming in passing, but to have someone put it right out there put them both on the spot.

When they reached the fourth floor, Steph waited for the others to exit the elevator first. "You all go on. My door is the closest to the elevator."

Not only that, she knew she couldn't walk another step with as much grace as she had faked so far.

"Have a good night, young lady," Mr. Newcomb said.

"Lovely meeting you, Steph." Mrs. Newcomb smiled and turned away with her husband.

"Okay, then. G'night." Kendall gave her a winning smile and joined the Newcombs.

With the three of them walking ahead of her, she was able to give in to the pain. She scrunched her face up with each step toward her door, and she found relief in walking as much on her tiptoes as possible to keep the backs of her shoes from rubbing on her heels. Also, for some reason drawing her shoulders up seemed to help. There was no logic to this. Her body simply did it all by itself.

It was because of the face scrunching that she didn't know Kendall had stopped to say something else to her. He made a kind of bursting-out-laughing sound before he caught himself, but Steph unscrunched her features quickly enough to see him.

"I'm sorry," he said. His expression sobered. "Are you in pain?"

Steph sighed in exasperation with herself. "No. I'm practicing my cat burglar walk." She reached down and pulled off her shoes. "I should have just taken these off in the elevator once I reached maximum-endurance capacity, but I wanted to be polite."

Mrs. Newcomb called down the hall from the door to their room. "Good for you, Steph. There's no substitute for good manners."

Kendall still held the Newcombs' luggage, but he walked toward Steph until he was close enough to speak quietly. He was clearly amused. "I'm all for good manners too, but the Fox and Hounds management hereby encourages you to run around shoeless for the remainder of your stay."

She laughed softly as he turned away.

One last time he looked back at her. With a glance at her feet and back to her face, he lifted his eyebrows and gave her a rakish smile. "Pretty feet."

As if she were a Victorian maiden, she felt a full-body flush of modesty. She let herself into her room as quickly as possible.

Once she had soaked in a warm tub her body was far more relaxed, and she knew her feet would be fine in the morning as long as she wore kinder shoes. She called room service for dinner so she wouldn't have to be seen eating alone. The meal was expensive, but she would have gone without eating rather than making herself presentable for public viewing again and trying to look content while chewing, drinking, and staring off into space.

She watched *The Philadelphia Story* on TV while she ate. Big mistake. She laughed in the appropriate places, and she appreciated the release in that. But the way Cary Grant and Jimmy Stewart doted on Katherine Hepburn? And *three* serious proposals of marriage? Not only did the contrast to her own situation hit home, but she would normally have called one of her girlfriends to talk out how she felt. After the way she stomped away from her two best friends, she'd be nothing but a self-centered user to impose upon them as sounding boards now.

When Hepburn's character removed her engagement ring to go for a swim, Steph looked down at her own ring. Simple and beautiful. And so pointless. Removing it required effort, because she knew she'd never wear it again. She tucked it away with the rest of her jewelry and tried to ignore how bare her finger felt.

She checked her cell phone messages. She checked her text messages. No one had tried to reach her. No one. Not her parents. Not her girlfriends. And especially not Rick.

She turned off the television and closed her eyes.

Lord, I know I'm not totally alone. I know You're here with me. And that does give me comfort in the grand scheme of things. But in the smaller scheme of things, I'm lonely. I've messed up so bad. And I'm way too embarrassed to crawl back home. I know that's pride. It's amazing how

I can be so ashamed and so full of pride at the same time.

Please help me sleep tonight, Lord. Please guide me in what to do next. And please get me through this night without more tears.

She thought she might manage to sleep, and she held out hope for decisiveness tomorrow.

But as she lay down and pulled the covers up to her chin, she already knew the prayer against crying was a no go.

SIX

Steph awoke to a nearly dark room, save the moonlight or streetlamp that glowed through the window's sheer blinds. She could tell by the soreness in her eyes that she hadn't slept much yet. The lit face of the clock on the nightstand confirmed as much. One o'clock in the morning.

She lay on her back and tried to keep her mind from kicking into gear, but it happened anyway. Once she started debating whether or not to work for Milly later on this morning, all the other debates kicked in. Whether or not to accept Christie and Liz's offer to stay with them, whether to keep trying to reach Rick, whether to beg her parents and friends for forgiveness, whether to wear her soft leather shoes today or break all the way down to a pair of sneakers, whether or not to get up and use the bathroom.

A groan of frustration punctuated her effort to sit up in bed. Sleep wasn't going to happen. But sometimes, when she had trouble sleeping, she managed to get sleepy again if she read a novel distracting enough to draw her mind away from real life. She was pretty sure she packed that bestseller about the quaint villagers in post-World War II England.

She got up and searched her luggage without success. Maybe she hadn't brought the book with her after all.

"But I did." She was sure of it. She was tired and not thinking clearly. She sat on the edge of the bed and scratched her head.

Memory dawned. "My car. It's in the car."

A mini debate, then. Should she bother to go get it? It was the middle of the night, but Middleburg seemed like a safe little town. And her car was just outside, parked on the street. Surely the front desk clerk would be willing to watch out for her if she stepped out to get her book.

She changed from her nightie into gym pants and a big T-shirt and ran a comb through her hair. After swishing mouthwash she checked herself in the mirror. Yes, her eyes were slightly swollen from crying herself to sleep, but God had actually drawn her into slumber before she went full-blown on the waterworks. She looked tired, not destroyed.

Her elevator opened to a quiet lobby, but Steph was sure someone would be at the front desk. She rounded the corner and gasped.

Kendall looked up from whatever he was reading. He stood the moment he saw her. "Steph! I assumed that was Jimmy at the elevator. Is everything all right?"

She ran her hands through her hair and remembered her image in the mirror minutes before. They were going to get her least attractive moments covered right off the bat, that was for sure. And here he stood in his casual perfection, as usual.

"I couldn't sleep. I was going to get a novel from my car." She crooked her thumb over her shoulder, toward the outdoors. "It's okay that I have my car parked right on the street, isn't it? I have a lot of my stuff in there."

"I'm sure it'll be fine. Middleburg is a safe place, and our police regularly patrol the area."

"Good, thanks." She frowned. "Do you actually live here in the inn?"

He laughed. "It definitely feels that way sometimes. No, Nathan was scheduled to work with Jimmy tonight, but his wife went into labor. And my other guy, Ted, has the flu. So I came back in to help Jimmy man the fort."

"So it's just you and three guys who run the place? That seems like a lot of work for a place this size."

"I have a full staff, but they all have their own work to do."

"Didn't I see a woman working the desk earlier?"

"Yeah, you saw either Catherine or Debra. They work the front desk too, but I don't like to schedule either of them at the desk at night." His rueful smile punctuated what he said. "I guess that's not a terribly liberated stance."

She shrugged. "Maybe, but I bet they're not complaining."

"No." He smiled.

They both turned when the elevator door opened. A young man with a marathon runner's build and hair like a red Brillo pad stopped in his tracks when he saw Steph. He looked from her to Kendall and back again.

"Jimmy," Kendall said, "this is Steph. She's one of our guests. I'm going to walk her to her car. Be back in a minute."

"Sure." Jimmy traded places with Kendall as he spoke. "Nice to meet you, Steph."

"You too." Steph was preoccupied with the fact that Kendall planned to escort her. Her car was an insane mess. In her rushed, melodramatic departure from family and friends, she had thrown armloads of her belongings into her car with no attention to order. This guy was going to take one look and imagine her a hoarding weirdo with twenty cats back home.

When he held the inn's door open for her, she said, "You really don't have to escort me. I'm not far down the street." She stepped out into the brisk night air.

"Then it won't be a bother for me to look out for you."

But it would be a bother for her. She'd look like Oscar the Grouch. In her case it was more like Oscar the Crybaby, of course, but it was the garbage can part of the character she was most uncomfortable about his seeing.

"But—"

"I'll walk ten paces behind you, how's that? We'll pretend it's a coincidence that the only two people walking around Middleburg at one thirty in the morning happen to be on the same sidewalk. No one will ever figure out we know each other. You really *are* a mystery woman, aren't you?"

Of course, they were already walking as they argued. She laughed. "No, that's not why—"

He suddenly plastered himself against the side of a building, as if he were in a cheesy spy film. He jerked his head from side to side, seeking imaginary adversaries.

"Oh, stop. I just didn't want you to see my sloppy car, that's all."

He fell back into step with her. "Why? What do you drive?"

"No, the inside of my car. It's chaos. I'm not always a slob." She looked down at herself. "Although, I guess that's the only side of me you've really seen."

He grinned and visibly checked her out. "This is you, sloppy? Very encouraging." He looked ahead and affected a proud, supercilious expression. "I can out-slob you with one hand tied behind my back, young lady."

But when she stopped at her little red Chevy Cobalt, stuffed with clothing, luggage, shoes, and even a lamp or two, she saw a moment of shock in his expression.

He blinked slowly and raised his eyebrows. "Wow."

"I warned you."

He bent over and peered into the car. Steph became even more uncomfortable. She gave him a little smack on the arm. "Stop. What are you doing?"

Without looking away from the car, he said, "I'm just looking to see if there's a bag lady in there."

"Okay. See, that's why I didn't want you to come out here with me. You're catching me at my worst in every respect."

He laughed and stood back up. "I'm flattered that you care, but what are you talking about? How have I caught you at your worst?"

She sighed and opened the car door to fish around for her book. Surprisingly, she found it right away, on the passenger-side floor, so she locked the car up and started back toward the inn. He joined her.

"It's bad enough to make a poor first impression," she said, "but every time you and I cross paths, I've just finished crying or I say something inane or I lead you to my car that has 'bag lady' written all over it." She gestured toward him as if she were presenting him as her next piece of evidence. "And you get to be all fresh and tidy and in your element and charming, with not a hair out of place."

By the time she stopped talking, she realized she

may have said too much. The contrasting silence—highlighted by Kendall's apparent surprise at what she had said—seemed another embarrassing moment on her quickly growing list.

And he was looking at her. What in the world was he thinking?

She stopped dead in her tracks. "What? Say something."

He suddenly reached up, put his hands in his hair, and went crazy like a monkey, messing himself up.

Now it was Steph's turn to be shocked.

Kendall stopped and looked slightly dizzy for a moment. One side of his shirt collar stuck straight up where he had hit it with his flailing hands. But the moment he shook his head against the dizziness, his tousled hair fell back into place almost perfectly.

"There you go," he said, his arms outstretched. "Hair out of place enough for you?"

She laughed. "No. But thanks for playing. We have some lovely parting gifts for you."

They walked back into the inn, and from the front desk Jimmy did a double take at Kendall. Steph realized Kendall looked nearly perfect to her, but to Jimmy he probably looked suspiciously disheveled for someone who supposedly just walked a guest to her car.

The implications brought heat to Steph's face, and she knew blushing could only make matters look worse. She prayed the soft lighting served as sufficient camouflage.

Kendall, of course, remained oblivious to the impression they gave Jimmy.

"Hey," he said to Steph, "if you're serious about trying to get back to sleep, I know exactly what you need. Follow me."

He walked through a door on the other side of the front desk, clearly assuming Steph would follow. She and Jimmy met eyes as she followed Kendall like a docile lemming.

What must Jimmy be thinking? What must Kendall?

SEVEN

Kendall held the door open for Steph. With relief she realized they were entering the inn's dining area. Not exactly a clandestine environment.

Still, the room had an intriguing atmosphere at night. Muted light seeped out from the kitchen and barely reflected off the dark wood tables and Windsor chairs. The stone walls were painted white, which made it easier to see the contrasting fireplace and rustic mantel adjacent to the kitchen. It wasn't romantic, but it was cozy. Steph loved the private take on such a public place.

Kendall straightened his collar, still askew from the deliberate mussing he had given himself. That was good. She had itched to straighten it for him but thought the gesture too intimate.

"My mother used to heat milk for me when I had sleep problems," Kendall said. "Worked every time."

Steph followed him into the kitchen, where he took a carton of milk from the industrial-sized refrigerator and held it up for her appraisal.

"You're not lactose intolerant, are you?"

"No. Just the opposite. Can't ever get enough

cheese." She frowned. Could she have said anything less attractive, maybe?

But her comment made Kendall laugh. "I don't think cheese works the same. Let's stick with the warm milk. Game?"

"Game."

He looked comfortable in the kitchen, as if he spent plenty of time there. Steph imagined herself in a mansion, watching a member of the upper crust performing a task typically reserved for his servants. Maybe that was what she watched. Certainly this inn thrived commercially. She noticed plenty of activity here both when she checked in yesterday morning and before she returned to her room last night. Maybe Kendall was loaded. But he didn't act snooty in any sense. Quite the contrary.

"Do you cook here sometimes? I mean, for customers?"

"Good grief, no. I'm not an utter failure in the kitchen—I can cook for myself pretty well. But Jean, our head chef, would probably open fire on me if I tried to horn in on his territory. He's very protective of this place. And he's the best, so I don't cross him." He wiggled his eyebrows at her. "We're being bad here. I'll keep it secret if you will."

Steph couldn't help the tug at her lips. This guy managed to make warm milk sound naughty. "I'm in. Our secret. Especially if it works, and you manage to get me to sleep."

She stopped again. Did that sound like a double entendre? She watched his reaction, but he seemed unfazed. She needed to relax. This guy was just friendly, not a tiresome flirt.

Her ex-fiancé came immediately to mind.

Well, well, well. Is that how she thought of Rick? A tiresome flirt? Maybe. But if so, what was wrong with her, to jump at the chance to marry him? Or maybe she would deliberately color Rick in an unattractive shade now, every chance she got. A defense mechanism.

Kendall poured her a mug of warm milk. "Come on into the dining room. I love it in the middle of the night like this." He approached a table for two and pulled out a chair for her. When he scooted her in, his hands just barely touched the sides of her arms, but in this setting she found herself hyperaware of his touch.

He sat across from her without a mug for himself.

"You're not going to join me?"

He gently lifted his hand. "I need to stay alert until the next front-desk shift comes on, and I haven't had any sleep since last night."

"I'm keeping you from your work—"

"No, not at all. Jimmy's fine manning the desk right now." He leaned back in his chair and gave her an appraising look. "What's keeping you from sleeping, anyway?"

She sipped her milk to buy some time. How

61

much did she want to tell him? Surprisingly, she found herself willing to tell him everything. But most guys preferred the bottom line—she knew that much.

"I'm struggling with events of the past twenty-four hours, basically. I was supposed to elope, and that didn't happen. He didn't show. So suddenly I have a lot of decisions to make."

He drew his head back ever so slightly, as if something had been shoved in his face. "Well."

She couldn't read his expression. Had she been too blunt?

"I can see how that could rob you of sleep," he said. "To have your wedding fall through."

"Yeah. And the relationship was the launching pad for a number of other things I did. Things I probably can't fix. And other things I have to make decisions about pretty quickly."

He gave her a warm smile. "That's a lot of things. Maybe you don't have to decide on everything tonight, though. You think?"

"That's easy to say, and perfectly logical. But when I'm lying there trying not to stress, I can't turn any of it off."

He nodded a few times and rubbed at his chin, as if the gesture would help him organize his thoughts. Then he stood and walked to the register, returning a moment later with a pad of paper and a pen.

"I've heard that women prefer to talk about their

problems but not actually do anything about them. Is that you, or would you like to tackle some of this stress right now?"

Steph laughed, nearly choking on her warm milk. "No, Kendall. Like all women, I'd much prefer to gather with the other hens and cluck all day without actually accomplishing anything." Of course, she wasn't about to admit she had just lumped him in the male, bottom-line stereotype moments before.

His crooked smile bought him a lot of forgiveness. "Okay, maybe I'm generalizing. I'm actually trying not to step on your toes. I've had the proverbial hand slap in the past for failing to be a good sounding board and going right to problem solving with my female friends—it's the manager in me." He held up the pad of paper. "And I love to make lists."

"A little structured, are we?"

He raised his chin, looked down at her, and adopted an arrogant tone. "I'm orderly, that's all." Were it not for the twinkle in his eye, he would have looked like that upper crust snob she thought of before. He relaxed back in his chair and lifted his pen, a secretary about to take notes. "Shall we?"

Now she leaned back as he did. She didn't know how he had managed to make organizing her life seem fun, but he had. She was as wide awake as ever, but right now she didn't mind that one bit.

"Why not? All right, manager man, solve away."

"Okay." He readied himself to write. "So the first problem is that some total moron didn't follow through on his promise of marriage. Correct?"

Suddenly, hearing it spoken like that—by a kind, attractive man—brought the seriousness of Rick's rejection back like a punch in the heart. Steph found herself unable to answer. And oddly embarrassed. The unpopular girl neglected at the dance.

Kendall looked up from his paper. When he looked her in the eyes, she realized she would cry again if she didn't get a grip very quickly.

"Steph, I'm sorry." He put the pen down and leaned forward in his chair. "That was insensitive. Really, I'm sorry."

Oh no. He mustn't be too nice or she would definitely lose it. But he kept on.

"I spoke so lightly about something so serious. Please forgive me."

She shook her head. "I don't expect everyone I meet to empathize anyway."

"Maybe not, but I should empathize. I've been through something similar."

"Have you?" She grabbed at the idea of focusing on him for a moment.

"Well, we weren't eloping, so she didn't get right up to the wedding day before she changed her mind. We were two months away from our ceremony. During our training. We took one of those premarital classes, you know?"

Steph nodded. The lump in her throat diminished. "We didn't do that. I think we were too impulsive about the whole thing." She huffed and held her palms up about her situation. "Obviously."

He smiled.

"What?" Steph asked.

He shook his head. "Do you tend to be impulsive?"

She sipped her milk and thought about that. "Not really, no. As a matter of fact, I usually have a hard time making decisions, so I'm probably the exact opposite of impulsive—what's the word for that?"

"Me." He laughed. "My fiancée decided I wasn't impulsive enough for her. And she was right."

"So I guess between the two of us, we'd never make a single decision."

"You may be on to something there." He had a visible sparkle in his eyes, even in the darkened room. "Or you may be wrong. I'm not sure. I'll have to think about it."

"Me too." She grinned. In the silence that followed, she realized they had just talked about how they would operate as a couple. She hadn't intended to insinuate that, and he probably hadn't either.

His smile lingered, but he looked away from her

and studied the empty pad of paper before him. "So . . ."

"Yes, so." Steph sat forward. "My initial problem was the moron. But now I'm here, and I need to decide whether or not to stick around after my reservation at your nice hotel runs out."

Kendall quickly jotted something down and looked back at her. "Okay. What's next?"

She craned her neck to try to read his notes, but the light wasn't good enough. "What do you mean, what's next? Are you just writing everything down, or have you already solved this one?"

"Oh, it's solved." He flipped the pad around so she could read it.

Stay? Yes X No __

Steph laughed. "I thought you said you weren't impulsive."

He turned the pad back in his direction and read what he had written. He looked at Steph and widened his wonderful brown eyes. "I'm cured. It's a miracle!"

She laughed out loud. "You're not exactly making me sleepy here, you know. No one ever fell asleep laughing."

"We're getting rid of what stresses you, aren't we?"

She had to agree there.

He didn't wait for her answer. "What's the next decision you have to make?"

"If I stay, I need to decide whether or not to work at Milly's. I mean, just until Jane returns. And whether to stay at Christie and Liz's place."

"Christie and Liz?"

"A couple of women Milly knows. She introduced me to them today. See, decisions like where to work and where to live—those aren't decisions to make impulsively."

"No, not in the long term. But both of those decisions sound temporary, right? And they both involve Milly and her trustworthy judgment. She's the finest woman I know in Middleburg." He glanced over his shoulder and slightly lowered his voice. "And, between you and me, that includes my mother. More warm milk?"

She had finished her mugful. She couldn't say she felt any closer to getting sleepy, but Kendall's positive spin on her problems certainly relieved some of her anxiety. She shook her head and stretched her arms forward.

"No, thanks. You know what? You've actually helped."

He feigned amazement. "Have I *actually? Me?"

Steph chuckled. "Yes. You're right. Those are probably two of the most pressing decisions I have to make—where to live and where to work—but I don't have to live with my decisions long term.

Maybe knowing that will help me fall back to sleep." She stood. "I should go."

"You sure?"

Just two little words, spoken softly. Not a hint of deliberate flirtation, but they certainly did the trick. She was not sure.

"Yes, I'm sure. Milly told me not to hurry in if I decided to work tomorrow—this morning, rather—but I'd like to show my appreciation by being a punctual employee. So I need to take another stab at falling asleep."

He smiled as they stood. "You're taking the job?"

"I guess I am!"

He put out his hand. "Then welcome to Middleburg, Steph."

But when she moved to shake his hand, he did that two-handed, gentle squeeze he had done before. It seemed to carry more affection than it had before, especially when he looked at her with such warmth. Her thoughts fumbled.

"You too."

You too? Welcome to Middleburg—You too? What was she talking about?

He laughed softly. "Thanks."

She rolled her eyes but kept her mouth shut. She'd probably babble if she tried to explain what she meant to say.

They walked back into the lobby, and it seemed Kendall meant to walk her to the elevator. This felt too much like an impromptu date.

68

Jimmy put a stop to that as soon as they passed the front desk.

"Hey, Kendall. Mind if I take a quick break?"

"No problem." Kendall tipped his head toward Steph. "Let me just walk Steph to the—"

"No, that's fine." Steph held up her hand and kept walking. She turned to smile at him. She shouldn't have been pleased to see a moment's disappointment in his face, but she was.

"Thanks for the milk," she said. "And the advice."

His disappointment passed. He gave her a teasing smile. "You too."

She had turned away before she realized he responded in the same awkward way she had. She had given him neither milk nor advice. She laughed softly to herself and kept going.

As she rode back up to her room, she struggled not to smile about him. She needed to get back on her feet, earn some money, decide where to live, and make right the things she had made wrong.

She was in this fix because she had focused too much on a man. What she did at present needed to be about her—not Kendall or anyone else.

Maybe You could help me with that, Lord. I don't think I've been listening to You much lately. Please show me what You want me to do.

By the time she had settled back into bed, she felt she would be able to get back to sleep without much trouble. She hoped that had more to do with God's attention to her than Kendall's.

EIGHT

Several hours later Steph rang the bell outside the tea shop. Milly came to the front door and gave her a smile and a warm hug. Other than a few new berry stains on her apron and flour-covered hands, Milly looked fresh and impeccable.

"How wonderful, Steph! You decided to join my ranks for a while?" She backed off. "Mind, I haven't gotten flour on you, have I?" She motioned for Steph to turn around for inspection, and Steph obeyed.

"I'm sure I'm fine, Milly. A little flour isn't going to kill me. I'd rather look like a battle-worn vet than a novice anyway."

"Then you've come to the right place, dear. Not a mark on you. Yet." Milly winked, turned, and headed toward the kitchen, speaking over her shoulder. "Do me a favor and lock the door before you head back here, will you? I'd prefer we didn't have any early walk-ins this morning. I have a few things to show you."

The scene in the kitchen surprised Steph. A wide variety of dishes, bowls, and pans already teetered in Milly's massive sink.

"Wow, I should have gotten here earlier, Milly. You've already been so busy."

Milly didn't seem to hear her. She had returned to her worktable, where three pie-sized rounds of dough sat. She had a knife in her hand, but she set it back down.

"Right, I'll wait on this and get you started. Normally, when Jane is gone, I'm more on top of the dishes and pans so they don't pile up like this. But I took a chance that you would join me today, and I focused on baking more than cleaning. I thought maybe you could help me by tidying up behind me first, and then when you catch up to me, I could teach you how to make some of the pastries and sandwiches and such."

"I don't want to make any of the food, do I? I mean, that could be catastrophic for you, Milly. I'm not a baker. Or a cook. I can barely *serve* food without wiping it all over myself. I never realized what a klutz I was before yesterday. When I worked at the *Konditorei*, I seemed coordinated enough, but—"

Milly held up a hand to stop Steph's rambling. "Don't you think yesterday was a bit of a fluster for you altogether, dear? The fact that you picked right up and made yourself busy, rather than going back to your room and wallowing, shows you're made of stronger stuff than you seem to realize. Now, you go on and set your attention to that sink, if you don't mind, and then I'll show you how to run a tea shop."

With a nod of finality, Milly turned back to her

work, cutting the rounds of dough into eighths. Steph recognized the triangular shape of the scones from yesterday and smiled. Maybe she *was* teachable. She took an apron from the hook on the wall and got down to work.

By the time Milly opened the shop, Steph had caught up to her. Milly assigned her berry duty and gave her instructions before going out front to unlock the door and make sure the tables were customer ready.

"Just finish cutting those strawberries, and then separate half of them into another bowl. We need half of the strawberries mashed up, and then we'll fold in the blueberries, raspberries, and the other half of the strawberries."

"Ah. Then they'll have juice from the smushed strawberries."

Milly smiled before she walked out of the kitchen. "What did I tell you? You're a natural."

Steph's confidence spiked, and she cheered herself on once she was alone. "I can certainly cut strawberries without burning down the shop." She made short work of the cutting while she allowed her mind to wander.

She wondered what her mother and father might be thinking about her. No doubt they assumed she was married by now and on her honeymoon with Rick. Even though they didn't want her to commit herself to him, she dreaded their finding out he had deemed her unworthy as a wife. She had always wanted them to be proud of her, but she never seemed able to measure up. They thought they knew better what was best for her. And now that she had finally struck out on her own, going against their instructions, she had done nothing but prove them right.

She retrieved the containers of blueberries and raspberries from the refrigerator. She rinsed them and nearly tossed them in with the strawberries before she remembered Milly's instructions.

"Oh, right. Separate the strawberries and mash up half of them."

She poured half of the strawberries into a shallow bowl and sought a utensil for mashing them. The closest thing she could find was a slotted spoon, but that was awkward. Too many of the berries slipped out from under the spoon, and a few shot right out of the bowl and onto the floor.

"I really need a potato masher."

She opened every drawer she found. Nothing. Then she noticed a hand-held mixer sitting on the counter near the berries. Of course. Milly meant for her to use that. That was why she left it out. None of this silly spoon smashing by hand. Milly ran a big-deal enterprise here, this tea shop. She didn't get this much work done every day by doing everything by hand.

It took Steph two seconds to shoot just about every berry out of the bowl at once. One quick switch of the speed dial on the mixer, straight to the highest setting, and she pelted everything in the kitchen—including herself—with fresh straw-berries and their juice. Steph was so surprised she froze in place, the mixer still running and berries splattered everywhere.

At that point Milly walked back into the kitchen, oblivious to the havoc. Just as she caught sight of Steph and the kitchen and started to react, her feet slipped on some strawberries on the floor. Unable to catch her balance, she fell sideways. Steph dropped the mixer on the counter and tried to stop Milly's fall. Instead, she found some berries of her own to slip on, and she managed to fall on top of Milly. To an uninformed observer, it might have looked as if Steph were actually trying to take Milly down.

Steph quickly rose to her knees. "Oh, shoot! I'm so sorry." She reached out to help Milly up, but she hesitated when she saw Milly's shoulders shaking. Visions of broken bones assaulted Steph's mind. "Are you hurt? I quit, I promise! I'll leave as soon as I get you to the hospital or—"

"Nonsense, Steph." Milly rolled the rest of the way over. She was laughing. She pushed herself upright and blew a curl out of her eyes before giving Steph a once-over. "You weren't kidding about wanting to look like a battle-worn vet, were you?"

Despite Milly's reaction, Steph didn't smile. "It

was the mixer." She stood and finally turned it off. "I don't know what I'm doing in here, Milly. I'm going to have you in traction at this rate."

"Stop. It's my own fault for not bringing in the floor mats this morning. I took them outside last night to rinse them off. It was a little dewy this morning, so they weren't quite dry. The floor is far too slippery without them. I should have warned you."

"You're not hurt? You didn't break a hip or anything?"

Milly stopped laughing and arched her brow. "Fifty-five, remember? I'm only fifty-five." She easily got to her feet. "I play tennis. Dance. I've even been known to amble to and fro from time to time."

Steph simply sighed and looked at the mess she'd already made of the kitchen.

Milly patted her on the shoulder. "Everything will be fine. We'll adapt. And no more quitting. I need you more than you need me, Steph. Why don't you tidy up in here as best you can for now. We'll do a thorough cleaning later. I don't have any tables to tend so far, and the bell over the door will jingle if anyone arrives. I'll take over with the berries for now."

"What's left of them," Steph muttered.

"Don't worry. The fellow who brings my produce is due today. We'll have more strawberries later. And we still have half of them to work with

75

now." She surveyed the room and lifted her eyebrows. "Why didn't you just use the masher?"

Steph shrugged her shoulders and raised her palms, as if trying to catch the missing potato masher as it fell from the sky. "I couldn't find it anywhere!" She looked around the room to reenact her search, and her eyes rested at once on the masher, which sat on the counter next to where she found the hand-held mixer. At the moment it even appeared as though displayed under a floodlight from above. She straightened and frowned before she looked at Milly. She knew how inane her next comment was, right on the heels of each word.

"Did you just put that there?"

Milly chuckled. "It's early. Sometimes my eyes don't serve me all that well first thing in the morning, either."

Steph sighed. "Thanks, Milly. I'll try to get it together."

"You'll do just fine. Let's get to work." She pointed toward a closet in the corner.

Steph walked around splotches of red on the floor and pulled some cleaning supplies from the closet.

Why did Milly assume Steph would do a better job than she had so far? Other than the fact that she couldn't do much worse, that is. Steph appreciated Milly's vote of confidence. Yes, she had fit easily into her last job in the men's suits department, but before that she had felt unqualified for nearly everything. Her math degree from college sat at home while she did nothing with it. She shuddered when she considered how serious the consequences would have been, had her mistake with the strawberries been a math or accounting error while working for some big-shot company.

Her parents always cautioned her against taking on more than she could handle, but it seemed that everything she could handle bored her to tears. She figured this job, if she ever mastered it, would eventually grow tedious too.

That was why Rick had seemed such a gift. His offer of marriage and a life of family bliss couldn't have come at a better time for her. Being a stay-at-home mother and wife would be more suitable for her. Or so she thought.

Lord, what did You design me to do?

She heard Milly talk with some people who had come into the shop. She shook herself out of her reverie. She needed to pay attention to what she was doing. Her wisecrack earlier, about burning down the tea shop, flashed through her mind. At this rate, anything was possible.

NINE

Steph felt quite a spring in her step. Despite her misgivings the day had gone beautifully. She *was* a decent student under Milly's tutelage, and she didn't cause any more fruit to explode or any other form of catastrophe to occur.

And she and Milly managed to clear all traces of her strawberry massacre with very little trouble. Milly closed early on Thursdays, so the day was still fairly young.

Now she was on a mission. Milly had given her the address for Liz's health food store, and it was supposedly right around the corner. The confidence Steph gained after a day under Milly's influence, coupled with Kendall's assurance last night, was all she needed to make yet another decision.

She definitely wanted to move herself and her carload of belongings into Liz and Christie's place. At least for the time being.

"You're so well suited to those two girls," Milly had said. "They're just regular people. Very kind and lots of fun. I trust them implicitly."

And Steph trusted Milly in the same way, so her word was valuable.

As Steph rounded the corner, she nearly smacked right into Kendall James. He stopped short of impact and brightened so obviously Steph couldn't help but brighten right back.

"What a nice surprise!" Kendall gave her arm an affectionate squeeze. He was dressed more casually than she had seen him before, in a simple gray T-shirt and jeans. She forced herself not to check out his arms, but her senses told her they were worth checking out.

She found comfort in the fact that she finally crossed paths with him when her appearance was less bedraggled. She might be a little dark under the eyes from lack of sleep, but at least she hadn't cried in the last several hours. Milly had suggested that she run back to the hotel to replace her strawberry-splattered shirt. Now Steph wore a new blouse she had bought for the honeymoon. Its simple elegance suggested feminine cool, and it went perfectly with her black pants.

Kendall said, "Where are you headed?"

"I'm not sure." She laughed. "I mean, I know where I want to go. I'm just not exactly sure where it is. I'm looking for the health food store."

"Yeah, that's on this block." He looked down the street and pointed while Steph studied the most attractive five o'clock shadow along his jawline. And it was only four o'clock. She sighed before she caught herself, and he looked back at her.

"Everything all right?"

"Sure. Everything's fine. I, uh, had my first official day at Milly's today."

He glanced at his wristwatch. "You're done already?"

She nodded. "She closes early on Thursdays."

"So you're free?"

Her heart pitter-patted at the anticipation in that question. Was she free? Was *he?*

"Um, actually, I need to go talk with Liz."

"Liz? Oh, you mentioned her yesterday. Friend of Milly's?"

"Yeah. I'm going to ask if she and her sister are still willing to let me move in with them."

"But not before you've stayed at the inn for the next few days."

"Right." That brought an absolute blush to her face, especially when he coughed self-consciously and glanced down at the ground, possibly embarrassed. He was clearly a confident man, but these brief displays of frank, humble interest bowled her right over.

Steph didn't know if she should speak, leave, or what. Finally Kendall spoke.

"Did you manage to fall back to sleep last night?"

"I did!"

"Or, I should say this morning, shouldn't I?"

She nodded. "Yeah, I only got to sleep for a few hours. But you must be especially tired after last night. You stayed up a lot later than I did."

He didn't answer that. He just looked at her and smiled. "What are you doing after you finish with Liz?"

She shrugged. "I'll probably just swing back to the inn and relax."

"I need to drive out to a local winery to meet with the owner. It will be a short trip. I have a large party dining at the inn tonight, so I'd like to be there. But I thought you might enjoy seeing a bit of the Middleburg countryside. Game?"

Steph chuckled. Game. That's what he said last night. She nodded once. "Sure, why not? Game."

"Great! I'll meet you back at the inn."

"See you then—"

Suddenly a black Porsche screeched to a halt at the curb, and a tall redhead jumped out with fire in her eyes. She stormed directly toward Kendall. Steph froze, unable to not watch, even though this was obviously none of her business.

Without a word the redhead stopped right in front of Kendall. He tilted his head in that innocent, curious way dogs have when watching television. And then the woman slapped him, hard, right across the face.

Steph gasped, but neither of them heard her.

"*That's* for Amy Eastman, you pig!" The woman turned quickly, rushed back to her Porsche, and peeled away.

Kendall raised his hand to his cheek, seemingly unaware of Steph's presence. He walked to the edge of the sidewalk and peered down the street, as if the reason for the incident lay there.

"Who's Amy Eastman?" Steph voiced the question without thinking, and she saw surprise in Kendall's face when he turned and saw her.

He shook his head, so she thought he might say he didn't know.

"She was my fiancée."

Wow. What did that say about the circumstances of their split? Kendall had told her . . . what? He had merely said his fiancée broke off the engagement two months before the wedding. And he had said his fiancée thought he wasn't impulsive enough.

But this hinted at way more than a lack of spontaneous imagination on his part.

"Who was that?" Steph pointed to where the Porsche had driven.

"I have no idea. Never saw her in my life."

And then they just faced each other, and neither appeared to know what to say.

"I'm . . . sorry." Kendall frowned as he spoke. "I'm sorry for—"

"Hey, you don't owe me an apology."

He nodded, but he still looked confused about what to do next. "I guess I'll see you back at the inn, then?"

"Okay." She hesitated a moment, and then she turned and walked a few steps away.

"Hey, uh, Steph?"

She looked back at him without speaking.

"I really don't know what that was about." He rubbed the back of his neck. "Not a clue."

She tried to give him an understanding smile, but she didn't quite know what she thought. "Okay. I'll see you later."

This time she turned and walked with purpose. She didn't want him to stop her again. She had just been dumped by one guy in whom she had foolishly put her trust. Now she was allowing herself to be charmed by another man who had complications in his life, whether he deserved them or not. She needed to focus on the small steps necessary to gain some independence while she figured out what God had in mind for her. Maybe that slap in the face was something God wanted her to see.

Maybe Kendall wasn't the only one getting slapped.

TEN

Steph was still thinking about the incident when she walked into the Good Life store at the end of the block. Nevertheless, her nostrils flared at that smell she always noticed in health food stores. An incense kind of odor that made her think of old perfume.

She saw Liz chatting with a customer, so she strolled the aisles and bided her time. She never felt quite at home in health food stores. There was nothing wrong with adding supplements to one's diet, in her opinion, and she liked the idea of cooking with organic ingredients and avoiding pesticides and all things processed. Still, if she thought she had to go through the rest of her life without shoving a big, juicy cheeseburger into her face once in a while, she'd be a bit depressed.

She already felt downhearted about what she witnessed outside. If the slap was out of line, she felt terrible for Kendall. If it was appropriate, she felt horrified about him. Then she wondered if, as a Christian, she would ever consider it appropriate to strike someone. Someone who wasn't physically threatening her or—

"Hey!" Liz breezed up to her. "Steph, right?"

Her troubled thoughts scurried to the back of her mind for later consideration.

Liz brought an air of comfort with her. She was such a natural, feminine, upbeat woman. Steph realized she expected all health store owners to be old hippies or New Age space cadets.

"Right. Hi, Liz." Steph smiled. "I wanted to chat with you when you had a chance. About the offer you and Christine made yesterday."

"Christie."

"Ugh. Yes, I knew that. Christie."

"Awesome! Are you going to move in with us?" Liz glanced toward the register, which her customer approached. She cocked her head in that direction, obviously meaning for Steph to come with her.

"I think so. Is that still cool with you?"

"Absolutely. We lost our last roommate when she—"

Steph couldn't tell if Liz stopped talking because of the customer or because she almost misspoke.

"Uh, hang on a minute." Liz turned her attention to her customer, so Steph browsed the shelves again. She wondered how Liz managed to keep track of the uses for all of these herbs. There were so many.

She picked up a bottle and read it. Kava Kava, an anti-anxiety supplement. She nodded. She could use that, for sure. She looked at another. St. John's Wort, to fight depression. Another nod. Right up her alley. A pretty pink label on another bottle said its contents, Brahmi, increased mental clarity.

She replaced the bottle and sighed. Was this place designed especially with her in mind? She seemed to have enough symptoms to keep Liz in business for months. Yet something told her none of this would help her because most of her problems were of her own making, not the result of any biological or chemical imbalance. She just needed to improve her judgment and decision-making abilities. And completely surrender to God's will.

She laughed softly. Yeah. That's all she needed to do. Simple, right?

The customer left the store, and Liz approached again. "What's so funny?"

Steph shook her head. "I'm just laughing at myself."

"An excellent ability, in my book. I laugh at myself all the time."

Steph smiled.

"If I don't, Christie will."

"She seems like quite a character."

"She's a big softie who tries to act tough. Our last roommate just loved her. They were best friends."

"Yeah, what were you starting to tell me? Why did the roommate leave?"

Again, Liz hesitated. Uh-oh.

"She got married." Liz grimaced. "Sorry. I know that's a sore spot right now."

Steph laughed before she realized how inappropriate she sounded. She saw Liz's eyebrows rise, so she shook her head.

"No, I didn't mean to laugh about your considerate comment. It's really sweet of you to be concerned. But I'm actually relieved your roommate left for a good reason. I don't begrudge anyone else's happiness because of my bad experience."

"Oh, good."

"It's just that I was afraid you were going to tell me some horror story about why she left. Something melodramatic. I think I've had enough melodrama today. You won't believe what happened outside right before I came in here. It kind of stunned me."

Liz glanced toward the front window. "What do you mean? What happened outside?"

"I was chatting with a friend, and this woman pulled up in her car and smacked him right in the face."

Liz gasped and looked out the window again, as if the scene were still playing itself out. "What? Are you kidding? That's so Jerry Springer!"

"I know! That's why I'm kind of—"

"What, did she just reach out the window and let him have it?"

"No. She parked, got out, and came right up to him."

Again, Liz raised her eyebrows. "Well, either

she's one crazy woman or she knows he's a gentleman."

"Why do you say that?"

"Just a hunch." Liz shrugged. "I think if she had any suspicion he might retaliate, she probably wouldn't have made herself so vulnerable by getting out of the car like that."

"But if she thought he was a gentleman, why would she hit him?"

"Who was this guy, anyway?"

Until this point Steph truly hadn't realized she was gossiping about Kendall.

"Good night, what am I doing? I shouldn't be blabbing like this. He was really embarrassed." She bit her lip. "Forget I said anything, okay? Let me make sure he's all right with my mentioning it, now that I've mentioned it to death."

"All right." But she looked disappointed.

"Really, Liz, could you keep it to yourself until I have a chance to talk with him about it?"

Liz held up her hand, making an oath. "Consider it kept. I won't tell a soul."

Christie's voice startled them both. "You won't tell a soul what?"

Steph gasped and spun around to face her. "Gosh! You ought to work for the CIA. That's twice you've snuck up on me."

Christie laughed, her bright blue eyes sparkling. "I'm not doing it on purpose. Maybe it's from clunking around in paddock boots all day and then slipping into sneakers." She glanced at her feet and up again. "I guess that's why they call them sneakers!"

The sneakers looked out of place with the rest of her ensemble. Steph would have expected leather boots up to Christie's knees to go with her sporty polo shirt and suede-kneed riding breeches. Still, her outfit was cool. Steph wasn't used to being around horse people, and she liked the English gentry look.

"Well, thanks for not wearing your boots here." Liz gave Steph a glance. "I had the hardest time convincing her that the health department would disapprove of her going from the barn to my store. I sell food!"

Steph said, "Still, I'll bet out here in horse country you get plenty of customers coming in that way, don't you?"

She apparently touched on a subject debated in the past because Christie jumped right on it.

"I *knew* you were a commonsense kind of girl!"

"She may be that," Liz said, "but actually most people are sensitive to where they go in their gear after riding." She pursed her lips at Christie. "Most people."

Christie grinned. "Anyway, don't try to distract me. You two already have a secret from me, don't you? Let me see if my CIA powers can detect what it is."

Steph kept her mouth shut. While she didn't

want to pitch sister against sister, she also hoped to show more respect to Kendall's personal business than she had so far.

Christie pointed at her. "You're going to move in with us, aren't you? Is that it?"

Steph clenched her jaw. *Don't lie. Don't lie.* "I *am* going to move in with you! Is that all right with you?" Maybe that would distract Christie away from Kendall's story.

"That's great, yeah! We're getting bored with each other." Christie folded her arms over her chest and studied Steph. "That's not the secret, though, is it?"

Drat.

"No, but—"

Liz spoke up. "We got carried away with gossip, Christie, so let's leave it at that. Remember our promise to Pastor Henry?" She shot a quick wink at Steph. "We've always had problems with gossip." To Christie, she said, "Steph saw something happen, and she doesn't want to discuss it just yet."

"She discussed it with you—"

Steph sighed in exasperation. "I saw a friend get slapped, okay? I was still kind of shaken up by it, and I told Liz, and then I realized it was my friend's personal business and not mine to share."

"Slapped? Do we need to report a wife beater or something? I mean, I'm all for minding my own business, but if some dude is hurting a woman—"

"Christie, no." Liz took hold of her sister's shoulders. "No women were harmed in the making of this scandal."

Christie stared into Liz's eyes. "Scandal?" She backed a few steps away. "Ah. So it was a woman smacking a man. Was it anyone we—"

Steph knew her face looked uncomfortable. Considering how she felt inside, there was no way she didn't reflect it on the outside.

Christie nodded at her. "Sorry. Okay, I'll drop it."

"Thanks."

"But if it's ever all right to tell me, please do."

"I promise."

"Especially if you're moving in. When is that happening? Today? Have you seen the house yet?"

"No. I have two more nights at the inn already paid for. I thought I'd enjoy the service and proximity while I can."

"Can't blame you for that," Liz said.

A customer walked into the store, and Liz glanced in that direction. "Hey, why don't we come get you at the inn and bring you over for dinner tonight? You can get a look at the place and see if you like your room and stuff."

Steph considered her plans to drive to the winery with Kendall. She assumed that was still on, slap or no slap. He did say he had to get back for a dinner party, though.

"Yeah, that's a great idea. Let's exchange phone numbers. I have an errand to run, but I should return in time for dinner. I could call you when we get back."

"We?" Christie tilted her head.

Drat again. "Uh . . ."

Christie laughed. "I'm teasing you." She patted at her pants. "I don't have any of my cards with me. No pockets! Liz, you want to write our cell numbers on one of your cards for Steph?"

Liz had already walked toward her customer. "Yeah. I have them at the register."

Christie turned to the front door. "I'll see you later, girls. I'm going to run over to the—" She suddenly lowered her voice and darted her eyes in the direction of Liz's customer. She spoke quietly to Steph. "I'm going to the butcher to pick up something for tonight."

"Why are you whispering?" Steph couldn't help smiling about Christie's personality.

Christie continued to whisper. She behaved as if she were the CIA agent Steph suggested earlier. "You're not a vegan or vegetarian, are you, Steph?"

"No. I'm fine with meat."

Christie nodded. "Perfect. We're not anti-vegetarian, mind you, but Liz has some real zealots for customers. I think more of them take issue with my eating habits than they do my paddock boots. I don't want to hurt Liz's business, so when I'm in here, I don't talk about the fact that she eats the occasional steak."

Steph nodded. "Her secret is safe with me."

"Hmm," Christie said as she walked out the door. "For someone who's only been in town a few days, it sounds as though you're collecting your fair share of secrets."

ELEVEN

Before Kendall knocked at the door to her room, Steph had just enough time to freshen up, change into jeans, and layer on a couple of light T-shirts. She based her look on the casual way Kendall was dressed when she ran into him on the street earlier. But what did she know? She'd never been to a winery before. Regardless, she had only brought part of her wardrobe with her when she left Maryland, so her choices were limited.

She needn't have been concerned. Kendall stood in her doorway looking fresh and informal. He still wore jeans, and he had only upgraded slightly to a light aqua T-shirt. His blond hair was so flawlessly ruffled, she wondered if he had taken time to make it that way.

"Ready for a ride in the country?"

You'd never know, looking at him, that he'd been assaulted an hour ago. He was the picture of calm perfection. Steph wondered what other conflicts in his life he managed to compartmentalize.

She still didn't quite trust her judgment, but he certainly didn't seem like the type to warrant face slapping on a regular basis.

"You sure you still want company, Kendall?"

He smiled and presented his arm, gentleman-style. "Not just any company."

They hooked arms and walked to the elevator, and then he stopped. "Oh, you might want to bring a little scarf or something. Or I could put the top back up on the car, if you prefer."

A convertible. Of course.

"No, I love riding with the top down." Steph dashed back to her room and grabbed the silver-streaked gauzy scarf she typically used more as an accessory than for practical purposes, such as jaunting around the countryside with a wealthy playboy.

When she saw his car, she found herself completely bowled over, even though she didn't gush about cars in general.

"What kind of car is that? That's the coolest car ever!"

Kendall's grin suggested more than personal pride. "That's my dad's 1961 Corvette. I don't take it out often, but today is too beautiful a day to pass up the drive."

Steph laughed. "Daddy doesn't let you take it out much, huh?"

He responded softly, as if he already knew how she would react. "He, um, died three years ago."

Steph sucked air through her clenched teeth. "What an idiot. I'm sorry, Kendall."

"Nothing to be sorry about." He shook his head and opened the car door for her. "You couldn't have known. Dad was only seventy. He left the car to me in his will. He used to let me work on it with him, so it always brings back happy memories."

Her heart ached at that. What kind of memories would she miss by avoiding her own father? Yes, she was a grown woman, and she didn't exactly have memory banks overflowing with Hallmark moments. Still, she would definitely never have them at this rate.

She noticed a brochure sitting on the passenger-side floor. She picked it up and scanned it. Ashby Gap Vineyards. It looked breathtaking in the photos.

By the time Kendall got in the car and pulled out onto the road, he had already moved on to another topic.

"Hey, Steph, I wanted to mention . . . you know, that scene on the street, with the woman who slapped me?"

As if she had forgotten. "Yes?"

"That's not typical. I like to think I haven't upset anyone to that extent."

She sighed. "Kendall, I have a confession about all of that."

"You do?"

"Yeah. When I walked into the health store after that happened, I kind of blurted out what happened to my friend. I don't usually blab like that. I was just shocked."

"You and me both."

"Do you know any more about who she was?"

She watched him check his rearview mirror. He really had the warmest brown eyes. "I'm still clueless," he said. "I put in a call to Amy—my ex-fiancée?"

As if she had forgotten that part too.

"I thought she might know what is going on," he said. "I had to leave a message, though, so I don't know anything yet. That redhead's anger doesn't make sense. Amy called off the wedding, not me."

They were on a lovely country road now, and Steph wasn't sure if either of them wanted to spend the entire drive talking about his old love. Yet she couldn't help wanting to know more.

Not that her sights were set on Kendall. But if she wanted to develop even a platonic relationship with him—or any man—she was determined to know more about him than she had about Rick. If a woman saw a reason to walk away from Kendall, she wanted to know why.

Still, her own fiancé must have had his reasons for ditching her. She wondered if Kendall was curious about that.

What was she thinking? It was too early for either of them to put serious thought into such things. She turned her attention to the gorgeous scenery—the grassy, rolling hills and idle horses grazing behind expansive gray fences.

Anyway, no doubt Kendall was thinking about

his business at the winery. He wasn't thinking about her.

"All right, enough about my would-be wedding," Kendall said. "Tell me something about yourself."

She widened her eyes at him. "What are you doing, reading my mind?"

He glanced at her and smiled. "Did I catch you dwelling on yourself?"

"No. I was dwelling on you." She frowned. "I mean . . ."

"I like the sound of that." He laughed. "Good thoughts, I hope?" He affected a cheesy, leading-man's voice, and a pompous expression to match. "Are you amazed? Impressed? It's the car, isn't it? The car gets 'em every time."

She shook her head and couldn't help laughing. "Piece of work, I'm telling you." She watched the countryside again as she spoke. "No, I honestly thought you probably had your mind on your business at the winery."

"Not really. I'm meeting their sommelier—just as a formality. We haven't done business with this winery before. My own sommelier, Gus, wants us to start."

"I'm sure this is a stupid question—"

"My favorite kind."

"What's a sommelier?"

"That's a wine steward. You know, an expert. Gus makes our purchases for us, manages our stock, makes recommendations to customers. That kind of thing." He met her eyes for a moment. "I don't drink, personally, so I need Gus as much as I need Jean, my chef."

She nodded. "Yeah, I don't drink either." She gazed at a quaintly weathered barn and silo. "I drank as a teenager. At parties and that kind of thing. I was a little out of control."

"But?"

"A close friend of mine did some serious damage to herself in a drunk-driving accident. After she got out of the hospital, she cleaned up her act. She started going to a church youth group, and she changed a lot." Steph shrugged. "One week she managed to drag me along." She studied him as she spoke, trying to gauge his reaction.

He kept his eyes focused ahead. "You became a believer."

He said it in such a casual tone, she wasn't sure she heard him right. He was a Christian?

"Uh, yeah. I did. I mean, I didn't stop drinking, not right away. I didn't change anything overnight, really. But after a while I looked back and realized I had walked away from some things that weren't fun anymore."

"Yeah." Kendall cracked a definite yet subtle smile. "I like that story. I have friends who say they don't want to give up all their fun, so they won't consider Christianity."

Steph sighed. "My parents are like that."

Kendall lifted his eyebrows.

"Not that they're wild partiers," she said.

They both chuckled.

"They just don't see the place for faith beyond Sunday morning church services. They worry I've set myself up to be ridiculed by making my faith more than that. They have always been the type not to rock the boat, regardless of which direction it sailed, and they think the whole Christian thing could make me seem weird. Less attractive. Less employable."

She considered their reasoning. Rick had claimed to be a Christian, but he had seemed a little put off by what he called her "churchyness." Maybe her parents were right.

"But they did like the cleaner-living part. I think I gave them a scare as a teen. They were just . . . well, they are always uncomfortable when I go in a direction other than theirs."

"Uncomfortable? Or annoyed?"

"Pushy, really."

He kept his eyes ahead. "Controlling?"

"Super controlling." She smiled. "Whose parents are we talking about, now? It sounds as though you've walked in my shoes."

"Not on your life. I saw what your shoes did to you the other night."

She saw him shoot a glance at her sandaled feet and remembered his saying they were pretty. When she looked back up at him, he gave her a sideways glance that almost said "pretty feet" all over again.

The boy knew how to use those eyes. She didn't realize she was fanning herself with the winery brochure until he casually turned on the fan. They were driving with the top down, for crying out loud. She stopped abruptly and appreciated his returning to their topic.

"Yeah, my parents were quite vocal about what I should do with my life," he said.

"They're both deceased?"

"No, my mother's very much alive. She was sixteen years younger than my dad, but they were like-minded about the path I should take. It was hard for them to accept my switching from law school to hotel management. But I never wanted to be an attorney. I only tried that for them."

She refrained from mentioning that her ex-fiancé was an attorney. The legal profession must be a big deal out here.

"It was fortunate for me that the inn succeeded so well," Kendall said. "That pleased both of them enough that they decided I could run my own life almost as well as they could have."

"So if they weren't supportive of your buying the inn, how did you—"

What was she doing? Was she actually going to stick her nose into his bank account? You couldn't get more gold diggerish than that.

"How did I pay for it?"

She grimaced. "I can't believe I went there, Kendall. Ignore me. You're just so young. I'm impressed."

"I'm thirty-two. But you're right, I wouldn't have been able to buy the inn six years ago if I hadn't inherited the money from my grandfather the year before. When the inn's former owner retired, I was in the right place at the right time."

They drove on past pristine farms, intricately landscaped stone manors, and the occasional scent of newly mowed grass and hedges of flowering bushes. Eventually Kendall turned onto a long gravel driveway that separated fields of vivid green grass and rows upon rows of thick, leafy grapevines. Full, white pear trees and delicate, pink-blossomed cherry trees dotted either side of the fence.

Steph sighed. "This is beautiful, Kendall. Are they all like this?"

"All wineries, you mean? You haven't been to a winery before?"

"No. I guess I never saw any point."

"That makes sense. But yes, in this part of the country and at this time of year, everything is rich and blooming like this. Gus and I recently visited a number of vineyards in Italy. Cuneo, Lombardy, and then down to Tuscany. Great trip. It's hard to compete with the views there, but Virginia's wine country has its own kind of beauty."

So Gus the sommelier was the companion on Kendall's trip. Not a woman.

"Our tree blossoms don't last long, though. One good windstorm, and they all fall like snowflakes. So we appreciate them all that much more while they're here." He turned to her, and she saw such pleasure in his smile. "The landscaping here is pretty amazing, isn't it?"

They stopped when they reached a spacious building surrounded by picnic tables and several gazebos. Kendall came around to open her door for her.

"I wish we had come earlier, then, since this is a first for you. The drive was all I planned to offer you today. Because I have to get back to the inn, we don't really have time to tour the vineyard."

"No, that's fine. You couldn't help that the winery is this far away. I have dinner plans anyway, so maybe we could do a tour another time. I'd like that."

"Dinner plans?"

They were interrupted before she had a chance to answer him.

"Well, now I know why I had to drive separately." A burly, dark-bearded man approached them, his eyes crinkled with amusement. He looked from Kendall to Steph.

"I'm sorry," she said. "I didn't mean to take your seat in the Corvette."

"I'm teasing you. It's only a ten-minute drive."

Ten minutes? They had driven three times that. She knew she had a question in her eyes when she turned to Kendall.

He looked like a young boy, busted for a minor prank. "I took the scenic route. I wanted to share more of the area around Middleburg with you." He arched a brow at the other man. "Steph, this troublemaker is Gus Abernathy, the inn's sommelier. Gus, this is my new friend, Steph Vandergrift."

"Steph! The one with insomnia." He gave her a wink.

"Jean gave me a hard time about leaving the milk out the other night," Kendall said. He looked back at Gus. "It looks as though Jean has loose lips."

Gus shrugged. "Comes from all that taste testing." He looked at Steph and did something with his lips that made him look like a duck.

Steph laughed out loud. She thought she was going to like Gus the troublemaker. When she looked back at Kendall, he was watching her with the same pleasure she saw before. To be appreciated, just for enjoying yourself? Well, she didn't see many people fake that kind of appreciation well. It was pretty charming. She held Kendall's gaze and felt a faint quiver in her breath.

Gus cleared his throat, and Kendall looked away from her.

"Come on in and meet Arthur," Gus said to him.

"You two will hit it off, and he has some nice blends I think we should add."

Kendall put his hand at the small of Steph's back to guide her inside. She knew he was just being a gentleman, but these days "just" didn't quite fit with "being a gentleman." She couldn't remember the last time she'd been around a man so courteous—at least, not one from her generation.

And Kendall's touch had a particular effect on her. She wouldn't have minded having that brochure in her hands at the moment. A little fanning was certainly in order.

TWELVE

B y the time Kendall and Steph arrived back at the inn, the special dinner party he had mentioned was clearly underway. Steph saw several elegantly dressed couples gliding into the restaurant entrance as Kendall drove around the corner toward the back of the building. She even spotted a limousine pulling up to the curb behind them.

"This looks like a serious event, Kendall."

"Yeah. It's a fund-raiser one of the local politicos is putting on for his favorite candidate."

"I hope we're not so late that your evening will be hectic." She knew she shouldn't feel responsible for their running longer than expected. Kendall had been the one to take the scenic route. Both ways. She smiled inwardly at that. Still, she didn't want him to have a stressful night.

He was the image of serenity. "Not a problem at all." If he was faking his calm, he did it well. His smile hinted at slyness. "The secret is to employ a staff that knows more than you do. I'm merely here as window dressing."

She was able to study him as he parked the car. He was definitely some of the finest-looking window dressing she had ever seen.

But, wait. What was she doing? She needed to leave the man alone. She knew way too little about him, and he didn't need to fill in as her rebound.

The moment they walked into the inn's lobby, Jimmy spoke to Kendall from behind the front desk.

"Marnie's looking for you, Kendall."

"Problem?" He still seemed calm, but Steph saw him promptly snap into business mode.

"I don't think so. I think she just wants to go over a few last-minute things with you."

"Okay. If you see her before I do, would you please have her call my cell? I'm going to walk Steph up and then change into my tux in the back room before I poke my head in there." He cocked his head toward the dining area.

Steph backed away. "No, Kendall, you don't need to walk me up. I'll—"

"Nonsense." He crooked his arm for her as he had done when he greeted her at her door earlier. "It's my pleasure."

She glanced at Jimmy, expecting him to look concerned about his employer's casual behavior, but Jimmy was comfortably absorbed in something on his computer screen. So she hooked her arm through Kendall's and relaxed.

"I don't know what I'm so nervous about. You would think this was my business. I think I inherited a little of my parents' buttinskyness."

"I'm flattered by your concern. You're being a considerate friend, that's all."

She loved the creases that appeared around his eyes when he smiled.

No, not love. She didn't love the creases. She liked them. Very, very much. The way a concerned, considerate friend would.

When the elevator door closed, they parted just enough to drop their arms from being entwined. They both faced the door, and in the silence she felt her body temperature rise, completely out of her control. Now that he had insisted on seeing her to her room, they had reached that stage she avoided before. Their drive to and from the winery had been the tiniest bit like a mini date. Was he supposed to give her a mini kiss at her door?

When they reached her floor, he put his hand to the small of her back again, and guided her out of the elevator. Like a bride marching to the altar, she measured her steps. She didn't want to rush away from his touch, but she didn't want to lean against it, either.

And why did she have to think of the whole bride thing? She couldn't have envisioned herself a bridesmaid? A flower girl? An elderly woman being escorted across the street by a Boy Scout?

"Are you all right?" Kendall's voice broke through her thoughts when they reached her door, and she realized her face hurt.

"Sure. Fine. Why do you ask?"

"You were frowning. Intensely. I was afraid you were developing a migraine or something."

She shook her head. "Wow, I'll bet that was attractive. No, I was just thinking too hard. Or too much, I guess."

He smiled infectiously. "Better than not thinking enough, right? Keeps us from drooling or walking into walls."

"Just barely." Steph laughed.

Okay, they were talking about drooling and other unattractive behavior. She could relax about the mini kiss thing—

And then he gently leaned in and brushed her cheek with his lips. He pulled back far more slowly, and it was all she could do to not take hold of his shoulders and go all fan-club crazy on him.

She considered it a blessing from God that she kept her cool.

He spoke softly and with so much composure that Steph realized his gesture had been far from relationship changing.

"Thanks for keeping me company this afternoon. We'll have to do that again sometime."

She nodded and waited for her voice to emerge.

Kendall stepped back. "I'd better get downstairs."

"Sure!" There it was—her voice. And as sophisticated as an eighth-grade girl's.

He turned and left, so she focused on getting inside her room as quickly as possible.

But then he walked back toward her. "Okay, this

is stupid, but I just have to ask. Whom did you say you were having dinner with tonight?"

Now that threw her.

"Um, I probably didn't say. I'm getting together with Christie and Liz—the two women I might move in with. The sisters?"

He gently pointed, as if his memory had just become clear. "Oh yeah. The sisters."

"I'm going to check out the room they're offering me, and we're having dinner together while I'm there."

He nodded. "Good. Good. Okay." He didn't seem quite as composed as before. He chuckled as he stepped back toward the elevator. "I guess I inherited some of my parents' buttinskyness too."

She laughed. "Not at all. I appreciate your concern. You're just being a considerate friend."

The elevator door opened, and he gave her a quick salute and a wink before he turned. He called out to her. "G'night."

"Good night." She stepped into her room and grinned. She was determined to become an independent woman, able to enjoy her life regardless of whether or not it involved a man. But she knew, thanks to that little interchange out in the hall, that this would, indeed, be a good night.

THIRTEEN

"Man, this is so much nicer than I expected." Steph stood in the foyer of Liz and Christie's home and viewed, openmouthed, the rooms on either side of her. It was as if she were a bumpkin at the White House.

"Well, thank you very much, I must say." Christie parked her hand on her hip and feigned insult. "You were expecting something more in the hovel-style, I take it? Is that because Liz is so slovenly in her dress, maybe?"

Liz rolled her eyes, and Steph laughed. "I'm sorry. That sounded horrible. I just can't believe you two . . . I mean, this place must be pretty expensive."

Christie and Liz's house was far newer and roomier than what Steph had envisioned. This was a family home; that much was clear. A full living room on one side of the foyer, and a formal dining room on the other. A broad staircase led upstairs, and, judging by the size of the place, there were probably three or four bedrooms on the second floor.

Liz said, "Between the two of us, we make enough to pay the mortgage. But this is actually our parents' place. We spent our teen years here, and we both came back to Middleburg after college. By then our parents wanted greener—"

"—or rather, warmer—" said Christie.

"—pastures," Liz said. "They moved to South Carolina and let us take over the mortgage payments. Eventually the place will belong to Christie and me."

"Of course, we're both assuming we'll meet our respective Prince Charmings," Christie said, "and have to work out some kind of split."

Liz smiled. "In my opinion, Christie is already dating her Prince Charming."

Christie put her hand on Steph's arm. "We'll talk later."

"But until then," Liz said, "this is the perfect setup for us. It would make life easier, though, to have another roommate."

Before Steph could respond, Christie put her arm around her. "And that, you poor, unsuspecting visitor, is where you come in. Please join us in the kitchen slash sunroom, where we will ply you with fine food and drink and cajole you into moving in and sharing our burden. And outrageous fun, of course. Always outrageous fun."

Steph laughed. "Well, as long as you're honest about your cajoling, how can I resist?"

The place did smell tempting. When Steph entered the kitchen, she realized why. They had put together a terrific spread. A Mediterranean array of olives, artichoke hearts, hummus, and pita chips sat on the table in the sunroom, and something Italian cooked in the oven, filling the room with the aroma of basil, oregano, cheese, and tomato.

"What is that I smell?" Steph sniffed toward the kitchen.

Christie wiggled her eyebrows. "That's my ultraspecial lasagna. Made with fresh stewing beef instead of ground. I got the recipe from the Countess Alagetti, one of my premiere horse clients here in Middleburg. And there's more tasty stuff where that came from. You will be putty in our hands, I'm warning you."

"Come on," Liz said. "Come see your room." She shrugged. "If you decide to move in, that is."

The room was wonderful. Steph walked inside and knew she would say yes. The pale peach walls and the distressed furniture suited her taste exactly.

Liz looked pleased. "You like it, don't you?" Judging by the proud way Liz surveyed the room, Steph imagined she had been the decorator.

"I do! I love it!"

"That's great, Steph." Christie gave Steph a warm, welcoming smile. "You just let us know when you're ready, and we'll help you move your things in."

"I don't have much with me. I left abruptly. But my car is full of my stuff, and I'll probably pick up more when I finally get in touch with my old roommates, assuming they haven't lost patience with me and sold everything on eBay."

They headed back downstairs. "I think you're going to feel at home here," Christie said. "We may not have a handsome proprietor like you do at—"

She stopped abruptly, as if something had just settled in her mind. She gasped and pointed at Steph.

"That's your friend, isn't it?"

Steph felt immediately embarrassed. "What do you mean?"

"The one who was slapped."

Now Steph gasped before she could stop herself.

Liz followed suit. "Mr. Cutie Pants? From the Fox and Hounds? He's the one who got slapped?"

"I . . . uh, I . . ."

Christie suddenly seemed angry. "Who would smack that fine young specimen? He seems like the sweetest guy—"

"Oh, he is!" Steph found herself completely caught up in their passion. "He's so nice—a real gentleman—and he doesn't know why she did that. He doesn't even know who she is!"

The oven bell dinged, and all three women looked toward the kitchen like Pavlovian dogs.

"Okay. Food." Christie led the way to the sunroom. "You just make yourself comfy in here. Have a seat."

She crossed over to the kitchen and removed the

lasagna from the oven, while Liz poured their drinks.

"Iced fruit tea. Stay there—I'll bring it in." Liz held a glass aloft, showing a burgundy-colored drink. "No caffeine. So your sleep shouldn't be interrupted."

Steph couldn't control the sly smile that slipped out as she sank onto the soft couch and popped a kalamata olive into her mouth.

Christie walked back toward the couches and pointed at her. "Okay, what's that smile for?"

Steph shrugged. "It's just that sometimes insomnia can be fun."

She could tell Christie thoroughly loved a good story just by the grin of anticipation that spread all the way to her eyes.

"I have no idea what that means," Christie said. She sat and scooped some hummus onto a pita chip. She spoke before she ate. "But no lasagna for you until I do."

Liz joined them and placed the drinks on the table. "Something tells me this doesn't have anything to do with the ex-fiancé."

"Oh, honey, no." Christie shook her head vigorously. "That boy had his chance with our girl." She darted a look at Steph. "Right?"

The two of them made her feel empowered. Between Kendall's kind attention and the sisters' sassy attitudes, she wondered what she ever saw in Rick.

"Absolutely right."

At the ring of the doorbell, Christie stood. "I'll get that. But no new news before I get back."

Steph heard Christie speaking softly to whoever came to the door, and she noticed Liz tilting her head as if to hear better.

Liz leaned toward Steph. "It sounds like Brant, Christie's boyfriend."

"Ah." Steph nodded. "Were they supposed to get together tonight? She doesn't need to stay home on my account."

Liz spoke softly. "No, as a matter of fact—"

She stopped talking when they heard both Christie and Brant walking back toward them.

"Steph, this is Brant. Brant, Steph." Christie had her arm around Brant's back. He was tall—almost a foot taller than Christie—but they looked perfect together. Both were dark haired and blue eyed, and he carried himself with the same confidence Christie did.

He stepped forward and shook hands with Steph. "Christie tells me you're going to try to put up with these two crazy women for a while."

Steph laughed. "We'll see who has to put up with whom."

Liz walked into the kitchen, grabbed a box from the counter, and handed it to Brant. "Okay, these are the steel oats I told you about. Just follow the directions on the box. They take longer to cook, but they're so worth it, dude. Try some pecans and cinnamon with them. And golden raisins. Awesome."

Christie gave his back an affectionate but rushed rub. "Okay, sweetie. You caught us in the middle of girl stuff, so I'm kicking you out and on your merry way." She cocked her head toward the front door. "Move along, folks. Show's over."

"You girls have fun." Brant gave Steph a smile and held up the box of oats when he looked at Liz. "Thanks for these, sis."

"Anytime, bro."

As soon as Christie walked him to the front door, Liz leaned back toward Steph. "He's a doll, but he drops by unannounced all the time. Christie doesn't want to encourage the habit."

"You got that right," Christie said. She walked back in, stuck a toothpick in a chunk of artichoke heart, and plopped back down on the sofa.

Steph laughed. "Boy, that was fast. Isn't he insulted by that?"

Christie shook her head and finished chewing. "He shouldn't be. I've told him plenty of times that he needs to respect my time as much as I respect his. I don't care how close we get, even if we get married—"

"Which they probably will," Liz said.

"Even if we do, I don't ever want to be taken for granted. I appreciate Brant, but I don't assume he's at my constant beck and call. I just ask for the same consideration in return."

Christie sipped from her glass of tea, and Steph realized she was staring in awe at her. "That makes perfect sense, but I didn't take that approach with Rick. It just seemed like the natural thing to always put him first, even if it meant canceling plans I had made before he called or showed up. I think I worried I might lose him otherwise."

A moment of silence followed. Both Christie and Liz looked at Steph, and her current circumstances hung between them like a blinding disco ball.

Steph spoke softly. "He totally took me for granted. Why wouldn't he?"

Liz reached over and gave Steph's knee a gentle squeeze. "Hey, don't start blaming yourself for his lack of moral strength. Yeah, maybe he skipped out because he took you for granted, but he might have just gotten cold feet. Or maybe he had daddy issues or something. You can't know for sure because he wasn't man enough to talk with you about it."

Christie stood and walked into the kitchen. "Which is the key thing to remember about little Ricky. He isn't man enough for you. It would have been awful to learn that after marrying him." She carried the lasagna and a bowl of salad to the table. "You've been blessed, Steph, whether you know it or not."

Liz fetched plates and silverware from the kitchen and returned to the sofa. "We eat in here a lot, rather than in the dining room. It's more comfy. And sometimes we have a show or movie we want to see."

Steph looked over her shoulder and saw the television. "Should I move out of the way?"

Christie smiled. "Only if you adamantly refuse to tell us about your new friend there at the Fox and Hounds. I'd love to know how insomnia plays into that whole story."

Regardless of the fresh hurt that had erupted when she thought about Rick, Steph found herself smiling too. She missed dishing with friends about interesting guys. She had only been in Middleburg for two days, and the reception she'd already experienced amazed her.

Yes, she'd been dumped, and she needed to tread very carefully with respect to anything that might be developing with Kendall. After all, she wanted to stand on her own two feet and be her own woman, the way Christie and Liz seemed to be. The last thing she needed was to let another charming man distract her from that.

But if nothing else, Kendall was one of several new friends she had already made here. And she had a job, however temporarily. And a room in a lovely home with two sharp, funny women.

Christie was right. She had most definitely been blessed.

FOURTEEN

R ight, Steph. You're on egg duty this morning."
Milly's greeting wasn't quite what Steph
expected when she arrived at the shop the next
morning. She must have shown her surprise,
because Milly laughed as she locked the door
behind them.

"I'm sorry. Good morning, by the way." Milly
adjusted the waistline of her apron as she went
back to the kitchen. "I'm going to teach you how
to make mayonnaise today, you lucky girl." She
spoke over her shoulder. "Unless you already
know how."

Steph lifted one shoulder. "If it involves more
than opening a jar, I definitely don't know how."

Milly pointed toward the refrigerator the
moment they entered the kitchen. "But first, you'll
find a bowl of boiled eggs in there, if you wouldn't
mind peeling them under cold water at the sink."
She began mashing strawberries in a bowl. The
fact that Milly had taken back that task wasn't lost
on Steph. "I'm not saying I don't use mayonnaise
from a jar, mind you. But for the tea sandwiches
you're going to make, I like to use a little of the
real deal to add richness. Have you had your
coffee? Your breakfast?"

"Uh, yes, thanks. What sandwiches? What am I making? Besides the real-deal mayo, I mean."

"Simple egg and watercress tea sandwiches."

"Simple." Steph smiled. "I like the sound of that." She looked at Milly's bowl of perfectly mashed strawberries. "I guess you considered mashed strawberries simple too, though, before I got ahold of them yesterday."

The tilt of Milly's head, coupled with a sweet smile, reminded Steph that those were mashed strawberries under the bridge.

"Right," Steph said, returning a smile of gratitude. "Moving on. But . . ."

Milly took a while to notice that Steph still watched her. "But?"

Steph pointed at the bowl of strawberry pulp. "You're making the same thing as yesterday, right? Please tell me that doesn't have anything to do with making mayonnaise."

Milly laughed out loud, prompting Steph to do the same. "Stephanie Vandergrift. I don't care how little experience you have in the kitchen, but you will not convince me you actually thought that."

Steph picked up an apron and tied it on. "Okay. I'll admit I would have been pretty freaked out if that was step one of making real mayo." She wrinkled her nose at the strong smell that wafted up as soon as she cracked the shells on the hard-boiled eggs. But she wasn't about to complain about such an elementary task. Any dimwit could peel eggs. She knew she would truly be of help to Milly this morning without risking a catastrophe.

"So, have you made arrangements with Christie and Liz?" Milly went to the refrigerator and pulled out two containers of fruit. "Did you find Liz's shop all right yesterday?"

"I did. The whole afternoon turned out really well, except—" Without thinking she almost launched right into blabbing about what had happened between Kendall and the redhead outside Liz's shop. What was her problem? She just itched to talk about Kendall's woes, didn't she?

"Except what?" Milly seemed more conversational than curious, only glancing in Steph's direction before returning her attention to the fresh berries before her.

"Nothing. Except nothing. It went perfectly." She cracked another egg. "Liz and Christie invited me to dinner at their place—"

"Lovely! When are you going?"

"I went already. Last night. Milly, I feel as though I've known them forever. They're so much fun."

"They are. I knew you'd all be good together. And the room for rent? Did you like—"

"The room is fantastic! And the house is nicer than anything I could have imagined."

Milly stirred the fruit together and smiled broadly. "I've only been there once, when their parents still lived here. Martin and Talia did quite well for themselves, and it worked out beautifully for the girls that their parents wanted them in the house after they retired. Both Christie and Liz really wanted to live in Middleburg after they returned home from college." She set the bowl aside and joined Steph at the sink so she could wash her hands. "I love to see parents helping their children like that, giving them a chance to get firmly on their feet when they're starting out in life."

Steph couldn't respond. She knew her parents wanted to help too, but their idea of help didn't seem as . . . well, as helpful as Steph would have liked. They had paid for her college education, for which she was eternally grateful. And, of course, she would never have expected them to turn their house over to her—nothing like that. But their help tended to come in the form of "advice." She realized they meant it to be supportive, yet somehow it always ended up feeling like criticism.

Milly's timer rang, and she left Steph at the sink to tend to whatever she had in the oven. By the time Steph had peeled the last of the eggs, Milly brought a bowl, containing a few raw egg yolks, and several other ingredients to the counter beside her. Dry mustard, olive oil, lemon juice—Steph shook her head.

"I can't imagine how that stuff relates at all with mayo."

"Prepare to amaze yourself, dear." Milly pulled a whisk from one of the drawers. "You're going to whip up a little miracle here."

And she did. Granted, she couldn't have done it without Milly's two hands contributing to the effort, but by whisking the eggs with a few of the other ingredients while Milly slowly added drops of oil and lemon, she saw the mixture thicken to a glistening, dense sauce.

"Excellent job, Steph. You've brought it to the perfect consistency."

"And toned my arms in the process!" She flexed a bicep and made Milly laugh.

"Now that you've accomplished this, I can tell you my secret." Milly looked over her shoulder as if she were a covert operative. "I usually use my electric mixer when I make mayonnaise."

"Then why did you make me do it—"

"It's important to know how to do things by hand, even if you don't always do so. Now you would be able to make mayonnaise even during a raging thunderstorm."

"Well, I can check that off my bucket list, can't I?"

Milly's eyes twinkled. "Oh, you'll be crossing quite a lot of things off of that list if I have anything to do with it."

"I don't really have a bucket list. I was just kidding."

"Mm-hmm. Maybe not. But my guess is—hold

on." Milly made yet another trip to the refrigerator and brought several more ingredients to her counter. Steph saw smoked salmon and a carton of heavy whipping cream.

Milly continued. "My guess is there are a number of things you'd like to accomplish—to see happen—during your lifetime. You just haven't taken the time to consider what they are. That doesn't mean the hopes aren't there."

Clearly the woman was no longer talking about handmade mayonnaise.

Steph wasn't used to having someone focus on what she wanted in her future. She wished she could spend much more time with Milly.

"When exactly is your assistant coming back?"

"Jane?" Milly glanced at the calendar next to the refrigerator. "She'll be back in, let me see, two weeks from yesterday."

Steph grimaced. "That's not much time."

"For you, you mean? To find another position?"

"Yeah. I suppose I'd better get busy looking. I'm not sure what I'm going to do. I have a small nest egg to lean on, but it isn't going to last me long. And I need to be able to pay for my room and my share of the groceries at Liz and Christie's. Is there a local paper that lists job openings in town?"

They both glanced at the door to the dining area when they heard the doorbell at the front of the shop.

Milly checked her watch. "Heavens, it's already

time to open, and me with salmon up to my elbows."

"I'll go." Steph quickly rinsed her hands at the sink.

"Thank you, dear. Let me know if you need me."

Steph barely patted her hands dry as she headed into the dining area. She stopped as soon as she glanced through the glass-paned front door.

Kendall had his head turned away, as if he were returning a morning greeting to someone. He'd look back any second and meet her eyes. She quickly fussed with her hair. Did she smell like hard-boiled eggs? Why hadn't she washed her hands with soap before coming out here? She whipped off her soiled apron and was in the middle of smelling her hands when he looked back. She jerked her hands down to her sides and then fussed with her hair again. She needed to get a grip. It was just Kendall.

He gave her a dazzling smile that didn't help her chill out, so she took a few deep breaths as she reached the door and unlocked it. She barely knew this guy. They were developing a friendship. She was newly dumped and cautious. Cautious, right?

It was that stupid mini kiss yesterday evening. It was like sprinkling salt on a perfectly fine steak. She could be satisfied with a good steak as it was, but she knew she'd like it better with a sprinkling of salt. It was just a little tastier, and so was her relationship with Kendall, now that he had added that little kiss.

"Morning!" His demeanor was purely friendly. Not a bit of flirtatiousness to it. "I'm on my way to the inn, and I thought I'd drop this by for you, in case you needed it today."

He held up the scarf she brought on their drive.

"Thanks!" She took it from him. "I didn't realize I'd left it behind. You didn't need to go out of your way, though. I doubt I'll need it today. You could have just left it for me at the front desk back at the inn."

He shrugged. "I suppose. You're a little sunnier than Jimmy in the morning, though. I think I prefer visiting you to visiting him. His beard is rougher."

She laughed and then realized that might have been a casual comment about that blasted kiss.

Something in her hair drew his focus. Oh no.

She resisted the urge to fuss further, but he reached up and gently removed something.

She grimaced. "Egg?"

He looked at what he held between his fingers. "Egg it is."

She probably didn't need to worry that he would obsess about kissing her. Girls with egg in their hair didn't usually have to fight boys off with a stick.

"Ah, good, Kendall. I thought that was you I heard."

They both turned at Milly's voice.

"You're exactly whom Steph needs today."

Steph's eye widened. Milly didn't seem like the type to embarrass anyone if she could help it. Regardless, the heat rose up Steph's cheeks as if it had barely been held in check until this moment.

"Am I?" Kendall's eyes met Steph's. Judging by the quick once-over he gave her, he could see the blush in her cheeks. His smile turned up on one side. He was enjoying the moment a little too much.

"Absolutely." Milly pulled both of them further into the shop and closed the door. "I was about to recommend you to her when you rang the bell."

He held his arms open and tilted his head. "I aim to please."

Milly wasn't as playful as he was. "Yes, well, she needs to find a position with someone before Jane returns in a couple of weeks. You could probably help her find something. You know all of the businesspeople here in town—"

"Don't you know them too?" Steph blurted that out without realizing she might be insulting Kendall. She wasn't sure she wanted to feel so obligated to him.

"Not the way this young man does, right, Kendall?"

He lifted his eyebrows and nodded. "I suppose . . ."

"I mean, most of them are men, and you do all of those men things together." Milly waved her hand in the air, as if she were flicking all of the men things away. "Golf and football games and such."

Kendall laughed. "My mother can golf rings around me, but I know what you mean."

Was he trying to back away from Milly's suggestion? Steph blushed yet again. She felt like the orphaned child no one wanted to take. She almost missed what Kendall said next.

"I think it's a great idea, if you don't mind spending the time with me, Steph."

"Huh? What? What, exactly, is the idea?"

"What are you doing this afternoon? We could just take a walk around town so I could introduce you to some of the local store owners. You never know what might come of it."

Steph looked at Milly. There was something else in Milly's eyes. Something more than bright British cheer. Steph squinted, as if it would help her see better. Milly promptly looked away as if she simply felt it was time to move on. "Right! Well, she can leave work early this afternoon, as far as I'm concerned. That is, if you're free, Kendall." She looked back at Steph, and the "something else" was gone. "As long as I'm not swamped, which I seldom am on a Friday afternoon. What do you say, dear?"

Milly and Kendall regarded Steph, energetic smiles on their faces. Who was she to rain all over their generous efforts on her behalf?

"Yeah. Sure. Thanks." She looked more specifically at Kendall. "Thanks."

He nodded once before turning toward the door. "Good. I gotta go. I'll call when I have a better feel for my schedule today." With a wave he left the shop.

Milly took Steph by the shoulders and turned her toward the kitchen. "And we'll get back to work on those sandwiches so it's easier for you to leave early. This little tour with Kendall will be very good for you. As he says, you never know what might come of it."

Steph couldn't get Milly to look her in the eye. At this point Steph wasn't sure whether or not Milly's comment actually had anything to do with looking for a job.

FIFTEEN

S o, if you know all the business owners in town, how come you don't know Liz?"

Steph and Kendall hadn't walked far from Millicent's Tea Shop, and it occurred to her that Liz and Kendall should have crossed paths before.

"I know *of* her, although I didn't know her name before you told me. I knew about her health food store, which was an Oriental rug store until this year." He shrugged. "We just haven't had occasion to meet yet." He smiled at her. "Despite what Milly says, I don't know all the business owners. Just many of them."

"Which are the mean ones?"

He laughed. "The *mean* ones?"

"Yeah. I don't even want to meet the mean ones if I might end up working for them. What's the point?"

"I guess that makes sense." He nodded and placed his hand on her shoulder, stopping her from their walk. "Well, Steph, you're in luck, then."

"Why is that?"

Kendall extended his arm toward the stores across the street. "All of the mean business owners are on that side of the street."

"Are they now? That's awfully convenient."

"We all thought it would be."

"We?"

"All of us business owners. Except for Liz, of course. Just us business owners who do all those men things." He waved his hand dismissively, as Milly had done earlier.

Steph gasped when she noticed the store beside them. "Middleburg Clothiers! My job back home was in the men's suits department at Macy's. I actually know what I'm doing in that environment. What's the owner like?"

Kendall frowned and gave a melodramatic shake of his head. "Vicious. He should really be across the street."

She laughed and gave him a little smack on the arm.

He grabbed at the spot. "Now you're going to be slapping me in the street as well, huh?"

The shop door opened, and an impeccably dressed middle-aged man smiled at both of them. His olive skin and luxuriant head of steel gray hair gave him a Mediterranean appearance, but Steph detected no accent when he spoke. "Is this reprobate bothering you, miss?"

He and Kendall laughed and reached to shake each other's hands.

"Steph Vandergrift, this is Herb Roth. Steph is new in town. I'm showing her some of the local businesses."

"Terrific. Come on in and see the best one, then."
He stepped back so Kendall and Steph could walk
past him.

She felt instantly confident when she entered the
shop. She didn't see nearly as many suits as she
was accustomed to, so she suspected Herb was a
custom tailor.

"You only deal in bespoke suits?"

She saw Herb's eyebrows lift. He cocked his
head. "I do a little made-to-measure too, but most
of my clients prefer the custom-made, yes. Our
man Kendall, for one."

Steph regarded Kendall, who shrugged as if he'd
been told on. She raised the sleeve of an elegant
charcoal suit and gently felt it between her thumb
and fingers. She looked at Herb. "Gorgeous.
Cashmere?"

He smiled at her as if she were his daughter.
"Very impressive. Yes, it is. You know your
haberdashery, I see."

"Steph worked with men's suits before moving
out here to Middleburg."

She almost corrected Kendall. She didn't feel she
had actually moved out here. But then she realized
that was exactly what she had done. At least for the
near future. Suddenly her spirits lifted, although
she wasn't sure why.

"Did you enjoy the work?" Herb asked.

She didn't want to lie. She couldn't say she
enjoyed the work, really. It was just a job. She was

certain she was meant to do something else. Still, this is what she could do right now.

"I was very comfortable with the job. I'm not a tailor, by any means, but I know a lot about fit and fabric."

Kendall leaned against the wall. "I don't suppose you're in the market for an assistant, Herb? Steph's a hard worker, and she's just helping Milly Jewell out until Jane returns."

"Oh." Herb scratched the back of his head. "I'm sorry, no. I have two assistants already, and I'm actually going to be letting one of them go. The business just isn't booming enough for me to keep them both busy." He made a sorry face at Steph. "I regret I can't help you out."

She shook her head. "Not a problem. I'm sure I'll find something." She wasn't sure of that in the slightest, but Herb couldn't do anything about that.

Kendall removed the discomfort she started to feel by placing his hand at her back again. She could grow to like this.

"We should get going, Steph. There are a lot of people who will want to meet you."

Herb smiled at her. "I think he's right."

And certainly everyone Kendall introduced her to that afternoon was wonderfully friendly, but they couldn't seem to find anyone who needed her help.

They visited the home decor store, Rooms.

"These displays are unbelievable!" She and

134

Kendall soon learned they didn't need help. She spoke without thought after they closed the door behind themselves. "I've never been in homes with decor that stylish. I guess people are really loaded here in Middleburg."

He laughed, and she realized he was probably one of the loaded ones.

"Some of them are," he said. "But one of my favorite things about Middleburg is the diverse socioeconomic makeup of the place."

Steph nodded but kept her next thought to herself. Rich people were usually the ones who said that. People who struggled financially weren't often all that charmed by the diverse socio-economic makeup of their hometowns.

She considered how backwoods she might sound to Kendall, but he didn't react that way. She was almost glad they didn't need help at Rooms. She would be like a Beverly Hillbilly working there.

He took her to a women's boutique called Gigi's. They offered the finest in scarves, hats, dresses, and costume jewelry. The shop was both chic and unique.

Steph sighed when she walked in. "Kendall, I'm in love. This stuff is great!" She grabbed a hat—a cloche with a side bow—and put it on, batting her eyelashes at him.

He laughed and sought out the owner. Only the manager, Trudy, was available, but she was around Steph's age and very affable.

Kendall asked her, "Do you know if Mikaela is looking for any help?"

"I don't think so." Trudy took a pad of paper from the counter and jotted on it. "But I'll ask her to call you." She looked at Steph. "Or she could just call you."

"No, have her call me," Kendall said. "I want her to know I recommend Steph as an employee." He looked at Steph. "Assuming that's all right with you."

Steph tried not to look at him as if he was her hero. But he was, kind of.

They visited the Wishing Well, a gift shop that had so much on display that it overwhelmed Steph when they walked in. Not that the shop wasn't adorable, but she wondered if she would ever be able to absorb enough about the merchandise to be a good salesperson there.

As it turned out, she needn't have worried.

"I wish I could help," said Jessica, the owner. "But I have plenty of employees. I'm not hurting for business, by any means, but I simply don't need more manpower than I have."

As she and Kendall walked on, Steph felt the slightest bit of panic coming on.

"What am I going to do, Kendall? I'm going to have to beg my parents to let me move into their house if I can't earn a living out here. After I beg their forgiveness for being such a headstrong daughter."

He shook his head with complete confidence. "That's not going to happen. You'll have employment here if I have to employ you myself."

Startled, she turned to him. She didn't know what she thought about that.

"Not that that's going to be necessary." He seemed to have startled himself.

And then they were both especially startled, when a small, crazed, sudsy dog ran toward them.

"No!" The cry came from the alley between the gift shop and the dog grooming shop. "Stop that mutt!"

Steph squatted down at once and grabbed up the dog. Her concern was that the dog would run out into the street and get hit. Of course, her next concern was how she would smell after she handed this sloppy wet critter back to whoever had yelled to them.

The dog was a mess. It had long, wet fur, a ratlike body, and a nasty little tongue that was going to town on Steph's neck. She was a dog lover, but this wasn't the best interaction she had ever had with a canine.

A middle-aged woman ran down the alley in their direction, and Kendall laughed.

"Daisy, it looks like you need help."

Daisy looked at Kendall and blew a lock of hair away from her eyes. "You're telling me, kiddo."

She reached for the dog and took great care to

settle it securely in her arms before saying anything to Steph.

"Thank you so much. Mrs. Rittenour would have had my hide if any harm had come to this little dickens, but he slipped out of my grip just as Beth was coming in from a cigarette break."

Kendall gave Steph a sideways glance and spoke softly. "What are your thoughts here? Yea or nay?"

Steph shrugged and wiped her neck with the back of her hand. "Yea, if she'll take me."

Kendall nodded at her and then turned back to the dog groomer. "Daisy, how would you like my good friend Steph to help you out for one day to see if both of you like the idea of her working here? Are you in the market?"

Steph read the name of the shop, displayed over the front door: A Lick and a Promise. She smiled and then met eyes with Daisy. She'd had the lick. Maybe this exchange held promise.

Daisy looked as if she would have hired the town derelict at this point. She cocked her head toward the back of the building. "Let's talk, Steph." She looked at Kendall. "You can come too, handsome."

SIXTEEN

Steph breathed with relief that Kendall was nowhere in sight the following day—Saturday—when she checked out of the Fox and Hounds and moved her belongings into Christie and Liz's home. Kendall had been so attentive and present for her the last few days that she worried he might think she expected his help in moving too. He had a business to run, and he had his own personal life going on. She had no intention of taking him for granted.

Neither did she relish saying goodbye to him, even if it was simply because she was moving a few miles away.

Still, she found herself feeling disappointed as the day progressed and she had no interaction with him at all. There was no reason for him to call her, really, or vice versa. And she and Milly were busy at the tea shop, so even if he had popped his head in at some point, she could very easily have missed seeing him.

Steph attended Liz and Christie's church Sunday morning. A visiting missionary was the speaker. As his well-meaning but rambling sermon finally neared its close, Steph was relieved by Liz's discreet whisper.

"Pastor Henry is much more riveting."

She'd give the church another try next week.

She went to the tea shop Sunday afternoon to do some extra prep work with Milly so she could work at the groomer's the next day without leaving Milly too short handed.

The busyness of her weekend helped, but in the Sunday night quiet of her pretty new room, her thoughts turned to Kendall. To Rick. To her mother and father. So many threads in her life were dangling. Or snipped short. Or tangled all around her heart. She fell asleep praying that God would knit everything together the way He knew best.

Steph arrived at A Lick and a Promise first thing Monday morning. She had to look twice at Daisy to be sure she was the same frazzled woman of Friday afternoon. This Daisy was tidy and perky and without a hint of dishevelment.

"You look great!" Steph said.

Daisy laughed. "I knew I was going to like you."

The shop was painted in springtime pastels and had very little doggy odor to it, which Steph found encouraging. Maybe tasks didn't get too nasty here. It wasn't the same as a boarding kennel, after all. Fido came in, got pretty, and got out. How bad could it be?

A heavy, stuffy voice preceded someone approaching from the back of the shop. "Aunt

Daisy, where did you want those two bigger kennels moved? I don't remember if—"

He stopped talking. He stopped walking. He stared at Steph as if she were an angel descended from heaven. She gauged him to be six foot five and flirting seriously with three hundred pounds. If she had been talking, she would have stopped too. His buzz cut was about a sixteenth of an inch long—barely a suggestion of hair growing above his oddly tiny ears. And his skin tone suggested he did plenty of work outside. Possibly on a farm. Or in some form of demolition.

Despite his daunting presence, Steph could tell he was a teddy bear. If he was a bright fellow, he hid it most humbly. She smiled at him and watched him melt. Uh-oh. She needed to tread carefully with this big bubba.

"Ernie, this is Steph," Daisy said. "She's just with us for today to see if she might like to work here in a couple of weeks."

Steph put out her hand, but Ernie didn't respond right away. In the silence she could hear him breathing through his mouth, Napoleon Dynamite-style.

Daisy spoke loudly, as if she needed to break through some kind of sound barrier. "Ernie!"

He started and then looked embarrassed, which made Steph melt a little herself.

"Sorry," he said. He shook her hand. Rather, his hand swallowed hers up like a fish on a worm. Yet he was as careful and gentle as Steph figured he would be. His smile was a little boy's. "Welcome."

Aw, Steph was going to love this guy, she could tell.

Daisy interrupted the moment. "Let's move those kennels into the alley for this morning, Ernie. Or, no. Just move one into the alley. I have two big dogs coming in this morning, both males. We'll need to keep them apart from each other until we're done with them."

Suddenly shy, he nodded at his aunt and ambled off to the back of the shop.

"Don't mind Ernie." Daisy spoke softly. "He's a big sweetie."

Steph nodded. "I can see that."

Daisy rubbed her hands together. "Okay. Normally I would have you work the front desk and gradually work you to the back, where we're more hands-on with the dogs." She walked toward the back of the shop, and Steph followed. "But since you're taking a one-day snapshot of the place, I'll try to give you a good feel for what you would be expected to do if you worked here full-time."

"All right." Steph wasn't sure what that meant. Was she going to be shaving dogs and clipping nails while squeezing her eyes shut, hoping for the best?

"I won't have you do anything that requires experience, but I'll have you get your hands dirty enough for both of us to come to a decision. How about that?"

Steph tried to smile, but she honestly wasn't sure if she was eager to get dirty the way she pictured getting dirty with regard to dogs. Still, what did she expect, coming to a groomer? Teasing poodle hair and clipping bows to collars?

The arrival of the first client dispelled all misconceptions. This must have been one of the big male dogs Daisy had mentioned to Ernie.

He was an extremely large Great Dane, and Daisy handed his leash to Steph as if she were the shop's professional handler.

"Please take PeeWee on back to Ernie, Steph. He knows what to do. I'll join you as soon as Mr. Dignon and I complete the paperwork."

Exactly who took whom to the back was debatable, but Ernie took over right away.

"There's my buddy PeeWee." He took a firm hold of the dog and hugged him up as if he were PeeWee's best friend. The dog practically smiled as Ernie lifted him to a table and hooked a leash to his collar. Ernie looked at Steph. "Uh, you could give him a quick brush down before we bathe him, if you want."

Steph followed the direction of Ernie's gaze to the brushes on the counter. She took one and held it up.

"This one okay?"

"Yep. PeeWee doesn't need a lot of brushing

before his bath since his hair's so short. Like mine." He grinned, and Steph laughed.

She had brushed PeeWee's front half and moved to his hind end when it dawned on her that Ernie had put on a big blue lab coat since she saw him up front.

"Oh. I guess I want to put on something like that, don't I?"

"Here you go, Steph." Daisy entered the room and went directly to a cabinet in the corner. She shook open a fresh blue coat for Steph and handed it to her. "You definitely want to have coverage while working here. Especially when expressing the dog's glands and things like that."

"Doing what?"

Daisy looked at Ernie. "You didn't express Pee-Wee yet?"

"Not yet."

Daisy promptly joined Steph at PeeWee's hindquarters and showed her why she would never be back for another day of dog grooming.

Steph glanced at the clock on the wall. She had made it through twenty minutes at this job. She was now ready to hang up her little blue lab coat and seek some way to erase her short-term memory.

"You don't even wear gloves?" She would have liked to play it cool, but she couldn't help remembering that she had shaken hands with Daisy yesterday afternoon and with Ernie just moments ago. Where was a tub of hydrogen peroxide when you really needed one?

"You get used to it." Daisy patted Steph on the back, and Steph sighed with relief that she wore that blue coat and wouldn't have to set fire to her shirt when she got home.

The bell jingled at the front of the shop, and Daisy left PeeWee in Steph's quaking, and Ernie's capable, hands.

Almost immediately a yappy barking started up front. Ernie murmured softly to PeeWee, which seemed to be all PeeWee needed to shrug off the barking of another dog.

"Sounds like Hildie is here," Ernie said in his adenoid-heavy voice.

"Poor thing sounds upset." She feebly brushed PeeWee some more, hoping she wouldn't be required to do much beyond that before she bailed.

"Nah. She barks like that the whole time she's here. She's like that. Persnickety."

Steph laughed to hear this bear of a man use such a term. He looked at her and laughed back.

"She is. You'll see."

And Steph did, indeed, see. Or rather, she heard. Hildie was the stereotypical Yorkshire terrier, and she appeared angry with everything and everyone in the world.

Another employee joined them, much to Steph's relief. More people here meant less chance she'd have to do anything truly horrible before the day was out.

"Hey. I'm Beth." Small and wiry, Beth looked as if she had been sitting in a tanning bed all of her life. She carried the barking Hildie like a football. A barking football. She held the dog toward Steph.

"Would you hold her for me so I can get my coat on?"

"Uh, sure." Steph took hold of Hildie on either side of her skinny little belly. She felt the belly jump with each bark. "How can you stand this constant barking?" She looked at Beth and then at Ernie. She even looked to PeeWee for an answer.

Beth took the Yorkie back from Steph and shrugged. "You get used to it."

That appeared to be the mantra for A Lick and a Promise. Steph had her doubts.

Still, she hung in there, even when her stomach churned as Daisy taught her how to clean the inside of a dog's ear. Or as Ernie showed her how to remove ticks.

She hung in there despite the brief time she spent with a bulldog named Rosco, who mistook her for a fire hydrant while she awaited instructions from Daisy.

She hung in there even after she nearly killed little Hildie. The owner was an hour late in picking her up, and Hildie—though hoarse—was diligent in her efforts to drive them all insane. Steph was ready to wrap a rubber band around her muzzle.

Instead she took the initiative of placing a bowl of kibble in Hildie's pen, and Hildie stopped barking long enough to take a mouthful. Steph basked in two seconds of pride before the dog started barking again. There was no one else in the room at the moment, so when Hildie inhaled and choked on her food, Steph didn't know what to do.

Could you perform the Heimlich on a Yorkie without crushing her rib cage? It was certainly a question Steph never envisioned asking. She ran into another room and found Ernie.

"Come quick, Ernie. Hildie's choking!"

Ernie wasn't one to move quickly, but he ambled with enthusiasm. By the time he and Steph reached Hildie's kennel, she shot out the lodged food on her own. The fact that the hard, wet kibble splattered on Steph's lab coat did little to dissuade Steph from hanging that coat up once and for all.

"Aaaaaand I'm done."

Hildie resumed barking.

Steph calmly walked to the laundry room in the rear of the shop, shook out the coat over the utility sink, and made a three-point shot into the hamper.

Ernie appeared in the doorway. "You're really quitting? Are you sure?"

He looked crestfallen.

Steph sighed and approached him. She reached up and patted his sturdy chest a couple of times. "You, Ernie, are a saint."

A sad smile worked its way into his expression. "Thanks."

Daisy walked into the laundry room and looked from Steph to the hamper. "No go?"

Steph laughed. "You mean you didn't come back here to fire me? I almost killed Hildie just now."

Daisy raised an eyebrow. "Merely a demonstration of common sense, my dear." She walked up and rested her hand on Steph's shoulder.

Steph wondered if she could bleach this particular shirt.

"But I understand," Daisy said. "This job just isn't for everyone. You have to love dogs more than the average person."

"You sure do." Steph loved dogs, but she didn't love the insides of their ears. Or many of their other areas. "I'm sorry, Daisy."

The tea shop was still open when Steph stopped by. "You're okay with my showing back up tomorrow, right?"

Milly stopped in the middle of emptying the little flower vases from her tables. "Of course! I was expecting you. Ah. It didn't go well at the dog groomer's, I take it?"

Steph picked up a couple of the vases and joined Milly in removing any flowers that had wilted. "I'm most definitely not cut out to be that intimate with animals."

"Not many people are. Why do you think groomers do such a booming business?"

Steph sighed. "I don't know what in the world I am cut out to do. I should know that by now."

"There's no 'should' about it," Milly said. She walked back to the kitchen, and Steph followed. "I've worked in a number of different fields in my lifetime, Steph. I didn't own the tea shop until . . . well, I suppose it was only nine years ago. Shortly after my husband died."

"Really?"

"Absolutely. I stopped working outside the home during my husband's latter years, but after losing him I found myself eager to start a business and spend more time around people each day."

"Huh. I'll bet when you were married you thought you would never return to the workforce again, right?"

Milly shrugged. "I didn't give it a great deal of thought. I've always tended to focus on life as it happens more than on what might happen. I mean, I'm always hopeful for good things in my future. But I leave 'what might happen' up to God."

Milly removed her apron and picked up her purse. She and Steph walked toward the front door. "By the way, Steph, your egg and cress sandwiches were a big hit today."

Steph grinned. "Were they?"

"I think you did even better the second time around. I keep telling you, you're a natural. If Jane ever leaves me for good, I'll come looking for you, that's for sure."

Not only did that comment lift Steph's mood, but so did the next one.

"In the meantime I suppose we'll need to ask Kendall to help you meet a few more business owners in town. What do you say?"

SEVENTEEN

Steph knew for sure she had done the right thing moving in with Liz and Christie when she arrived home early that evening and described her dog-grooming fiasco to them.

"What you need is dinner out with the girls," Christie said. Without a moment's delay, the sisters marched her right back out the door and into Christie's SUV. They drove back into town, arriving at the Hidden Horse, an 1886 tavern down the street from Kendall's inn. They walked past wisteria-covered stone walls under a forest green awning and then stepped down into a surprisingly well-lit restaurant. The street-level window allowed light to shine against the thick stone walls painted a cozy, creamy white.

"Okay, don't even think about what happened at the groomer's today," Liz said, leading the way to one of the tables by the window. "You tried it, you didn't like it, let's move on."

Steph thanked the waitress for her menu and looked from Liz to Christie. "It's just that the grooming job was the only one Kendall and I came across yesterday. There don't seem to be oodles of opportunities out there."

"Didn't you say you stopped looking once Daisy

said she'd give you a chance?" Christie asked, setting her menu aside without even reading it. "There might be five other possible positions you just haven't come across yet. I might even be able to get you a job working with horses if you're interested."

Both Steph and Liz looked at Christie as if she were crazy.

Christie laughed in response. "I guess I just don't see animals the same way you do." She shrugged and opened her menu. "They're just part of nature."

"So are tsunamis and the bubonic plague," Steph said. "I don't want to work around them, either."

"You're such a *girlie* girl." Christie gave Steph a playful shove in the arm.

"Thank you." Steph sighed. "I'm an unemployed girlie girl, to be more exact."

Liz set her menu down. "You have almost two weeks before Jane returns to Milly's. Isn't that what you said?"

"Yes. Or, rather, no. I think we're down to nine or ten days."

Christie patted Steph once on the hand. "I'll bet you find something before then. And it's not as if we're going to be sticklers about the rent right away." She looked at Liz and back at Steph. "We'll give you a good two days before we chuck your sorry behind out on the sidewalk, won't we, Liz?"

"You betcha, hon." Liz studied her menu again.

"But for now, I would like to turn your attention to the crab cakes, Steph. This place has the best crab cakes ever, if you're into that kind of thing."

"Love good crab cakes." Steph finally opened her menu, but when Christie gasped, she jerked her head back up.

"It's him!" Christie lifted her chin toward the window and gave Steph another little shove.

Steph looked out the window and saw Kendall approaching. Her stomach actually flipped. For goodness' sake, she really was a girlie girl. He was just a friend. She should be able to have a good-looking friend without reacting to him so biologically. She forced a nonchalant shrug. "It makes sense he'd be around here. His inn is right on the cor—"

She stopped abruptly when Christie reached up and banged on the window to get his attention.

"Christie!" Steph's face must have turned ten degrees warmer in half as many seconds.

Christie laughed. "Hey, we've been wanting to meet this guy for ages." She looked at Liz. "Haven't we, sis?"

"Afraid so, Steph."

"You're our Kevin Bacon," Christie said. "And we're cashing in."

Steph frowned at her. "What in the world are you talking about?"

Outside, Kendall finally seemed to focus on Steph. He broke into a captivating grin.

Steph smiled back, but she cringed inside. He was sure to think she was the one who had banged on the window. How groupie was *that?* In the background she heard Christie explaining herself.

"*You* know. They say everyone can be traced to the actor Kevin Bacon within six acquaintances or something like that. You're our Kevin Bacon connection to Mr. Cutie Pants."

Steph's frown returned. "I'm not sure that even makes sense."

Christie enthusiastically waved Kendall into the restaurant.

"Christie!" Steph physically sank down in her chair. "I'm going to kill you! This is really embarrassing!"

"Oh, shucks, *I'm* the one acting embarrassing," Christie said. "He sees that."

"Anyway," Steph said, finally considering Christie's Kevin Bacon comment. "You've probably been within six acquaintances of Kendall forever. Why are you—?"

But she stopped arguing with Christie. Kendall had turned toward the entrance. He was coming in.

Steph moaned. "Why are you guys doing this?"

Liz leaned forward. "Actually, Christie's the one doing this, but I'll admit that's only because I'm not as blatant as she is. Maybe he wants to have dinner with us!"

Christie leaned forward too, and she and Liz had a little chuckle together.

Steph had to laugh, despite being humiliated and a little angry. These two were horrible and fun at the same time.

And then he stood at their table.

"Hey, it's my favorite dog groomer! How did it go today?" He looked directly at Steph, but she imagined they all three sighed a little. He was freshly showered, and his hair was slightly damp with several blond locks dropping casually to his forehead. He wore a fitted black suit with a black shirt, open at the collar. No tie. If he stuck his hand in his pocket and looked off into the distance, he could sell that suit and many others right off the pages of a fashion magazine.

Steph didn't know what he asked. She just said what she thought. "Terrific."

"Great!" He absolutely beamed. "I knew you would do well there. From the way you scooped up that runaway dog, I could tell you would blend right in."

Steph sat upright. What were they talking about? "Wait . . . no, I didn't do well at the groomer's. It's not going to work out, Kendall. I stink at working with stink. And all things that make stink possible."

He laughed. He introduced himself to Christie and Liz, both of whom behaved as nonchalantly as Steph strived to. He could have been a big homely woman, and they would have acted the same from all appearances. You'd never know they thought of him as Mr. Cutie Pants.

Christie sat back and regarded Kendall politely. "Would you like to join us for dinner?"

"Thanks!" His expression was just as polite as Christie's. "But I'm on my way to work." He looked out the window, toward the inn. "I own the Fox and Hounds, on the corner." He turned his smile on Steph. "That's how Steph and I met, isn't it, Steph? When she first got to town."

As if she wouldn't have already told them all about him. He had clearly forgotten she blathered to them about the redhead's slap in the street. She gulped. Humility was pretty attractive, especially when freshly showered and dressed in a dark shirt and suit.

"That's right." She spoke to Liz and Christie and used wide eyes to warn them not to embarrass her any further. "Kendall tried to help me find a job." She looked back at him and sighed. "I appreciate your efforts, even if it didn't work out."

"Hey, we're only getting started." He checked his watch. "I have to run, but I'll swing by the tea shop tomorrow. You're going to be there, right?"

"Uh, yeah."

"Great. Maybe we can take another little tour and see what else is available. Sound good?"

"That is so sweet." Christie spoke to Kendall, but she had a teasing glint in her eye when she turned to Steph. It was all Steph could do to concentrate. "Isn't that sweet, Steph?"

Without answering Christie, Steph smiled up at

Kendall as comfortably as she could. "Sounds really good. Thanks."

Kendall nodded at Christie and Liz. "Nice meeting you, ladies. Enjoy your evening." He saved his parting smile for Steph. Yes, it was merely friendly, as far as Steph could tell. But it was markedly different from how he looked at her roomies.

She imagined they had noticed, but she couldn't tell because both of them watched him walk away until he was completely out of sight.

She burrowed into her menu and spoke before they turned back to her. "Crab cakes, you say?"

Liz reached over and slowly lowered Steph's menu. "Word of advice. You take as long as possible finding that job, you hear?"

"Amen to that, sweetie," Christie said. "You tour all of Loudoun County with him if necessary." She picked up her napkin and dabbed at her forehead. "It's warm in here."

Liz's cell phone rang. She checked the ID. "Sorry. I have to take this." As she stepped away from the table, Steph heard her try to calm whoever spoke on the other end of the line. "Wait. Slow down, Isabel. Speak English."

Steph and Christie had barely looked at their menus before Liz returned, raising her index finger as if her caller said something noteworthy. She responded in front of them.

"You really need to hire an assistant, Isabel."

She winked at Steph. "Yeah, well I might know someone who could help you out. Let me get back to you in an hour or so, okay? Don't worry. Bye."

Before she could tell them anything, their server came by with water and took their order—crab cakes, all. The moment she left, Liz's eyes lit up.

"Okay, I was supposed to take a Pilates class tomorrow afternoon with my friend Isabel." She looked at Christie. "From Country Garden Florists?"

"Right."

"But that was her, calling to cancel. She just found out she has to do twice as many table centerpieces as she thought for an engagement party tomorrow. I mean, she has to put them together tomorrow. The party is the next day."

Christie sipped her water and raised her eyebrows at Steph. "And?"

Liz answered Steph rather than Christie. "And she needs help. She needs it bad. Tomorrow afternoon. Would you like to try your hand at working at a florist's?"

It was certainly a timely problem for someone to have. Timely for Steph, anyway. And she did love flowers, although she'd never considered herself particularly adept at arranging. Still, there was probably a strict design to follow for centerpieces. How hard could it be?

"Yeah. Definitely. I just need to make sure

Milly's all right with my taking the afternoon off, but I'm sure she will be."

Their server brought homemade bread and fresh mixed-green salads to them. Steph's stomach growled. She hadn't had much of an appetite while working at the groomer's, but it was back in full force now.

"Hey, but wait a minute." Christie tore off a piece of bread as she spoke. "If you work at Country Garden, you won't be able to resume your tour with Kendall."

Steph laughed. "No. But the point of touring with him is so I can find a job. I haven't paid enough attention to God's guidance lately. This might be an opportunity He wants me to take."

Christie shrugged, her face fallen. "If you say so."

Steph finally had a reason to give Christie a playful shove—a little of her own behavior right back at her. "Why, Christie Burnham. I do believe you're a soft little romantic."

Christie rolled her eyes. "Whatever."

Steph grinned at Liz. "She's such a *girlie* girl!"

EIGHTEEN

O h, you save my *life,* Esteph." Isabel gave
Steph a hug the moment she walked into the
florist's and identified herself. A lovely scent
lingered after Isabel stepped back, as fragrant as
any of the flowers in the shop.

Latina bombshell. That was the thought that
went through Steph's mind the moment she saw
Isabel. For that matter, it seemed there were
quite a few very attractive women in Middleburg. She saw that Isabel wore a wedding ring,
but still. It was curious Kendall hadn't been
snatched up yet, considering how many striking
and successful women there seemed to be
here.

And why was she thinking of Kendall? Was it
simply because she hadn't been able to talk with
him about canceling their tour this afternoon?

No. She was thinking about him in connection
with his being snatched up. Ridiculous. She
focused on Isabel.

"Liz says you might need someone full-time. Is
that right?"

"Yes, yes. We make this your interview, no? I
pay you for your time today and we talk about full
time after. Come to the back. I show you how the

centerpieces look. If you have question, you ask, okay?"

Steph nodded. "Sure." She followed Isabel to the workroom, just beyond the shop front.

Isabel removed a beautiful arrangement from the refrigerated case. Steph didn't recognize any of the flowers in it other than the pink roses. The other flowers included delicate, waxy, coral-colored blooms and small white . . . lilies, maybe? They were arranged around a saucer-style champagne glass, but she couldn't tell what held the flowers there.

"That's gorgeous, Isabel!"

"Yes, but we need twenty more like this, and I have no one but you. You see why you save my life, *muchacha marvillosa*?"

Steph laughed. She didn't know what Isabel called her, but she did it with such passion that there was no doubt it was a compliment.

Isabel put a shallow bowl on the table before Steph and placed one in front of herself. She poured water into the bowls and then centered a champagne glass in each. She handed Steph a spool of green tape and a box cutter before she picked up similar items for herself. "You watch me do this, and you do it with me, okay? Do not be afraid. You can do it."

"Wow. You don't mess around, do you?" Steph wasn't even going to have time to get intimidated by this task, which was probably for the best. At

161

least there were no critters to emit bodily fluids or anything else around her. Today's job was a definite step up.

Isabel patiently taught her to form a grid of tape across the shallow bowl, which allowed her to arrange the various flowers around the stem of the glass. The flowers lay nearly horizontal, but the tape held them in place. Isabel identified each one as she snipped its stem and added it to the arrangement. "Mokara orchid. Calla lily. The, um, English rose." By the time Isabel finished, only the bowl of the champagne glass showed, surrounded by a lovely floral wreath. "Tomorrow we put water in the champagne glass and float the little candles in them. Pretty, no?" She put her arrangement in the refrigerated case.

"So pretty." Steph's arrangement wasn't quite up to par with Isabel's. "What am I doing wrong?"

"You just needs more flowers. You needs more tightness in there."

They heard someone enter the shop. Isabel wiped her hands and stepped back from the table. "Do not forget to trim the stems before you put the flowers in, okay?"

"Okay."

Isabel went up front, and Steph could hear her greet a customer in a nearly musical voice.

"Mrs. Manfred, I do not see you for a long time!"

Steph froze right in the middle of snipping a

stem. Mrs. Manfred? As in Rick Manfred? Was this her jilting fiancé's mother?

"Yes, it's been a busy couple of weeks, Isabel. I just thought I'd stop in for a little something for the foyer while I'm in town. What do you have that's already done?"

Steph didn't know much about Rick's mother. Or his father, for that matter. Rick had always hinted at their being overly concerned with social appearances, but other than that he usually changed the subject whenever Steph had mentioned his parents. Still, just hearing Mrs. Manfred's voice made Steph picture a pigeon-shaped socialite with her nose in the air.

"That one, with the birds of paradise. That's perfect."

"It has been so busy for me too," Isabel said. "I had a big order *double* last night. Centerpieces for . . . um . . . for engagement party tomorrow. I do not know if I get them all done. So difficult when the people change their minds like that, you know?"

Mrs. Manfred's voice lowered just slightly. "Whose engagement? Is it the Stetson girl?"

"No. The Millers. Their oldest. Pretty girl."

"Yes. I know the one. I wouldn't have minded my son meeting someone like that young lady. Lucinda. Very refined. Well educated. And good family, the Millers."

"Very nice family."

Steph heard Isabel sliding display doors open and closed between snippets of conversation. "So your son—"

"Richard."

"Yes. He is your only children?"

"My only child. Yes."

"And he is married?"

Mrs. Manfred's sigh was forceful enough to travel back and condemn Steph.

"That's what's made life so hectic these last two weeks." She lowered her voice again, and Steph leaned toward the doorway to listen. "He very nearly *eloped* last week."

"*Madre mia!* Who was the girl?"

Steph wiped beads of sweat from the top of her lip and then realized her forehead was just as damp.

"Some girl he didn't even want us to meet, can you imagine? I don't know what in the world he was thinking. He's just about to begin his whole life. His father was livid. Richard is to be the newest associate with his father's law firm, you know."

"Ah, good for him."

"Certainly, good for him. But does he look to the many excellent families here in town when he considers marriage? No. He picks up some common . . . oh, I can't even talk about it without getting upset."

Steph didn't hear a verbal reaction from Isabel.

She wondered if Isabel hailed from one of the many excellent families in town or if maybe Mrs. Manfred was insulting her too.

"You can imagine, Isabel, how vigorously his father and I had to interfere. His father had to threaten the loss of his future with the firm, as well as a possible severance from his inheritance. A good social standing is of utmost importance to a family's future, you know. To tell you the truth, I don't know if Mr. M would have followed through on his threats or not, but we were desperate. We sent him away until we could be certain the entire fiasco had blown over."

No response from Isabel, other than a barely audible "Mm-hmm."

"Oh yes, that arrangement is perfect. Let me pay you for that and get going. Put it in a box or something so it doesn't tilt in the car, will you?"

Steph stopped listening at that point. She allowed her mind to digest this news. These answers. His parents had driven him away from her. He had been given a choice, and he didn't choose her.

Did she blame him? Given the choice, would she have given up everything for him?

But . . . that's exactly what she had done. She had walked away from her job, her family, her friends, and her home for him. Her loss was no less important than his would have been.

She wasn't aware she was crying until Isabel walked back into the workroom.

"Esteph, why you crying? What is the—"

The next sound Isabel made was a mix between a squeak and a scream. It snapped Steph out of her self-absorbed trance.

"What did you do?" Isabel ran her hands through her hair and held them there, as if she were afraid her head might explode. "Why do you *do* this?"

Steph looked around her work area and gasped. Had *she* wreaked this havoc? A couple dozen of the orchids lay across the table. She must have gone onto autopilot while engrossed in Mrs. Manfred's comments. But she wasn't a florist—she had no autopilot in this field. She had taken Isabel's parting instructions to an extreme, trimming the stems but not placing the flowers into any arrangements. So she continued to snip the same flowers repeatedly, until they barely had stems left at all. She had destroyed nearly every orchid.

"Isabel, I . . . I don't know what to say. Can we still use them? I was distracted . . ."

She could tell Isabel was struggling not to cry. Or erupt. Steph wasn't sure which.

"How can I make this better, Isabel? Can I run to another florist and get more orchids? Can we make some of the centerpieces different, maybe? With different flowers? But matching?"

She didn't know what else to say.

Isabel walked quietly out the back door of the shop.

What should Steph do? She removed her cell phone from her purse with the intention of calling Liz and getting her advice.

But Isabel returned before Liz's number came up. She spoke calmly, but she obviously held something like panic or anger just below the surface.

"Okay, here is what we do. We rearrange the ones I already done." She went to the refrigerated cases and pulled a large vase of flowers out. Different flowers from what they had used so far.

"We remove some of the orchids from the finished ones and use them in the ones we do not make yet." She pulled one of the different flowers from its vase. Its color mimicked that of the coral orchids, with a touch of yellow in the petals. "We fill in the holes with these Gerbera daisies. We can fix this, but now it takes us longer."

She looked Steph in the eye. She obviously wasn't seeking Steph's approval, but she waited for Steph's acknowledgement and agreement.

"Definitely," Steph said. "Let's get to it."

"We will be here into the night."

"Yes. I'm sorry, Isabel. So sorry."

"And when we finish?"

Steph looked up from the arrangement she was already changing. "Yes?"

"When we finish, you are fired. I pay you, but you go. You understand, no?"

Steph sighed. "Yes. I understand completely."

So much for saving Isabel's life. And so much for employment. One more day gone. At this rate she might not have to make a choice between staying in Middleburg and crawling back to Maryland. There were only just so many employers she could disappoint. Her choice might be made whether she liked it or not.

NINETEEN

By the time Steph got home that night, she knew what she had to do. The time had come to call her parents, if only to touch base. And to apologize for the way she left the last time they spoke. She needed to find out how they felt toward her, in case she couldn't make her way here in Middleburg. She didn't want to presume they would welcome her home after the way their last encounter had ended. They hadn't tried to call her this past week, which made her call to them that much harder to make.

She sat on the edge of her bed, the bedroom door closed. She hugged herself with her free arm, suddenly chilled in the normally warm room.

"Hello?" Her mother's voice reminded her of her teen years. Steph was fifteen before she recognized disappointment in her mother's voice. Rather, before she recognized her mother's disappointment in her. There wasn't much judgment, just sadness. Fatigue.

"Mom? Did I wake you?" Steph fought to keep her tone steady, but she could tell she spoke higher than normal. Like a younger girl.

A moment's hesitation. Then, "Stephanie?" Almost whispered, as if trying to keep Steph's father from hearing.

"Yeah, it's me, Mom. Are you all right?"

In the silence Steph strained to hear. Was her mother crying?

"Mom?"

"Honey, are . . . are you . . ."

"Mom, please don't cry. I'm sorry."

"Is he there, Steph? Is Rick there with you?"

Steph cringed. Then a clattering on the extension interrupted them.

"Stephanie?" Her father. "Is that you?" Stern, but not all business. She knew him well enough to recognize concern there as well.

"Hi, Dad."

"Where are you?"

"I'm in Middleburg. I know I should have called sooner—"

Her mother said, "No, we didn't expect—"

"We assumed you wouldn't call until after your honeymoon," her father said. "If that soon."

Steph rested her head in her hand. "No. We didn't go on a honeymoon."

Silence.

"We, um, we didn't get married."

Could two people have expressed more relief merely by sighing? It was as if neither had exhaled since the day she left.

"Good girl," her mother said.

She almost heard a smile in her father's voice. "I knew you'd come to your senses."

She didn't relish explaining her circumstances.

No one wants to tell her parents she's unwanted.

"But why are you still in Middleburg then?" There was no mistaking the hint of growing panic in her mother's voice.

"Stephanie." The smile had vanished from her father's tone, and he had already launched into lecture mode. "You're not living with him, are you?"

Steph's mouth dropped open. She may have gone against their wishes by eloping—or attempting to elope—with Rick, but she never gave them cause to suspect her morals. That was one of their standards she had lived up to. And it had been no easy feat. Of all people, they should know that. In a moment of extreme honesty last year, Steph's mother had confessed to her about their premarital mistakes. She had done so to let Steph know she understood how hard it was to wait.

Well, Steph had waited. She spoke before checking her anger. "No, Dad, I'm definitely not living with him. I don't even know where he is."

Her mother gasped. "Oh, honey! What happened? Did you—"

"I'd like to wring his greasy little neck."

"Dad, don't get all worked up. Please. It's just . . . well, he wasn't even here when I arrived. I didn't know for sure what had happened until yesterday. His parents were against it—"

"That didn't stop you," her father said.

She could hear the tightness in his lips. "No, it

didn't stop me. I'm twenty-five, Dad. When you were my age, did you do everything your parents told you to do? Didn't you make decisions for yourself at twenty-five?"

After some silence she heard him exhale, resigned. "So why are you still there?"

"Yes, you should come home." Her mother's eagerness broke her heart. "You know your room is always available for you."

Steph closed her eyes. Relief washed over her, but not without a healthy dose of dread. She didn't want to give up, tuck in her tail, and sniffle back to her childhood room.

"That's right, sweetheart." The softening of her father's voice caught her in the throat. Tears sprang to her eyes. "Come home and regroup. Get away from that place."

"I might. Thanks." It would be so easy. And she wouldn't even have to rush to find employment. She could go back to school. Get a master's degree. Or find training in some field. She probably wouldn't even have to cook her—

Her eyes shot open. What was she doing? It was almost like being hypnotized. Her parents' suggestions were like intergalactic tractor beams, drawing her back to the mother ship. She couldn't give up after failing only a couple of times. She still had nine days before Jane returned to the tea shop. She could fit all kinds of failure into that much time.

"The thing is, I really like Middleburg. I think I'd like to see if there isn't a profession that suits me out here before I make a decision."

"But why there? Where are you living?" her mother asked.

"I moved in with a couple of friends."

Her father asked, "Female friends?"

"Of course female friends, Dad. I'm still the same person you've always known. It's not a nunnery, but you'd approve, trust me."

"And what about money?" he asked. "What are you doing for money? Should we send you—"

"Thanks, Dad." Steph smiled. "I appreciate the offer, but I have a bit to live on, and I'm working a short-term job at a little tea shop here. I'm filling in for someone who's on vacation. I'm trying to find a regular job before she gets back."

Her mother asked, "Doing what? I mean, what kind of job are you hoping to find? And when does this person get back?"

Steph shrugged. "I'm not sure yet where I fit, job-wise. I've tried a couple of things that, um, weren't for me. I'm still looking. And Jane returns to the shop in nine days."

"Good." Her father sounded completely at ease now. "That's not too long. We'll see you in nine days, then. Your room will be ready."

She rolled her eyes and silently thanked her dad for the vote of confidence.

"I'll call you in a few days. I love you."

Her parents spoke over one another with their *I love you too*s.

She closed her phone and stared at the wall. They did love her. And they were definitely there for her. She knew plenty of people who lacked that kind of familial support. She felt a measure of relief. If she failed miserably in Middleburg, she had a place to go.

The first part of that condition hung heavily over her. She didn't want to fail miserably here. She was smart. She had done really well in college. She had a math degree, which would be great if she could stand the idea of being an accountant or a statistician or a mathematical technician. Mercy, she had almost fallen asleep out of boredom just considering her possibilities.

How did she manage to get a degree she had no interest in using? That might not have been so smart.

She stood up and frowned with concentration. *Enough of this nonsense.* That was it for the "poor me," the counting down of days, the focus on failure, the pining after Rick—or Kendall, for that matter. Even if she had to recommit daily, she would. Tomorrow she would get back out there and meet some more employers. Okay, Kendall was instrumental in that, so she wasn't going to knock him totally out of the equation. But she would keep their relationship purely friendly.

He was definitely a Mr. Cutie Pants, but she

would make her own mark in the world—or at least in Middleburg—before even glancing in romance's direction. If someone else snatched him up, so be it. Then God didn't mean him for her, and that was just fine.

Still, when she found the note from Christie on her nightstand, she couldn't fight a grin.

Milly called. Says Kendall stopped by tea shop. Will come by tomorrow to take you on another job tour. You lucky girl, you.

Christie

P.S. Remember to take your time.

TWENTY

Milly carried a tray of used dishes into the kitchen the next afternoon as Steph conducted her own personal taste test.

"Mm-hmm," Steph said. "I definitely prefer the American version of these cucumber sandwiches."

Milly delicately picked one up and took a nibble. "Frankly, I do too. I think the cream cheese improves the taste. We'll serve these with the Darjeeling or the Nilgiri this afternoon. We have quite a few sticklers for the classic cucumber sandwiches in our clientele, though. Let's go ahead and make up a batch of the plain cucumber as well."

Steph grinned. "Already done." She opened the refrigerator door and extended a hand to present the tray she completed earlier. She basked in the glow of Milly's appreciation. "I'm getting better at this, aren't I, Milly?"

"You are! Did I not say you would? You're a quick study."

"At this, maybe." Steph sighed. "I do enjoy this job. I know I haven't met your regular assistant—"

"Jane."

"Right, Jane. I wish her all the best, but I sure wouldn't raise a fuss if she was discovered by a

Hollywood talent scout or something while she's on vacation and decided to move to the other side of the country."

Milly gave Steph's arm a gentle squeeze. "You're going to like Jane, regardless of her reclaiming her job. Anyway, God has the perfect spot in mind for you. Just keep looking." She shrugged. "Or not. Perhaps Jane will be discovered, although that's highly unlikely while she's in England. And I don't know if she's ever had an interest in acting or anything else along the Hollywood lines. Maybe she'll fall in love with a young man overseas and decide against getting on that plane."

"Have you heard from her while she's been gone?"

A slight grimace. "Um, yes. She sent me a postcard saying she'd be home according to plan. But it was sent last week, so I thought I might dream along with you for a moment."

"Nothing wrong with propping up my hopes, right?" Steph mustered a smile.

"Exactly." Milly continued to the back of the kitchen and picked up her purse. "Listen, Steph, I need to run to the bank for a moment. I won't be long. Will you linger up front while I'm gone?"

"Sure. Go on ahead." She returned the sand-wiches to the refrigerator. "I'll just wash my hands and get out there."

When Steph walked back up front, the shop

was empty, save for a boy of maybe sixteen sitting alone at one of the tables. He focused so intently on the textbook in front of him that he didn't even look up as she entered the room. He was thin and fairly pale, but he didn't look sickly. Just Anglo to the max. He wore his blond hair short but unruly. She was glad he didn't notice her, because she couldn't keep from doing a double take on his legs. He wore a prosthesis in place of his left leg. Rather, it looked as if it started at his knee. And it was one of those sporty, springlike legs she had seen on the news—never before in real life.

She looked at his face, and then he seemed to sense her. He looked up, frowning about whatever he was working on.

"Hi," Steph said. "Would you like some tea or juice or something? Some food?"

He shook his head and relaxed his frown. "No, thanks. Milly brought me some stuff already." He leaned back in his chair. "You're new."

"Yeah. And on my way out, I'm afraid."

"Right now? Milly left too, you know."

"No, I mean in another week or so I'm on my way out."

He chuckled. "Milly fired you already?"

"No, she didn't fire me already." Steph laughed. "Jane's only gone for a while longer, and I've been filling in for her." She approached him and put out her hand. "I'm Steph."

He shook her hand. "Chip." He grinned. "You're prettier than Jane."

"Ah, you're a shy one, huh?"

He laughed and then he did look shy.

"It's kind of early in the day for school to be out, isn't it? Are you a homeschooler?"

"No. We closed early for a teacher workday. They do that at the end of the grading period. We get report cards pretty soon."

Steph looked at his textbook. "Calculus homework?"

The frown quickly returned, and he leaned over the problem, head in hand. "Yeah. I'm stuck. I've done this problem about five hundred times, and I can't figure out what I'm doing wrong. And my friends are coming to get me for Ultimate Frisbee pretty soon. If I don't get this done, my mom's going to freak. She dropped me off here on her way to a meeting and made me promise I wouldn't go to the game if I wasn't done with my homework."

Steph pulled up a chair next to him. "Well, young man, you must have been praying, because I am your answer."

He leaned back and assessed her. "Huh?"

"I defy you to find a calculus problem I can't teach you. It's my thing. Did it with my friends in high school, did it with my friends in college."

He studied her for a moment and narrowed his eyes, as if trying to determine whether or not she was playing a joke on her. "Okay. How about this?" He turned his textbook so she could read it, and he pointed to a word problem. "The one about measuring farmland." He placed his paper next to the book. She could tell he watched to see if she understood what she read.

She must have passed muster, because he proceeded to discuss his work with her. "See, I do better when I can draw a picture with problems like these."

"Me too." She nodded and looked from the book to his paper. "Yeah, that's right. And you figured out the area."

"Okay," Chip said, "but how do I use that to find the length of the optimized field? I can't get past that."

She took his pencil and another piece of paper. "That's because first you need to find the derivative and set it equal to zero, like this." She worked through another equation. "See? That gives you ninety feet for your width. And then—"

"Oh!" Chip grabbed the pencil from her. "And then substitute ninety for w in this one!" He worked an additional equation and turned to her. "Right? Is that right?"

"Absolutely correct."

He smiled at the problem and smacked his hand on the table. "You are the coolest girl ever!"

She laughed. "Are there other problems you need help with? It's not exactly busy here right now."

"Let me try these last two and see."

She left him alone and tidied up the rest of the shop. At one point she heard him quietly exclaim. "Awesome!"

Ten minutes later he said, "Could you just take a look at this last one to see if I did it right? I think I did. It was a lot like the farmland one."

She looked over his shoulder and studied his work. "Perfect."

He pulled his fist down in the universal winner's gesture. "Yes!"

The shop bell jingled, and two more teenage boys poked their heads in. One of them called out, "Chip! You finished?"

"Yeah. Hang on. I just have to pack my bag."

He stood and shoved his books and papers into his bookbag. He gave Steph a triumphant smile. "You're awesome. Thanks, Steph."

"Anytime." She felt as if she had just saved the world.

This day was working out beautifully. As long as no one asked for her help with flora or fauna, she thought the afternoon might be a winner.

Milly returned minutes after Chip and his friends left, and before Steph could say anything about him, two groups of ladies seated themselves at the tables. Steph didn't even have to play at pleasantry with them. She was in such a good mood she found her attitude infectious. They seemed to enjoy her as much as she enjoyed them.

The only thing that could further brighten her day was getting a job.

Steph corrected that thought half an hour later, when the front bell jingled again and she met eyes with Kendall James. His smile was definitely a mood lifter.

Yet he brought bad news. He stood just inside the door and waited for her to approach him. He seemed to be in a hurry, and he spoke to her softly, his manner private.

"I'm so sorry. I have to reschedule for tomorrow, if you're free. We've had a minor crisis at the inn, and I need to be there."

She tamped down her disappointment. Hadn't she canceled on him just the day before? It was best to embrace Milly's belief that God had the best job waiting for her. If that was the case, He'd surely hold it for another day.

Kendall spoke again before she could.

"Or did the florist job work out?"

"Noooo, indeedy, it did *not* work out. I think we can safely cross dogs and flowers off the list."

He looked almost happy about that. "Then the search continues!" A brief grimace. "But I'm sorry it will have to wait until tomorrow. Okay with you?"

"Not a problem at all." She glanced at another table as it filled with customers. "Actually, it looks like it would have been unfair to leave Milly this

182

afternoon. She's busier than she expected to be, I think."

When she looked back at him she caught him studying her face. He hadn't followed her eyes when she looked at the new customers, but had focused on her instead. Now he gave her a fetching smile.

"Tomorrow, then?"

She nodded. "Right. But call before coming to the shop so I can make sure it's okay with Milly."

Milly happened to walk by at that moment. "It's okay with Milly." She gave Steph a grin. Clearly Steph and Kendall weren't speaking as quietly as they thought they were.

Steph called after her. "Tomorrow afternoon, Milly? You want to commit to that already?"

"I close early on Thursdays, remember? You go on and plan for anytime." With that Milly turned her back on them and tended to her customers.

"Wow," Steph said. "That means I've worked here a week, Kendall. We closed the shop early on my first day. I can't believe how quickly the time is passing."

"Yeah, but it seems as though we've known each other longer than that, don't you think?"

That stopped her. Did she feel that way? She hadn't learned much about him, really. But he did have an easy way about him that often brought out the most relaxed feelings in her. She didn't usually experience that—not around such attractive men—until she had known them quite a while.

She realized she was squinting as she considered his comment.

"I didn't mean to stump you there."

"No." She laughed. "You didn't. I think you're right."

A customer squeezed past them, and Steph realized they were becoming conspicuous. Kendall must have done the same.

"I'd better go." He hesitated, as if debating whether to do something beyond turning and walking away. But turning and walking away won out, apparently. He spoke over his shoulder as he left. "I'll see you tomorrow, Steph."

She knew he was in a hurry, and she and Milly were busy. Still, something about his departure felt abrupt. He closed the door behind himself, but then he glanced back in through the glass. He must not have expected her to still be there, watching him. The pleasure in his eyes when he gave her a parting smile was enough to last her the rest of the day, and quite possibly until his return tomorrow.

TWENTY-ONE

The following morning passed swiftly, thanks to two separate, bustling parties of women who visited the shop. The first group, a local book club, carried on a lively discussion about their book between rounds of tea and savories. They broke out in rowdy peals of laughter during a number of their exchanges. Steph made a note to ask what they were reading before they left the shop. She couldn't remember having that much fun with a book for a long time.

The second party appeared to be a women's counseling group. Their conversation was no less animated, while clearly more serious. Steph took care not to listen too carefully as she served them or passed by.

Would she ever come to that point? Would she become so frustrated or confused that she needed to get professional guidance? Sometimes it sounded downright tempting, and it would probably do her good.

As the women's counseling group finished their meeting and paid their bill, a sharp, blond woman strode into the shop, unable to fully mask an air of entitlement. Steph guessed she was Milly's age, somewhere in her fifties. Her sleek, shoulder-length hair perfectly complemented her charcoal-gray suit and elegant cream satin blouse. Steph thought she might be an attorney or banker. There was that kind of gravity about her. No humor whatsoever.

Milly walked out of the kitchen just as Steph approached the woman, and Steph froze when she heard what Milly said.

"Well, Mrs. James, how lovely to see you again."

Mrs. James. This had to be Kendall's mother. Yes, Steph could see the resemblance now, although Kendall had a constant hint of humor about himself. Steph wondered if this woman was anything like Rick's image-conscious mother. But the moment Mrs. James met eyes with Milly and broke into a smile, it became clear she was a different type of woman altogether. And she was less rigid than Steph had originally thought.

"Milly, you know I prefer you call me Silvie. You make me feel like an old woman, showing all that deference."

They gave each other polite hugs.

"Silvie, then. Have you come to relax with a nice cup of tea?" Milly turned to include Steph in the conversation—at least as a subject, if not a participant. "Steph just made some lovely tea sandwiches that go beautifully with Darjeeling."

The woman's eyes opened slightly at the mention of Steph's name. She took Steph in with an up-and-down glance so speedy many others might have missed it. Steph only noticed because of this being Kendall's mother. She couldn't help but wonder if he had ever told his mother anything about her. What were the chances of that?

"So you're Steph. My son raves to me about you."

Hmm. Apparently the chances of his discussing her were pretty good. She found herself both flattered and concerned.

"He does? Um, well—"

"That's actually why I stopped by. I thought it would be good for me to meet you."

Gracious, this was moving just a tad quickly. Meeting the mother already? Weren't she and Kendall just friends? Steph turned to seek assistance of some kind from Milly, but Milly seemed to have vanished from the room in a puff of smoke. She must have gone back to the kitchen to give them some privacy.

Steph didn't know what else to do, so she stepped forward and extended her hand. "Well, then, it's very nice to meet you, Mrs. James." She waited for the correction, for Mrs. James to tell her to call her Silvie.

Nope.

Mrs. James shook her hand. "And you are Steph . . . ?"

"Vandergrift. It's a Dutch name. My father's grandfather came over in the early nineteen hundreds. He was a cobbler."

Now, why had she volunteered that? Had the woman given any indication she was conducting genealogical research?

Mrs. James did, in fact, frown almost negligibly, as if she had just mentally marked a jot on the "weirdo" side of Steph's personality scoreboard. "I see." She glanced around the shop. You'd think she had never been there before. "And this is where you work?"

Now Steph frowned. Was she being interviewed? Or maybe Mrs. James didn't know what else to say. But how strange would it be to come all the way here to meet her and not have more in mind than whether or not she worked at the tea shop?

"I'm just working here temporarily. Milly's assistant, Jane, is away on vacation. I'm filling in for her."

"And when she returns? Where will you be then?"

"I'm . . . not sure, actually. I've been looking for another job here in town. Kendall has been helping me in that regard. He's—"

"Kendall has?"

Uh-oh. She looked inordinately surprised by that information. What, exactly, did she think Steph and Kendall were doing together? She took a deep breath. She might as well get right down to it.

"May I ask what this is about, Mrs. James? You have obviously come here specifically to meet me. Why?"

The slightest raise of one eyebrow. Too forward? Well, that would just have to be all right, because Steph hadn't done anything with Kendall that she needed to explain to anyone, not even his mother.

"I wanted to see about hiring you. For my son."

Struck momentarily speechless, Steph started at a crash in the kitchen. It sounded as though a tray of silverware was dropped. She felt certain the accident happened just on the other side of the door.

"You . . . you want to hire me for . . . excuse me, but what exactly are you talking about? Why would *you* hire me for *him?* Isn't that something he should talk with me about?"

Mrs. James tilted her head and narrowed her eyes. "I'm sure he will, once I give him permission."

Permission? What kind of "Mommy Dearest" were they dealing with here? Steph started searching her memory banks to recall what Kendall may have said about his mother since they had met. He really didn't seem like a mama's boy.

Perhaps because Steph didn't respond, Mrs. James forged on.

"Certainly you wouldn't expect me to allow him to meet with you regularly without my making sure you were above board. And qualified."

Steph's heart pounded. Who did this woman think she was? "Qualified?"

"Indeed. Do you have a college degree, for instance?"

A college degree? At least she didn't ask if she was a Vandergrift "as in the New England Vandergrifts," or something snooty like that. Then again, Steph had already helpfully volunteered the lowdown on her family's roots.

"I . . . yes, I have a college degree. You know, I don't mean to be rude, Mrs. James, but I don't even think Kendall has asked if I have a college degree."

"And why would he? He knows nothing about this."

"Well, I'm glad to hear that. I would hope he'd find all of this pretty odd. And embarrassing. And—"

The front door opened at the same time the kitchen door did. Milly hurried in just as Steph's friend from yesterday, young Chip, walked into the shop. Steph was distracted by how minor a limp he had when he walked. She gave him a smile and decided this conversation with Mrs. James was over. She didn't want Chip to witness an unpleasant scene.

But he strode directly to them and planted a kiss on Mrs. James' cheek. "Hey, Mom."

He returned Steph's smile, even though hers had swiftly been replaced, she was sure, by a look of stupefaction.

"See?" He spoke to his mother. "Didn't I tell you she was cool?"

Mrs. James spoke, and Steph forced herself to look her in the eyes. "Yes, honey. You did."

For the second time in the last few minutes, Steph found herself rewinding mentally. What, exactly had she said to this woman while under the wrong impression? This had been about Chip, not about Kendall.

Milly jumped into the conversation. In the recesses of her mind, Steph noticed that Milly held several pieces of silverware. "Silvie, I have to apologize. I don't think Steph knew that Kendall and Chip were brothers. I should have mentioned that when you came in." She looked at Steph. "I didn't realize you and Chip knew each other, Steph."

Steph still battled the words and images bouncing around her head. How rude had she just been to Kendall's mother?

Chip said, "Yeah, we met yesterday afternoon after you left the shop, Milly. Remember? Steph is the most awesome calculus tutor."

Milly's eyes widened, and she smiled at Steph. "Are you? I had no idea, dear."

Steph sighed. It confused her too much to try to remember what she had already said. "Mrs. James, I'm sorry. I thought you came here to hire me to be with Kendall."

Uh, no. That didn't sound good at all. No one spoke, so Steph jumped back in.

"I mean, I thought you were talking about Kendall the whole time you meant Chip." She chuckled, although she struggled to sound sane as she did so. "I couldn't imagine why you were sticking your nose into Kendall's business."

No. That wasn't any better. Now she was insinuating something more serious about her relationship with Kendall than what really existed. And she kind of called Mrs. James a busybody. And she told her to mind her own business, in so many words.

"Not that I'm Kendall's business. He's not into me that way."

So tell us, Steph. How, exactly is he into you?

"I mean, he's not into me at all. We're just friends."

Mrs. James breathed in. Held it. Breathed out. She looked at Steph and said nothing.

Finally Chip spoke to Steph. "So are you going to do it?"

Steph tore her eyes away from Mrs. James' to look at Chip with total confusion. "Do what?"

"Are you going to tutor me? Please say yes. I don't need help all that often. I'm just going through a rough patch right now, but if it gets past me, I'm going to completely mess up this year. I need to keep up, and sometimes I'm too confused to even know what I don't know."

Steph loved his obliviousness to the discomfort the adults all felt. She smiled at him and gained confidence in his innocence. She looked back at Mrs. James and awaited her comment.

Mrs. James sighed again. "Perhaps we should

start over. Would you be willing to tutor Chip in calculus every other day for an hour or so? I'll pay you forty dollars an hour. If you could meet him at the library after school, I would appreciate it. The library is right down the street. I'm assuming, of course, that your degree qualifies you."

Ah, yes, the college degree. That made much more sense now. "My degree is in math, yes." Steph smiled at Chip. "I'd be happy to help Chip. You don't have to pay—"

"I think forty dollars is a fine rate," Milly said. She gave Steph a subtle, private, crazy-eyed expression. "And I can attest to Steph's character, Silvie. I'm sure she's exactly what your boy needs."

The front door opened, and one Kendall James stepped in. Steph noticed he looked first at her, and his smile broadened immediately.

Mrs. James must have noticed too. She looked at Steph as she answered Milly. "We're still talking about Chip, right?"

TWENTY-TWO

O nce they were alone together, Kendall's laugh brought enormous relief to Steph. He had played it very straight when he entered the tea shop and found his mother and brother there. But the moment he and Steph left for another tour of Middleburg, Steph started filling him in.

She punched him on the arm.

"Why didn't you tell me about Chip? Are there any more siblings out there?"

"A sister, Jenna. She's older. Married. Living in New York." He shrugged. "It's not as if you filled me in on your family situation right away. I don't know anything about your siblings, either."

"I don't have any siblings! I sounded like an idiot to your mother, I'm sure. I thought she was trying to hire me as your escort or something."

They both laughed at that.

"You mean, like my date?"

"Yes! She said you raved about me. Well, it wasn't you. It was Chip who raved about me."

"I would have been happy to rave about you, given the chance."

She hesitated only long enough to tuck that away with a smile. "She wanted to make sure I was qualified. For *you,* I thought. Qualified!"

He studied his nails like a self-absorbed dandy. "I do have my standards, you know."

She couldn't believe how attractive he was when he played around like this. As embarrassed as she had been, she found herself enjoying the fact that they could share this together.

He had shown such respect for his mother when he found her in the shop, yet he hadn't seemed intimidated by her in any way. Steph knew she shouldn't make comparisons, but she remembered listening to Rick's demanding mother in the florist's shop. Rick had certainly gone running when his parents had ordered him to. Somehow she couldn't picture Kendall doing the same.

Of course, Rick had depended upon his parents for his position at the law firm, and Kendall already had his own business. But Kendall had achieved his success despite a struggle between his wishes and his parents'. He had stood his ground, like a man—not cowered, like a child.

They were clearly different from one another.

She checked herself. One big difference was that she and Rick had been romantically involved. She and Kendall were not. She needed to mosey that little thought back into the corral.

"So you're going to tutor Chip in calculus?"

"Yeah, but he doesn't need much assistance. Sometimes people just miss one step in solving problems, and the whole process becomes overwhelming. It's smart of your mother to get him help."

"Especially from you." He wiggled his eyebrows at her.

She blushed immediately. Drat. "Why do you say that?"

"My guess is that Chip has—or will have—a little crush on you. He's going to want to give those tutoring sessions everything he has just to impress you."

She frowned. "Not at all. He . . ." She suddenly remembered Chip promptly mentioning that she was prettier than Jane. "Oh. Maybe you're right."

"I know my little bro."

"What, um . . . is it all right for me to ask about his leg?"

"Sure. He's never known anything else, so he's pretty jaded by it. I guess we all are, especially people who have lived here for the past sixteen years."

"What happened?"

"He was born without a fibula." He squatted at her feet and ran his hand down the shin of her jeans. "That's the thinner of the two leg bones, right here."

She started at his touch. He wasn't being romantic, but she hadn't expected it. He stood as quickly as he had squatted. Her voice was unnervingly breathy when she said, "Uh-huh." If he noticed, he didn't let on.

"By the time he was one, the doctors said it would be best to amputate at the knee and have him use prosthetics."

She exhaled and thought of a one-year-old, rather than the Chip she had met. "Poor baby."

"Yeah." He frowned and fell silent for a moment. "I was a teenager at the time. I remember that being the first time I had cried since I was a little kid. He was so small."

"I can't imagine what that must have been like for your parents too."

"Yeah, they tried to be tough about it. They needed to be. But I heard both of them cry behind closed doors while all of that was going on. They leaned on each other. And I think their faith helped them out a lot."

He took a big breath and released it. "Anyway, it all worked out really well. Chip's a confident, thriving athlete, believe me."

She smiled. "He was headed to an Ultimate Frisbee game when I met him."

"Mm-hmm. He has never let anything get in his way. I have a lot of respect for him."

Oh, she liked this guy. Respect for his little brother. Emotion he wasn't afraid of.

"What?" He smiled at her.

She had been staring at him, probably as if he were on a pedestal. She shook her head. "Nothing."

He lingered for a moment. It looked as if maybe he knew her thoughts, but she'd never know.

Then he turned and regarded the shop front beside them. "You want to see if my Realtor friend needs any help? I don't know what they pay, but—"

"Yeah, let's check it out. I'm running out of time."

"Right. We want to keep you here." He opened the door for her, and they walked in together.

They repeated that process at the bank, the art gallery, and the town newspaper office. There were absolutely no jobs available. By the time they left the last place, Steph was fighting tears.

"It just isn't happening for me here, Kendall. I don't think God wants me to stay."

He shook his head. "The only thing we know for sure is that He doesn't want you working at those jobs."

"Well, I hope He has a big windfall in mind for me soon. I'm getting worried." She looked at him and sighed. "I really don't want to move back to Maryland and live with my parents."

He draped his arm around her shoulders. The gesture would have fit even if she were a male friend, but she immediately hoped she still smelled fresh enough for him to be that close. It had been a long, stressful day.

"I have two things to say about that," he said.

"You do?" His face was so close to hers. He had amazing lips. And he smelled wonderful, like cedar and cloves.

"Yeah. One, that is definitely not going to happen."

"Uh-huh. What isn't going to happen?"

He chuckled. "You will not have to move back to Maryland. Trust me. You need to stop worrying."

"Okay." From this proximity he could have ordered her to shave her head, and she would have responded the same.

"Two, let me take you to dinner. I will keep you from worrying. At least for tonight."

Oh. Was . . . was he asking her on a date? Or was this just a buddy kind of thing?

He pulled back, apparently to gauge the meaning of her silence. "No? Not a good idea?"

"No. Yes, I mean! A good idea, that is. Go to dinner we should." Why was she talking like Yoda?

"Good. We'll go to the French Bistro. I promised to stop by anyway. Excellent place. They have a great menu."

"Do I need to go home and change?" She looked down at her clothing, which seemed too casual for anywhere French, as far as she could imagine.

"No, I've been there in jeans before." He studied his nails again. "Anyway, you're with me. That will compensate for countless errors on your part."

"Well, aren't I fortunate?"

He looked her in the eye, and somehow his eyes looked darker than moments before. "No, the fortune is all mine."

TWENTY-THREE

O h, Kendall, I *am* too casual. This place is so elegant."

The restaurant was right around the corner from Kendall's inn, as so many lovely spots seemed to be. Although dusk had barely settled in, diners already filled the bistro. Clearly a popular site, it boasted a light, French, classy atmosphere. Framed prints by Toulouse-Lautrec and Seurat on antiqued yellow walls. Arched doorways and white crown molding. Heavenly aromas and French country dinnerware. It all added up to a place far more fancy than Steph's simple blouse and jeans. She felt herself shrink around the shoulders, as if she could disappear by doing so.

"I'm no dressier than you are," Kendall said. "We're fine, believe me."

Of course he was dressier than she was. He wore smart black trousers and a spotless white golf shirt—designer, no doubt. Yet when he draped his arm over her shoulders again, he made her a part of his little sphere of acceptability. The maitre d' approached them and didn't so much as glance at her jeans.

"Mr. James! We haven't seen you for a while."

"David." Kendall shook his hand. "I'm sorry, but I didn't make a reservation."

David looked as if he would hear no more of it. He cocked his head and walked deeper into the restaurant. "Right this way."

Kendall removed his arm to let Steph follow the maitre d'. She murmured to him over her shoulder. "Man, you really do have pull, don't you?"

"Are you impressed?"

She laughed softly. "I think I am." She was so busy flirting over her shoulder that she walked right past the table to which David led them. Kendall had to speed up and catch her by the arm.

"You are going to sit with me, aren't you?" He smiled at her.

Her face flushed immediately, but she joked to cover her awkwardness. She glanced around at all of the other diners before sighing in resignation. She tilted her head to the side and tsked when she looked at him. "I guess so."

There was that crinkle at the corners of his eyes. Her awkward feeling faded away.

She breathed in the delicious aromas. "Mmm, I don't know what they have on their new menu, but I think I approve. Smells so good."

"I think that might be me." He gave her the silliest sly grin, one eyebrow raised like a bad actor in an equally bad film.

Steph laughed. "Idiot."

That made him laugh out loud.

They ordered and shared *steak frites*—grilled filet mignon and amazing fries—and *gigot d'agneau*—roasted leg of lamb with lentils and a creamed garlic sauce. Steph didn't know if she was inordinately hungry or if the food just tasted so wonderful she couldn't stop eating.

"You liked it." Kendall smiled as she ate the last bite from her plate.

"Oh my goodness, I'm sorry, but there was no way I could pretend to be a dainty eater with those two dishes. They were phenomenal."

He laughed. "Dainty eaters are overrated. Passionate people are more fun."

Is that what she was? A passionate person?

"I thought I was just piggy. You sure know how to put a nice spin on things."

"No, I mean it. Can't you tell, sometimes, when you come across someone who's passionate? I mean, I realize you're shy sometimes, and you're careful when you first meet a person. I see that."

Well, he had her pegged there.

"But I'm getting pretty good at seeing the signs."

"The signs?" She leaned back in her seat and crossed her arms. She gave him a crooked smile, unconvinced.

He lifted his palm to present her as his case in point. "Like that, for instance."

She looked down at herself. "What?"

"You're sitting back and crossing your arms. Both of those gestures would normally signal your not wanting to talk about this." He leaned toward her and she instinctively loosened her arms. He mirrored her crooked smile. "But that expression on your face is sheer challenge. Like you're ready to just take me on."

She didn't know exactly what he meant by that, but she felt herself flush. "Take you on?"

"Yeah. Spar. Thrust and parry. Verbally wrestle with me. You do it all the time, once you get comfortable around me."

She suddenly realized she had lowered her arms and leaned forward just as he did.

He grinned. "I really like that about you. That's a passionate person, as far as I'm concerned. Much more interesting than 'dainty.' "

What happened next felt so out of place, Steph would have thought she had imagined it if not for prior circumstances. From her perspective, one moment Kendall was charming her socks off and complimenting her for not being dainty, for being passionate as opposed to piggy. And the next moment he was doused in water.

Or, rather, not water at all, but more likely alcohol. Something pink and fruity.

His face registered as much shock as Steph felt, and the two of them seemed to move in slow motion. By the time he shook off the drink and they turned their heads, they were just able to see the last of a redhead dashing out of the restaurant.

"Are you all right, Steph?" Kendall showed more

concern for her than curiosity about the woman. "Me? Yeah, I'm fine. She was aiming for you."

He glanced down at himself. "Well, she should be very happy, then."

Steph stood. "Let's go!"

He looked up at her and grinned. "You mean, go get her?"

"Well, at least we should go see if we can figure out what her problem is."

He stood. "You stay here. We don't know how unbalanced she is. For all we know she's waiting out there with a bazooka aimed at the front door."

Their server approached, a solicitous smile on his face. He stopped in his tracks when he saw Kendall. "What happened? Let me get a towel to mop that up."

"Thanks. I'll be right back."

Steph sat back down and watched him walk out. She knew Kendall was joking about the bazooka, but who knew what this woman had going on in her head? Talk about passionate. This was passion run amok. Steph couldn't believe the redhead had managed to throw her drink at Kendall without anyone else noticing. You would think she did this sort of thing all the time.

Kendall walked back to the table at the same time the server did, and he took the towel to dry off his shirt. "Thanks." He looked at Steph and shook his head. "She tore away in that same Porsche from before. I'm going to have to call Amy again."

"She never called you back?"

"No. And I didn't follow through. I figured it was a one-time thing, so I stopped thinking about it."

"Man. I wonder if it was a coincidence she was here. Maybe she's stalking you."

"We'll find out soon enough. I'll be more assertive with Amy. I have a feeling there's something she doesn't want to tell me."

He took care of the bill, and they stepped outside. Steph couldn't help glancing around for the Porsche. How could Kendall stand it?

But the street was peaceful, the night beautiful.

They soon neared Kendall's inn. "Do you mind if I stop in to put on a clean shirt before walking you to your car? Or did you walk to work today? I could take you home."

"No, I drove. But sure, get out of that wet shirt."

Jimmy was behind the desk when they walked in.

He smiled and seemed to recognize her, but then he noticed Kendall. "What happened to you? Someone throw a drink in your face?"

Kendall and Steph met eyes and then looked back at him.

"Yeah," Kendall said. "That's exactly what happened."

A shocked look hit Jimmy. "Really?" He looked at Steph, a question in his eyes.

She held up her hands. "Not me. Some crazy redhead."

"Crazy redhead?" Jimmy pointed at Kendall. "Is this the same one who belted you last week?"

Kendall pulled a packaged T-shirt from behind the front desk. It had the Fox and Hounds logo on its front. He laughed. "I certainly hope so. If there's a legion of crazy redheads out there aiming for a target painted over my face, I may have to leave town."

Then, without ceremony, he lifted his own shirt over his head and replaced it with the clean one. He did it within seconds, but it was, again, like slow motion for Steph.

Somehow, in the midst of running a restaurant and an inn and whatever socializing he did to know all the businesspeople in town and escorting her all over the place and keeping in touch with his mother and brother and who knows whom else, Kendall James found time to work out.

Just as the image of a flashbulb remains imprinted on one's eyes after having a picture taken, the brief image of Kendall's upper torso remained for Steph, even after he covered it up. He, of course, was completely oblivious to what he had done. He came out from behind the desk, holding his soiled shirt in his hands.

"Okay, see you tomorrow, Jimmy." Kendall placed his hand in the small of Steph's back. "Let me walk you to your car."

"G'night, Steph," Jimmy called.

Huh. She didn't even know he knew her name. "Bye, Jimmy. Have a nice chest!"

And she froze. No. She did *not* say that. "I-I mean, have a nice night!"

They walked out of the inn, and she didn't know whether to cover her face in her hands and admit her embarrassment or just pretend she hadn't said what she had. In silence they neared her car, and she cautiously glanced over at Kendall, who had no expression on his face whatsoever. But then the slightest creasing started near his eyes, and his struggle not to smile became clear.

Right. Face in hands it was, then. She stopped and nearly screamed through her fingers. "I can't believe I said that, Kendall. Please forgive me."

"Forgive you? Just because you think Jimmy has a nice chest?"

She jerked her head up. "Not Jimmy—" But then she realized he was teasing her, and she had just embarrassed herself again. This time, though, he had played a role in it, so she lowered her head and gave him a little pounding on that nice chest. "That wasn't fair."

He laughed and held her hands to keep her from pounding him. "I'm sorry. I'm just playing with you."

She didn't want to look him in the eye.

Still chuckling, Kendall released one of her hands to lift her chin. "Look, can I, can I just . . ." He managed to get her to look at him. But he didn't say anything else. In what seemed as big a surprise to him as it was to her, he leaned down and almost kissed her. He stopped less than an inch from her, and she heard her own gulp as they both hesitated.

She saw decision cross his eyes. He whispered one word. "Impulsive."

They had established it earlier—neither of them was impulsive like this.

A smile would have formed on Steph's lips, had Kendall not suddenly, softly, and most impulsively kissed her good night.

TWENTY-FOUR

Now, Steph knew not to put too much store in that kiss. They had only been on one date, really, and it had been a mere eight days since she was, essentially, left at the altar by another man. So this incident had rebound written all over it, the result of infatuation, pure and simple. But as infatuations went, this was one of the better ones. Kendall was charming, but he wasn't slick. Everything she had seen so far indicated he was kind and noble. Everything but the angry redhead's unexplained indignation, that is.

Still, Steph got all kinds of smile mileage—smileage—the following morning at work.

In the middle of teaching her how to make smoked salmon tea sandwiches, Milly stopped and tilted her head to give Steph a good look.

"Young lady, I think the last time you looked this happy was . . . well, before you came to Middleburg." Milly smiled too. "What happened?"

Steph shook her head. "Nothing, really. I'm being silly."

Milly returned to mincing the smoked salmon. "Well, then I can only surmise this nothing has something to do with Kendall."

Steph lifted both her head and her eyebrows. "How do you figure that?"

"Most women aren't *silly* about much, but if they are, it's usually about things like spiders and vanity. And men."

Steph chuckled but volunteered nothing. She concentrated on her salmon-mincing efforts as if she were restoring the Sistine Chapel.

"The way I see it," Milly continued, "were you silly about spiders, I'd see one or two around here. And you wouldn't be smiling, you'd be screaming and jumping up on the furniture. And were you silly about vanity, you would have noticed by now that you have mashed strawberries in your bangs."

Steph looked up at Milly, who nodded. A quick glance in the mirror near the sink confirmed it. She sighed.

"I'm *never* going to get the hang of that stupid hand mixer. I'm using the masher from now on."

Milly would not be diverted. "And since Kendall is the only man you have spent time with recently—as far as I know—I assume he's said or done something to make you . . . silly." She pointed to a bowl of whipped cream on the counter beside Steph. "Here, bring that over here, will you? We're going to fold that in with the salmon."

Steph did as Milly asked. "We, um, went on a date last night after an unsuccessful afternoon of job hunting."

"Did you? I take it the date went better than the job hunting?"

Steph sighed again. "Much better."

Milly's smile was the kind Steph would have liked to see on her own mother's face more often. Not calculating about husband material. Just pleased that Steph was pleased. "Lovely, Steph. So what now?"

"Now?"

The bell at the front door rang. Milly checked the clock on the wall. "Someone's early."

"I'll go." Steph already had her apron off and dashed her hands under the faucet before walking out.

"If that's Christie, let me know," Milly said. "That little stinker has been coming by to grab breakfast every morning without a moment's how-do-you-do. I'm withholding crumpets from her until she makes time to pay a real visit."

But it wasn't Christie. Steph froze halfway to the door when she saw who it was.

Milly poked her head out the kitchen door, still playful. "Is it Christie? Not a single scone for her . . . Steph?"

Steph approached the door and opened it. Her mother and father poured into the shop like molten lava.

"Honey!" Her mother smothered her with her hug. "Thank God you're all right. You are all right, aren't you? Look at you. You're so thin!"

Steph gently pulled back from her mother. "Thin? Mom. I've only been gone a week, and I've been eating like a linebacker. How did you find me?"

"This is the only tea shop in Middleburg." Her mother raised her arms to encompass their surroundings.

"You gave us quite a scare, Stephanie." Her father looked as if he expected an apology. And maybe she owed him that. She felt she had done that on the phone, but here they were. In person. In Middleburg. Very much in her current situation. What did this mean?

"I'm sorry, Dad. I told you what I was doing when we spoke on the phone—"

"Yes," her mom said, "but you didn't do what you said you were doing, did you, sweetie." Her mother tended to end her criticisms with endearments. It always seemed to make them sting a little more sharply.

"Not for lack of trying, Mom, believe me. I expected to be married by now."

Her father crossed his arms. "What your mother means, Stephanie, is that we don't quite understand why you're still here."

Steph sighed. "Dad, I thought I explained that. I like Middleburg. I'd like to see if there's something here for me. Job-wise, I mean. And life-wise."

Milly walked out from the kitchen. Steph suspected she had heard what was going on, just as she had heard Kendall's mother yesterday. Milly had a lot of class, and she was the type to use her apparently superhuman hearing for good, rather than for evil.

"Steph? Are these lovely people your parents?"

Both of Steph's parents assumed friendly stances and smiled kindly enough at Milly. Steph did love them. They were good people and only wanted the best for her. They just wanted it so bad that sometimes Steph could barely breathe.

She faced Milly. "Yes. Milly, these are—"

"John and Peggy Vandergrift." Steph's father shook Milly's hand, and Steph cringed at how openly he surveyed Milly. It wasn't clear whether he approved or disapproved, but he obviously took her measure. Her parents were both in their Sunday best, as if they had anticipated the need to impress whomever they might meet here in Middleburg.

Milly's charm never faltered. "Milly Jewell. What a pleasure to meet you. Of course, I would have expected no less, considering how pleasant your daughter is. She's been such a delight to have working here this past week." She extended her hand toward one of the tables. "Won't you make yourselves comfortable? I'll bring you some tea. And a few nibbles, maybe?"

"Nothing to eat for me, thanks." Steph's mother finally spoke, and her smile for Milly looked genuine. "But I'd love a cup of tea."

"Yes." Steph's father hesitated. Then he said, "I suppose we could sit a while. Thank you. And just tea would be fine."

"I'll get it, Milly." Steph headed toward the kitchen.

Milly put up her hand to stop her. "No, no. You sit, Steph."

Steph pleaded otherwise with her eyes. Milly gave her an understanding nod, all but reassuring her out loud.

Steph's father chose a table and her mother followed. Steph allowed herself the smallest of sighs before she joined them. John spoke the moment Milly left the room.

"Stephanie, please tell me this isn't the extent of your aspirations. Waiting on tables in a coffee shop?"

"Tea shop." She bit her lip too late. What did it matter—tea or coffee? It wasn't as if he would approve of either. She sat across from him.

"Fine. Tea shop. Is this why we spent eighty thousand dollars on your college education, so you could wait tables?"

She shook her head. "No, Dad. This is only temporary." But then she felt horrible. She didn't mean to sound as if she belittled what Milly did. Everyone loved Milly and what she did.

"I know you expect more, Dad. And I'm only filling in here thanks to Milly's generosity. I've been looking for other jobs for the last few days. I just haven't found anything yet. I told you all of this on the phone just the other day."

"Why here, honey?" Her mother put her hand on top of Stephanie's. "Why don't you just come on home and look for something there? How long are you going to—"

"We didn't want to wait the nine days you suggested." Her father's expression held something deeper than his sternness. Steph sensed worry. "We would just as soon have you come home now, rather than starting at some job that will tie you up for an indefinite period of time. It will be that much harder for you to leave if you start a full-time job all the way out here."

Steph studied his face. He hated the idea of her being two hours away from them. Was that out of love or the need to run her life? The fact that she couldn't tell pressed heavily upon her.

The front door opened and all three of them turned their heads. Kendall stepped in without looking their way at first. The sunlight streamed in with him, and Steph's heart lifted. Her parents weren't dragons by any means, but at the moment he surely did look like a knight in shining armor.

Milly entered from the kitchen with a tea tray. Steph saw her smile at once when she saw Kendall. Then she shot her eyes at Steph to assess the situation. Kendall followed Milly's eyes, and his face lit up. He took several steps toward Steph before he noticed her parents and slowed down.

Milly spoke up. "Kendall! Good morning! Have you come by for a little tea and breakfast?"

He turned toward her. "Sure, thanks, Milly." He pulled out a chair at a different table, but he glanced Steph's way. She could tell he wanted to make sure he wasn't putting her in an uncomfortable situation by introducing himself. She smiled at his gallantry and subtly cocked her head in invitation. That was all he needed.

He approached her father as he spoke to Steph.

"How are you this morning, Steph? Working hard, as usual?"

She could tell she wasn't going to have to do a thing on his behalf. The man was confidence personified. "Hi, Kendall. Not working very hard yet, really."

He put his hand out to her father. "Good morning. I'm Kendall James, a friend of Steph's."

Milly managed to set the pot and cups on the table, and Steph could tell she preferred to stick around rather than retreat to the kitchen. But she simply gave Steph a wide-eyed glance and a smile before she left.

"John Vandergrift." He shook Kendall's hand and nodded toward Steph's mother. "My wife, Peggy."

Kendall shook her hand too. "Welcome to Middleburg, Mrs. Vandergrift. I take it you're Steph's parents?"

That was when Steph saw the look in her mother's eyes. Charmed. Immediately.

Steph nearly laughed out loud. Wait till she got a load of his financial status. Steph could already hear the change of tune coming with regard to her future in Middleburg.

"And how do you know our Stephanie?" Her father crossed his arms and ignored his cup of tea.

The proprietary tone of "our Stephanie" was not lost on her.

Kendall smiled at Steph as he spoke. "I met her right here in the tea shop, didn't I, Steph?"

"That's right." She pushed at the leg of the spare chair, scooting it out from the table. "Join us."

She liked that he smiled at her parents but still joined them, according to her wishes. She appreciated his show of respect for them, but his deference to her wishes filled her with confidence she didn't feel before he walked in.

"Kendall has been introducing me to many of the business owners in town. He's trying to help me find something permanent."

She watched her father's brow crease even further. "And how is it you know so many of the business owners?"

"My family has lived in Middleburg for years. And I own the Fox and Hounds inn and restaurant a few blocks down."

Peggy gasped softly. "The big one on the corner, you mean?"

"Yes." Kendall smiled. "So you've seen it. Would you let me treat you to lunch while you're here?"

217

Steph could see her mother nearly jump at the offer, but her father interrupted.

"I'm afraid we won't be around that long, but thank you." A moment of silence ensued to the point of awkwardness. Steph searched for something to say, but Kendall saved the day by glancing at his watch.

"Well, please stop in if you change your plans. Just tell the maitre d' to let me know you're there." He looked at Steph. "I have to run, but I wanted to . . . to say good morning."

Steph smiled. "Good morning." The intimacy of the grin they shared dawned on her the moment her father cleared his throat.

Kendall rose from the table. "Mr. and Mrs. Vandergrift, it was a real pleasure to meet you. I hope to cross paths with you again sometime."

"Definitely," Peggy said.

Kendall gave Steph a quick smile and a nod before he walked out the door. As soon as it had closed her mother began to gush.

"So that's why you want to set yourself up here. I can't say I blame you, honey. He's wonderful!"

Steph rubbed the back of her neck and frowned. "No, Mom, that's not the reason at all."

"Are you sure about that, Stephanie?" John had found something new to frown about. "You already let one man get your head in the clouds. Are you sure it isn't just happening all over again?"

"Yes, I'm sure. Kendall and I are . . . well, we're becoming very good friends, but I'm in no rush to get involved again. Not seriously. I want to stand on my own two feet before I try that again."

"What do you mean, stand on your own two feet?" John said. "Do you honestly think you're in a position to support yourself? And what kind of job is he helping you find? Another waitress-type position?"

Now was probably not the best time to tell them she'd flunked dog grooming and flower snipping.

"I'm looking at all the possibilities, Dad. You're the one who constantly dissuades me from looking into accounting firms and other places where I might be able to apply my math degree. So I don't know what, exactly, you expect me to do."

"Now that's not totally fair, sweetie," Peggy said. "You told us you weren't all that interested in—"

"Yes, I know. The idea of sitting at a desk balancing columns all day doesn't appeal to me, Mom. You're right. But Dad keeps telling me I'm not ready to assume the responsibility it takes to work in a firm that would hire a newly graduated math major. Maybe that's true, but . . . oh, I don't know. I'm sorry, but I want to prove to myself that I am responsible enough to make my own choices. About where I'll live. Where I'll work. Whom I'll love."

"Well, good luck with that last one." Her father's

lips drew tight, and he grasped his hands together on the table. "Your track record hasn't been—"

"John, now stop." Peggy placed her hand on his arm, quieting him. She turned back to her daughter, and Steph nearly cried, seeing her mother's love after her father's criticism. She couldn't speak.

"I'm sorry, Stephanie. I shouldn't have said that. And I don't mean to imply you have no sense of responsibility. I just worry about your being hurt or unemployed or . . ." He heaved a resigned sigh and focused on his hands as he spoke. "Look. We'll go home and give you time. Just let us know what you're doing, all right?" He finally looked at her. "Don't let so much time pass without calling us." He stood, and the women followed suit.

"Okay, Dad." She went into his embrace and clenched her teeth to keep from tearing up. She didn't know why it was so important to her that she not cry in front of him, but she fought it with everything she had.

Her father pulled back and reached for his wallet.

"I'll cover the check, Dad."

He nodded but pulled out two one-hundred-dollar bills and handed them to Steph.

She held up her hands. "I'm fine, Dad. You don't need to—"

"Just make your father happy and take this, will you, please?" He pushed them into her hand, and she took them.

She walked them to the door, and her mother gave her a hug and whispered in her ear. "Do let me know what develops with that adorable Kendall."

Steph simply smiled and nodded.

She stood at the closed door after they left, trying to unravel her thoughts. Her father had little faith in her ability to develop a career, yet he expected her to find a position of which he would approve. Her mother criticized less than he did, but she simply sounded eager to marry Steph off. No wonder she didn't know what to do with herself, either professionally or emotionally.

She was twenty-five, a college graduate, and able bodied. She knew it was time to step back from her parents' influences and support, especially because they confused her so much. She finally understood why Middleburg appealed to her. It was a two-hour step back from her parents.

Obviously, a geographic departure wasn't going to do the trick. Steph could see she would have to step back in more ways than one.

TWENTY-FIVE

I think you are completely right, Steph." Liz stood and cleared the dinner dishes off the table in the sunroom that evening. "If you don't set some boundaries for your parents, it won't matter how far away you move. It's too easy for people to stick their noses in your business with all the technology we have today. People can all but teleport into your living room if they want. I'm surprised your parents didn't call your cell phone before you contacted them earlier this week."

Steph shrugged. "I think they needed to cool off a little after I defied them. And they also thought I was on my honeymoon."

"Hmm." Christie pushed her lips out and raised her eyebrows. "At least that shows some respect, don't you think?"

"Yeah." Steph stood to help Liz. "It's not like they are ogres or anything. They really love me—"

"That always makes it harder to ask them to back off, doesn't it?" Christie said.

Steph nodded and carried salad bowls into the kitchen. "That and the fact that they put me through four years of college. It just wouldn't be right for me to say, 'Thanks loads, now get lost.'"

Liz carried a box of truffles into the room and sat next to Christie on the couch. "Well, we can see that your efforts to get lost yourself have not panned out very well. So you're right to insist that they allow you to use all of that education and experience to start living as an independent adult." She put her hands up, a physical caveat. "Insist lovingly, but insist."

Steph grimaced. "Did you two have to do that with your parents?"

Liz and Christie looked at each other for two seconds before they both laughed out loud.

"Hardly," Liz said. "Mom and Dad love us, but they were really eager for an empty nest, even if it meant moving into a new one down south." She cocked her thumb at Christie. "This one took it all out of them. They needed a break."

Christie had reclined slightly and now shoved at Liz's leg with her feet. "Not exactly. Miss Healthfood USA was so busy forcing fiber and tofu on them that they retreated to the land of retirees, eggs, and scrapple."

Liz grimaced and produced an exaggerated shudder.

Steph's phone rang. She excused herself and walked into the kitchen while Liz and Christie started channel surfing for a good film.

It was Kendall, and he wasted no time referring to the meeting with her parents. "I hope the rest of your day was a little less strained."

"Oh, you were able to recognize the strain, were you?"

"The vein throbbing in your dad's temple kind of clued me in, yes."

"Yeah, he's worried I'll end up living all alone underneath a bridge somewhere. But everything will work out—"

She heard the clatter of something being dropped, apparently in the restaurant's kitchen.

"Sheesh." Kendall said something quietly to someone, his hand over the phone, before talking to Steph again. "I'd better go or I'll be living under that bridge with you."

Steph felt a half smile twitch and looked up to see Christie and Liz watching her. She rolled her eyes and turned her back to them. "Okay, I'll let you go."

"But hang on a second. I called because I wanted to talk with you about something. Is it all right if I stop by tomorrow when you finish work? Six-ish?"

Had Kendall not sounded rushed the night before, Steph would have gladly stayed on the line with him to hear what he had to say. She had never been very good about waiting for things. During her childhood, her mother always faced a challenge keeping Christmas and birthday surprises secret. Steph was no better now, focusing far too much effort on trying to figure out what Kendall had in mind to tell her.

So she was thrilled when no customers were lingering in the tea shop near the closing hour. She and Milly had the place in tip-top shape by the time Kendall came by. A quick hello and goodbye between Kendall and Milly, and then he could tell her what he wanted to talk about.

There was still plenty of sun left before dusk would descend, so Kendall and Steph took a comfortable stroll down Washington Street while they talked.

"I finally got a call from Amy yesterday." Kendall put both his hands in his pockets. Steph had become accustomed to his occasionally pressing his hand against the small of her back as they walked around town, so she found the change intriguing. What was he feeling?

"Oh. How did that go?"

He shrugged at first. "It was a little weirder than I expected, I have to admit. It's odd to be on such formal terms with someone you thought you were going to marry, you know?"

He looked at her, and she wasn't sure how to respond. "Um, yeah. I can imagine. I mean, I haven't talked with Rick since he took off, but—"

"Right, right." He nodded. "It will be weird for you too, I'm sure."

"Assuming I ever hear from him again."

Another nod. "Yeah." He took in a deep breath and exhaled. It felt like a signal that they could retire Rick as conversation fodder for now.

"Anyway. Amy called to explain the redhead."

"Oh!" Of course. Steph had been so distracted by Kendall's reaction to Amy's call that she almost forgot why he had initiated contact in the first place. "What did she say?"

"Well, I understand now why she didn't call me back the first time I left her a message. She was pretty embarrassed."

"I would think so. If someone behaved that way and said she was doing it on my behalf, I'd be embarrassed too."

"No, it wasn't—" Kendall shook his head. "Yeah, Amy probably never would have thought that Jessica—I think that's her name—would slap me or throw a drink in my face on her behalf. But what embarrassed her most was the lie she told that blew up the way it did."

Why Steph felt a frisson of pleasure over the news that Amy lied, she didn't know. She didn't want to know. She had no illusion about it's being a Christian emotion.

"What do you mean? What lie did she tell?"

Kendall actually looked embarrassed on Amy's behalf. Again, Steph rankled with the emotion she experienced—was it jealousy?

"Jessica is Amy's cousin, and for some reason Amy was hesitant to admit that she had called off our engagement. As far as I'm concerned, if she wasn't comfortable about our marrying, that was reason enough for us not to go through with it."

"Sure," Steph said. She knew immediately that, had Rick given that as a reason for calling off their elopement, she would have been crushed, but she would have understood. Eventually.

"But apparently Amy felt that wouldn't be the case with her family. So she told them all that I broke off the engagement. And when they pressed her for my reason, she told them I was interested in a number of other women, that I wasn't ready to settle down. And they all believed her. This, despite a year's worth of my demonstrating devotion to her with absolutely no indication of my having that straying kind of temperament."

Even though hours had passed since he heard this news, the pain he felt over Amy's betrayal was so clear Steph wanted to hug him up.

"I'm sorry, Kendall. That's so unfair."

"From what Amy says, her cousin Jessica had seen my picture, knew I lived here, and is prone to histrionic reactions like the ones she showed here. The screeching of tires, jumping out of the car, smacking me in the face—"

"Tossing a drink in your face," Steph added.

"Right." He looked at Steph in dead earnest. "I mean, she *really* doesn't like my face."

Steph tried not to burst into laughter, but she did erupt just a little, and Kendall followed suit. Still he nudged her as if she were the only one finding humor in the situation. "You're not supposed to think this is funny."

Steph sobered immediately. "No. It's not funny. You know, my friends tell me Jessica must have known you were a gentleman who wouldn't come after her—wouldn't retaliate—or she probably wouldn't have done what she did."

He frowned. "Your friends?"

"Well, not all of them. Just Christie and Liz. My roommates."

His frown remained. "You told them about this?"

Uh-oh. "Well, I've told them a lot of stuff about you, not just this."

The ensuing silence bothered her. Right on the heels of finding out his ex-fiancée was a big fat liar, and his ex-family-in-law thought he was a cold-hearted Casanova, he finds out his new friend was, essentially, a gossip. But what was a girl to do? She had to be able to converse with her girlfriends, didn't she? Were they to stick strictly to discussions about world events, housekeeping hints, and Bible verses?

Finally he spoke, and to Steph's surprise and utter satisfaction, he struggled not to smile. "So . . . what else have you told them about me?"

Steph grinned and felt her face redden. She looked away from him and watched her feet walking, one step at a time. "I don't know."

He took his hand from his pocket and draped his arm over her shoulders again.

She absolutely adored his doing this—she had

228

come to that conclusion. She appreciated that this was clearly a default position of his with her.

"Come on, now," he teased. "If you've truly told your roommates a lot of stuff about me, surely you can come up with one other thing you've said. What is it?"

The way he turned into their huddle, she didn't have to look far to meet his eyes. Very warm eyes, with definite twinkle at the moment.

"I might have told them . . ."

He squeezed her shoulder. "What?"

"Well, that you're an excellent driver. And you have quite admirable posture."

His hand moved swiftly from her shoulders to her ribs, and he tickled her before she could move away. Both of them laughed and jerked toward and apart from each other in one quick motion.

"*Don't* tickle me!" She was laughing but completely serious. "I hate being tickled. Really, Kendall. Okay?"

He put up his hands, as if she threatened to punch him. "Okay. I promise."

Once they settled down Steph realized she still had a question for him. "So, did Amy come clean with her family? Did you ask her to?"

He sighed. "She said she would. I asked her to at least talk with her psychotic cousin, since she's the one who feels the need to act upon her indignation."

They crossed the street and headed back in the direction of the shop and Steph's car.

"Listen," Kendall said. "There's something else I wanted to discuss with you."

Of course, her heart did that little flip she'd experienced a few times while talking with him. "Okay."

He looked in the direction of the inn, even though it wasn't possible to see it from where they were standing. "I'm not sure if I've mentioned it during the last couple of days, but I'm a little short staffed at the inn. In the restaurant."

Oh. Boring. "I think you mentioned that."

He nodded. "Well, we have a banquet going on late tomorrow afternoon, and since the tea shop is closed on Sundays—"

"You want me to help out?"

He became more animated. "What I'm thinking is that we haven't had much success yet, you and I, in finding somewhere for you to work after Jane returns to the tea shop. And she returns pretty soon, right?"

Steph nodded. "In five days or so."

"So I thought, if you liked working at the inn, you could work there until something more appropriate comes along."

Her grin was unavoidable. He wanted to make sure she didn't have to go back to Maryland. Regardless of his feelings—or lack of them— toward her, this was such a kind gesture she wanted to hug him. Again, she wanted to hug him. She was beginning to suspect she just wanted to find a valid reason to hug the man.

"I don't know anything about working in a restaurant, though."

"But you look perfectly at ease at the tea shop."

"Well, I'm not, really. And I suspect the pace is a little more complicated at the inn. Are you sure you want—"

"I'm sure it will work out just fine. What could go wrong? As I said, we've been shorthanded lately. We've already had trays dropped, orders forgotten—we've even had the till slightly off, thanks to my manager, having to do more than her usual tasks. Marnie asked me to find her a few warm bodies. You're that, at least. I know, because I just tickled you."

She laughed and then pointed at him with as stern an expression as she could muster. "For the last time."

"Yes, for the last time." He lifted his eyebrows. "So? Tomorrow at one?"

She crossed her arms over her chest. He was right. She'd just have to do as she was told. It would mean more money for her and a possible position to depend upon until she could find a job better suited to her talents.

She smiled and gave him a nod. "I'll be there. Thanks, Kendall."

"My pleasure. Now, let's head back. I need to make an appearance this evening or Marnie will be just slightly put out." He placed his hand at the small of Steph's back.

Ah, yes. That was more like it.

TWENTY-SIX

Steph had done well to get up early enough for the first service at Liz and Christie's church the next morning. As Liz had promised, Pastor Henry's sermon rivited and inspired her. She needed to feel divine protection once she entered the fray at Kendall's restaurant.

She was completely right. The pace at the Fox and Hounds was far more hectic, and the work far more complicated, than it had been at the tea shop. Not that she was called upon to whip up tea sandwiches or fruit shortcakes here. She didn't have to worry about baking or cooking at all, and that was a blessing.

But working a banquet was an entirely different challenge. There were so many more employees, for one thing. This was short staffed? She felt she was forever in someone's way and that everyone else knew what they were doing, in stark contrast to her bumbling approach to her tasks. She shuddered to think Kendall could walk in at any moment and catch her looking useless.

Marnie, the restaurant manager, came to the rescue and had her get out of the kitchen to help set up the tables for the upcoming banquet. She could set a table easily enough, as long as she had a model to copy. She needed a little help figuring out how to fold the napkins, which was harder than it sounded.

"We're just using the basic bishop's mitre pattern," Marnie said, right before someone called out to her from the kitchen and she dashed away.

Steph grabbed one of the servers before he could get past her. "Bishop's mitre?"

"What?"

She held up one of the cloth napkins. "How do I do a basic bishop's mitre pattern?" It sounded like a combination of sewing, organized religion, and carpentry.

He set down the empty wine glass crate he held and took the napkin from her. Within seconds he had folded it into the shape of the hat the pope wore. "Like that." He stood it up on the table. "You put it in the center of the plate."

If he had managed to conjure an actual bishop standing under the thing, he couldn't have confused Steph any more than he had.

She frowned. "Ummm, could you do it again, but slow it down to idiot speed?"

"Okay. Watch closely. No, actually, do it along with me."

After showing her slowly how it was done and waiting until she had actually produced an acceptable specimen, he hurried off. Steph found a spot at one of the tables where she could fold to her heart's content without being in anyone's way. By the time a busboy set the plates on the tables, Steph crowned them with her masterpieces. She spent only a moment considering how sad it was that the achievement of napkin folding made her feel so successful.

Within an hour the entire restaurant smelled divine. Whatever masterpiece Jean was creating in there, it was sure to be delicious if it tasted as hearty as it smelled. Banquet guests began to arrive, and Steph graduated to more lofty duties, such as serving baskets of fresh-baked bread and filling water glasses. Kendall had yet to make an appearance, but she was ready for him now. She imagined herself the picture of poise, floating about the room, delivering bread to the tuxedoed masses like a little bakery fairy. Lilting, classical music being piped into the room accompanied what she envisioned as gracefulness of near-balletic proportions. Working for Kendall just might work out after all.

When all of the guests had settled at the tables, and a boisterous, rotund man—apparently the head of the group—had made several announcements and toasts, Marnie enlisted Steph to help distribute salads. This was the point in the evening when Steph finally caught sight of Kendall as he passed among the restaurant employees and guests. He looked as cool as could be. Kendall was in charge of everything going on this evening, but he looked as if there were nowhere he'd rather be than right in the thick of the action.

He did a double take when she met eyes with him, and his friendly smile just made her evening. There was really nowhere she'd rather be at the moment. Then he moved on, doing his ownerly thing. Maybe they would get a chance to chat at evening's end.

It wasn't until the dessert portion of the meal that Steph heard a voice among the banquet guests that leadened her wings just a little. Who was that voice attached to? And why did it bring her down? She looked at the woman but didn't recognize her. An attractive woman who was probably younger than she appeared this evening, her dark hair all caught up in a teased hurricane of formality. Could she be some friend of Steph's parents? She was about that age. But no, that didn't feel right. Surely they would have mentioned knowing someone out here.

Steph was too busy retrieving orange-chocolate mousse from the kitchen to linger and listen more carefully. Besides, it seemed that every guest spoke at once. It was difficult to listen without leaning in more obviously than she could casually do, although she gave it a good effort. Once all the guests had their desserts and coffees, she chose to linger directly behind the woman while surveying the tables, supposedly seeking diners who might need her help in some fashion. Unfortunately, the woman's right-hand neighbor—an older, thin, smoky-voiced matron—monopolized the conversation at that moment.

Marnie spoke from behind Steph, and Steph jumped as if she had been caught holding a glass against a hotel room wall.

"Steph, would you please refresh water glasses for me? I see a few that are nearly empty."

"Oh, sure. Right away."

When Steph came back out of the kitchen, water pitcher in hand, she was pleased to see numerous empty water glasses at that woman's table. The server who taught Steph to fold napkins headed in the same direction, also holding a pitcher.

"No!" Steph didn't yell the word, but the force of her stage whisper caused her coworker to frown at her. She smiled quickly. "I'll get them. I think that table over there needs water too."

He shrugged. "Whatever."

The timing couldn't have been better. Steph began to fill water glasses. The woman was fully animated by whatever she shared with her skinny neighbor, who reacted to what she heard with wide, froggy-looking eyes.

"Honestly, Susan!" Hurricane hair said. "He told her he'd *marry* her. She was one of those lunatic, radical religious types, and our Rick tried to convince us he'd had some 'spiritual awakening.'"

Steph's smile froze on her face, and her wings dropped to the ground with a thud. No.

"His father and I know better. I'm telling you, the boy absolutely worries us to death. If he's religious, I'm Joan of Arc."

In the far recesses of her mind, Steph held the image of orchids snipped to smithereens. She had been in the flower shop destroying centerpieces the last time she heard this voice.

"I think he'd say anything to get . . . well, cooperation from a girl. But I suspect he didn't have to go to such great lengths with this one. I think the sweet, virginal act was just that."

Rick's mother. Steph could have been floating around the ceiling for all the connection she currently felt with what her body was actually doing. Had she been floating around the ceiling, she would have looked down and watched herself lift Mrs. Manfred's water glass from the table right before she poured the entire contents of the pitcher into Mrs. Manfred's mean-spirited, heartless, gossiping lap.

The ensuing panic that erupted included Steph dashing from the room and into the ladies' room, as if escaping herself in some way. She hadn't been drunk since her wild teenage years, but this mental fog reminded her of those days. Completely disoriented, she looked in the mirror and finally realized what she had just done.

"Oh. Oh no." She spoke to her image, and her image just stared back at her, pale and beaded with sweat. She lowered her head.

"Dear Lord, help me, please. What do I do?"

And wouldn't you know, this was one of those times when the Lord answered right away. Steph knew immediately that she had to walk back in there, take responsibility for her actions, and apologize. But, just in case, she lowered her head again, whispering this time.

"You sure, Lord?"

She waited for a different answer, or to come to an understanding that her answer came from her own head, not God's heart.

Nope.

But then she also knew, like a vapor in the midst of her dread, that everything would work out all right. She would suffer some embarrassing consequences, but the right thing was the right thing, and she would ultimately be rewarded.

She just kind of hoped her reward wasn't waiting for her in heaven. She much preferred to get this one here on earth.

She splashed some water on her face, blotted it dry, and walked back into the dining area.

Kendall.

She saw him before anyone else. She nearly started crying. He was trying to calm Rick's mother down. Steph had caused him this problem. Mrs. Manfred was flustered and yelling at him and possibly crying.

"I absolutely *demand* you fire that girl, do you hear me? Otherwise, you will bitterly regret it.

Make no mistake about that! My husband is the senior partner in the firm of Manfred and Chase. You will make this right immediately, do you understand me?"

Kendall nodded. "Yes, I understand. I promise you I'll get to the bottom of this. I'll dismiss whoever did this to you if it was done on purpose."

Steph felt as if she needed a shower, she was so damp with stress. She closed her eyes for a moment, and then she walked toward the fray and cleared her throat. The continued hubbub drowned her out, so she had to raise her voice. "Excuse me?"

Mrs. Manfred and Kendall and everyone else in the room turned to look at her. Mrs. Manfred stretched out a bejeweled arm, pointed her manicured index finger, and assumed the stance of a soap-opera diva from a bad courtroom scene.

"There! That's the one!"

Steph watched Kendall's face. He realized whom he was looking at and closed his eyes in utter dismay. He collected himself swiftly.

Steph's voice could barely break through the chaos, but she gave it a good shot.

"I-I'm so sorry, Mrs. Manfred. I'll pay to have your dress cleaned—"

"What?" Mrs. Manfred couldn't hear above the din. She looked around at Kendall and her companions. "What is she saying?"

The thin, froggy woman spoke up. "Evelyn, I

240

think she said she'd pay your cleaning bill."

Mrs. Manfred erupted in a sardonic laugh. "*Cleaning* bill? You stupid girl! This is one hundred percent dupioni silk. You've probably destroyed this dress with your little stunt, do you realize that? You don't make enough in a year to pay for this dress."

Kendall stepped forward. "Mrs.—Manfred, was it?—the Fox and Hounds will reimburse you the value of your dress." He glanced at Steph with such stress in his expression that she wasn't sure if he felt protective of her or was full of anger.

But she wasn't able to stay and find out. Marnie pulled on her arm.

"Come with me, please. Quickly, now."

Steph looked from Marnie to Kendall one last time. He didn't look back. He was still struggling to reason with Rick's mother. Steph turned and followed the manager into the kitchen.

Marnie handed her a slip of paper. A check. "Here are your wages for your work tonight. I'm sure you understand that we have to let you go, yes?"

Tears sprang to Steph's eyes. Other employees quickly turned away, obviously embarrassed for her. She held the check back toward Marnie.

"I couldn't possibly take this money, Marnie. I'm so sorry for causing this trouble. Please tell Kendall—"

"Kendall leaves these decisions up to me. He has his hands full out there. I'm sure he knows you would take back your actions if you could."

True. What in the world was she thinking, pulling a stunt like that?

Marnie said, "I think it would be a good idea for you to leave before the banquet completely breaks up, don't you? It's best if you go through the lobby rather than going through the restaurant again. Would you like someone to walk you to your car?"

Steph shook her head, unable to speak around the lump in her throat. She reached behind herself and untied her apron, which she handed to Marnie. She set the check on the counter and walked back to the employee storeroom to retrieve her purse. Marnie didn't follow her back, but her surveillance made it clear she didn't plan to move on until Steph had left.

Just as Steph headed for the door to the inn's lobby, Marnie put her hand on her shoulder. "Stephanie, don't be too hard on yourself about this, okay? We all make mistakes."

Well, that just did Steph in. Marnie had said she acted on Kendall's behalf, so her kindness felt as if it had Kendall's sanction. She merely nodded at Marnie and walked into the lobby, her head down. Jimmy called her name as she passed the front desk. She raised a hand and waved in an effort to be polite, but she didn't look at him. She couldn't get to the anonymous space inside her little red Cobalt soon enough.

TWENTY-SEVEN

A re you kidding me?" Christie had her arm around Steph as they sat on the couch back home. "You're beating yourself up over dousing that old biddy with water after she besmirched your honor like that? Man, if that had been me, she would have been lucky if I didn't fire up the crème brûlée torch and set her doopy poopy silk dress on fire."

"Dupioni," Steph muttered. "It is fine silk, and I probably ruined it."

Liz carried a tray of mugs to the coffee table and sat in the chair on Steph's other side. The comforting aroma of hot chocolate surrounded the three women. "Steph, I'm not going to say it was the right thing to do, because I know we're supposed to turn the other cheek and all that. But, honey, I think if you had to get fired from Kendall's restaurant, this was the way to go."

"But I didn't have to get fired. I could have made a different choice."

"Yeah, and if you hadn't been so disoriented, so shocked by who she was, you probably would have," Liz said. "What a horrible woman. Aren't you glad she isn't going to be your mother-in-law?"

That was a good point. "Yes, I am. Of course, she didn't realize who I was. She might not have said those things if she did."

Christie snorted. "Right. She would have waited until you went back to the kitchen before bad-mouthing you. Girl, you have heard her talking you down twice now. How many times has she done that when you haven't heard her? Does the woman have nothing else to talk about?"

"Middleburg isn't all that big." Liz frowned. "It's just so wrong of her to keep slandering you. Eventually her nasty comments are going to be heard by someone who knows you. If she knows your name, sooner or later people will know she's talking about you."

Steph looked at Liz. "Yeah, well, I probably lit a fire under that eventuality, don't you think? There's a very good chance she learned my name tonight, and I'm assuming Rick told his parents my name when he said he planned to marry me." She blew out a frustrated little breath. "Anyway, what are people getting to know about me? I choke defenseless dogs and destroy expensive floral arrangements. And now I assault society matrons in fine restaurants. I've caused Kendall all sorts of trouble."

"Aw, he's a big boy." Christie squeezed Steph's shoulder. "I'm sure he's experienced worse."

"Not at my hands, he hasn't." Steph grabbed yet another tissue and blotted her nose. "Some friend I turned out to be. I'm so embarrassed. And here I fussed about that weirdo redhead throwing her drink in his face. Who's the weirdo now? And he doesn't even know why I did it."

"Hmm," Liz said.

Steph looked over at her. "What?"

"This will be very interesting. Kendall has no idea what might have prompted you to do something like that. But of all the people you've met here in town over the past two weeks, he's come to know you pretty well, hasn't he?"

Steph shrugged. "I suppose so."

Liz nodded. "It will be enlightening to see how he handles this. He just fired you, yes, but he pretty much had to. Now will he, as your friend, try to find out what this was all about?"

Steph sighed. "I certainly didn't do this to test Kendall's worth as a friend."

"No, you didn't." Christie gave her a rueful smile. "Still, his worth as a friend is going to come into play, regardless. Let's see how deep Mr. Cutie Pants wants to take your friendship."

"I don't know if that's fair." Steph pressed her fingertips under her sore eyes. "He's innocent in this. It seems like my responsibility to contact him and explain myself."

Liz leaned forward and dropped mini marsh-mallows into the mugs. "Yeah, you're probably right, but give it some time. You're all defensive right now, and he's . . . well, what do you think he is? Do you think he's mad at you?"

"I have no idea. I'm sure he's confused, at least." She shook her head, trying to rid herself of her own uncertainty about what to do next. "Who knows? This probably isn't a very good moment for me to make decisions. I need to do like you said, Liz, and wait a while. A couple of days. You see? This is why I'm not a naturally impulsive person. I stink at impulse."

"How do you figure that?" Christie took up two mugs and handed one to Steph. "I mean, apart from your trying to melt the Wicked Witch of the West tonight, what other impulsive things have gone wrong?"

Steph held out her free hand, suddenly animated. "I'm here, in Middleburg, thanks to a terrible impulse. I clearly didn't give enough thought to the whole elopement idea."

Liz smiled in sympathy. "Yeah, that was a mess, but God brought some good out of that. If you hadn't acted on that impulse, we would never have met you. And you would still be selling men's suits at that department store—"

"Which you said you really didn't enjoy," Christie added.

"And," Liz continued, "you wouldn't have met Milly."

"Or Kendall, for that matter." Christie grimaced slightly, as if maybe she shouldn't have mentioned that one.

Steph couldn't help a little smile at Christie's expression.

"And you respectfully faced down your parents in the aftermath," Liz said. "Your decisions have been other than what they wanted, yeah, but it was probably good that you were forced to stand your ground. You're twenty-five, right? You needed to shake things up a little, I think."

"I didn't need to do it impulsively, though." Steph took a tentative sip of her hot chocolate. Still too hot. She set it back on the table.

Christie shrugged. "Maybe you did."

Both Liz and Steph looked at her.

"What do you mean?" Steph asked.

Christie took a gulp of her hot chocolate and struggled with the heat of it before swallowing it down. "Mercy, that's hot! Maybe you do things on impulse when you're afraid you won't do them otherwise. If you think about them too much, you might talk yourself out of doing them. And you *want* to do them."

Steph stared at the bowl of marshmallows on the tray before her. Was Christie right? Is that what she was doing when she acted impulsively? "Gosh, that sounds so irresponsible. Like people who booze it up and then do or say inappropriate things they always wanted to, claiming later they were just drunk."

"I don't know that it's irresponsible." Liz pulled her legs up to sit cross-legged. "But I think there's a chance you don't trust your judgment all that much."

Steph said, "You think right. It's been difficult to get a decision in edgewise with my mom and dad. I'm kind of inexperienced."

"Only one way to get experienced." Christie lifted her eyebrows.

"Yep," Steph said. "As Nike says: Just Do It."

Liz laughed. "Maybe a prayer or two beforehand and *then* just do it. I'll bet you've made plenty of well-thought-out decisions you don't give yourself credit for."

"Honestly, though," Christie said. "There's something to be said for spontaneity. It does have its place." She picked up a handful of marshmallows and brought them to her mouth.

"Yeah." Steph sighed. "I guess my one good impulse was kissing Kendall. Or, rather, he kissed me. But I did kiss him back. If I thought too much before that one—"

Both Liz and Christie sat stock still, staring at her. Marshmallows protruded from Christie's lips, save the two that silently tumbled into her lap.

Liz broke into a huge grin. "You did not tell us about that, young lady."

"Didn't I? Are you sure?"

Christie frantically finished her mouthful, grunting a noise as if she feared she would miss something, even though no one was going anywhere. She made Steph laugh.

"Christie, you have marshmallow powder all over your chin."

Christie grabbed a napkin but talked while she dusted off the powder. "When did this happen? I can't believe you didn't mention it."

Liz gave Steph a little shove. "Come on. There's no way you accidentally didn't tell us. You had to be thrilled. Why didn't you say anything?"

"It's so soon after what happened with Rick. I'll admit I'm attracted to Kendall, but . . ." She sighed again, exasperated. "To tell you the truth, I didn't want you two influencing me."

Two mouths dropped open at once. Four eyes sent shock in her direction. She had to laugh, but she didn't get a chance to speak.

"Us?" Liz looked at Christie—obviously to ensure they were both equally affronted—and then faced Steph again. "Influence you? Why would you think we'd try to influence you?"

"And why wouldn't you want us to?" Christie said. "We're absolute pillars of romantic wisdom!"

Steph laughed again. "Come on. You two aren't exactly impartial. I can't imagine either of you doing anything but encouraging me to storm straight ahead with Mr. Cutie Pants. I need to have a clearer head about him. And look at you." She gestured toward Christie. "You're practically foaming at the mouth over the idea that we kissed."

Christie wiped at her chin again and mocked

wounded pride. "That's marshmallow powder, I'll have you know."

"But . . . but . . ." Liz opened her mouth to argue but chuckled instead. "Okay, you're probably right. We forgive you for holding out." She looked at her sister. "Don't we, Christie?"

Christie picked up the two stray marshmallows from her lap, popped them into her mouth, and sniffed. "Maybe later. We'll see how well you present yourself from here on out."

"It doesn't matter now, anyway." Steph picked up her mug and sat back against the couch, her hands cradling the warmth. "Today I blew the chance of our friendship becoming anything more than that. I'll be lucky if he's even willing to just be friends after he gets the bill for that dress." She sighed. "And the whole kissing thing will probably never happen again."

As she had earlier in their talk, Christie leaned over and put her arm around Steph's shoulders. "Never say never, Stephanie." She cocked her head toward Liz to include her. "We may not be impartial, and we may not be subtle, but when it comes to you and Kendall James, we are ever hopeful."

Liz lifted her mug in a salute to Steph, who smiled in resignation, clinked mugs with both women, and drank the warm chocolate all the way down.

TWENTY-EIGHT

The tea shop buzzed with activity the next morning. Soothing music flowed from Milly's CD player, but the *William Tell Overture* might have been more fitting.

"Unusual for a Monday!" Milly said as she and Steph passed each other with trays full of teapots and pastries.

Steph considered it a blessing to have so many customers to serve. The distraction helped the hours to pass quickly, and she had little time available to think about her behavior of the day before. But because Middleburg was a small town, she couldn't shake the feeling that a customer or two today might have witnessed her bit of melodrama yesterday.

Additionally, while Milly never delved into Steph's business the way Christie and Liz did, she had clearly enjoyed seeing Steph as happy as she had been the last couple of days. If the shop weren't so busy, Milly might have time to notice the spring in Steph's step had sprung and landed in a dull clunk on the ground. As it was, neither one of them spent enough time with the other to carry on much of a conversation.

Business slowed down in the early afternoon, and

Steph grew nervous that Milly might ask how the banquet went. But what Milly said when she finally stopped to have her own cup of tea and chat for moment nearly brought on a panic attack for Steph.

"Didn't you have plans today to meet young Chip at the library?" Milly ran her finger across the calendar posted next to the refrigerator. "I thought your tutoring sessions were—"

"Oh, for crying out loud!" Steph ripped off her apron and ran to the sink to wash her hands. "I completely forgot about Chip. Milly, can you spare me for an hour, do you think?"

"Certainly. I can spare you for two. I didn't plan for you to be here because of the tutoring. And you can see how much slower the afternoon is shaping up."

Steph grabbed her purse and gave Milly a quick hug. "You're the best. I'll be back."

Milly's laugh was full of fondness and a gentle lilt. "Take your time, dear."

Chip arrived at the door to the library at the same time Steph did. He laughed when he saw her.

"Why are you breathing so hard?"

She fanned at her face with her hand, which accomplished absolutely nothing. "Wow. I need to get back to the gym." She patted the moisture from her forehead with the back of her hand. Even if the day weren't sunny, it would have felt so to her. "I almost forgot about you, dude."

He shrugged. "No problem. Anytime that happens, I'll give you a call. Or you can call me if you can't make it. What's your number?" He pulled a cell phone from his backpack, and they exchanged numbers.

Steph smiled to herself as he punched his contact information into her phone for her. He was a take-charge type, just like his brother.

The thought of Kendall hurt, a thornlike reminder of Kendall's obvious disappointment when he saw she was the troublemaker in the midst of his employees.

They walked in and found an empty table in a far corner. Chip sat and sprawled in teenage boy fashion, as if he were trying to claim as much territory as possible.

Steph glanced at his leg. "Hey, you're wearing a different one today." She almost gasped the moment the words came out. Why had she spoken so bluntly?

He looked at his leg as if he hadn't noticed it before now. "Yeah, I had on the Cheetah leg when I met you 'cause of my Ultimate Frisbee game with my friends after."

"Cheetah?"

"Sprinting legs, yeah. But I normally wear this one if I'm not doing sports or running or stuff. This one's more comfortable. Looks more natural too."

She didn't know why, but her throat suddenly closed tight with the swelling that happens right before crying. And then she had to fight tears.

Chip pulled his textbook out from his backpack and frowned when he looked at her. "You all right?"

This situation—his leg—would never get better. Of course it wouldn't. She had known that.

"Yeah. Fine." She laughed softly and leaned forward, trying to focus on his book. But she couldn't help looking at him as he flipped pages in his binder. She could see what he must have looked like as a one-year-old, prior to his surgery.

What was wrong with her? Was this a hormonal thing?

"Okay, here we are." Chip laid the binder flat on the table and looked up. "Hey, are you crying?" He stared at her now, a worried tilt to his head.

She wasn't crying, really. Only one or two tears had escaped. She wiped them away with a broad stroke of her hand. "I'm not. I'm fine. Show me what you're working on. What's giving you trouble?"

Chip hesitated and continued to meet her eyes. She forced herself to look right back, a smile plastered on. She watched something happen—a realization on Chip's part, and his brown eyes warmed up, just as Kendall's had in the past. He leaned forward, across the table. He lifted his eyebrows. "I'm okay, you know."

The kid was too smart. "Sure. I know that."

"Hi, Chip." Two girls' voices chimed together as they passed the table. They were both adorable, slim, and working the eyelashes to beat the band.

Steph saw Chip turn from her and watch the girls. He raised his hand and gave them a broad white smile. "Hey, guys. Courtney, I owe you three dollars."

The girl spoke over her shoulder, a little coquette. "I'll trust you for it."

Her friend giggled.

Chip turned back to Steph. When she grinned at him, he shrugged, embarrassed.

He really *was* all right. She felt relieved and blessed to have seen that brief exchange. Kendall had told her Chip and everyone who knew him were jaded about his leg. She needed to forget about the little boy of the past and focus on the confident young man of the present.

"Okay, here's one I need help with. This one about the tree. I'm supposed to figure out how much support wire would be needed without knowing the tree's height. I know it's surrounded by seven-foot support posts—"

"Right, I see that," Steph said. "Each is fifteen feet from the tree."

They discussed the remainder of the problem, all of the given information, the various equations, derivatives, and substitutions. Steph guided Chip in every step of the problem when he needed it. She loved watching the confusion melt away from his features. She couldn't believe how much fun she had with him.

Evidently, the feeling was mutual. After they went over several problems, Chip raved. "You make it so much clearer than my teacher does! You should be a teacher."

She laughed. "Ugh, no. I could never handle a whole classroom full of kids." She thought about the rush of the restaurant yesterday. Yes, she had created her own catastrophe there, but even before that, she hadn't felt quite at home with so many people depending upon her at once. At least, that was how it felt. "I don't think I do crowds very well."

Chip's attention moved beyond her. "There's my mom."

Steph's stomach flipped. Did Mrs. James know what she had done at the Fox and Hounds yesterday? Obviously Chip didn't know. She assumed he would have teased her about it. But would Kendall have mentioned it to his mother?

"Am I too early?" Mrs. James stopped and smiled at both of them. Not only did she look at ease—dressed in elegant but casual pants and a fine-knit top—but she seemed happy to see Steph. Kendall had apparently kept yesterday's incident to himself.

Another woman caught up to them. It seemed she had arrived with Mrs. James but found something to delay her. She had a scattered way about her. "There you are, Silvie. Hi, Chip, honey. Silvie, is this the young lady you told me about?" She smiled at Steph and extended her hand. "Kitty Henderson."

Steph was touched by her friendliness, and by the fact that Mrs. James had discussed her with a friend, apparently in a positive way. "Hi. Steph Vandergrift." They shook hands.

"Kitty's daughter is struggling with algebra," Mrs. James said.

Kitty nodded. "Yes, really struggling. Do you do algebra?"

"Do it?"

Chip spoke up. "Tutor it."

"Oh." Steph sat up straight. "Well, I—"

"She's an awesome tutor," Chip said. He packed his books away as he spoke. "Hannah will love her."

"Fabulous!" Kitty clenched her tiny hands and looked to the skies before addressing Steph again. "You charge by the hour, then?"

Steph wasn't sure what to say. She was just thrilled to have another paying gig, especially since she was so close to losing her job at Milly's shop. Should she ask for forty dollars? Yes, that's what Mrs. James paid, but was that exorbitant? "Uh, yes. I charge—"

"Fifty per hour," Mrs. James said. "And she's worth every penny of it, believe me."

Steph knew her eyes flashed for a moment

before she looked at Mrs. James. There was no mistaking the wink Mrs. James gave her. Steph almost laughed, but she collected herself quickly.

"That's great." Kitty put her hand on Steph's shoulder. "How soon can I have Hannah meet with you? I'll bring her here, or to your place, or wherever. You can even come to our house if you want."

And just like that, Steph had a second tutoring position. Tutoring alone wouldn't support her, but it would help.

After Kitty left Mrs. James spoke softly. "Kitty is a dear, and her daughter Hannah is a sweet girl, but I happen to know they pay more than forty dollars an hour to have that awful dog of theirs—Hildie— walked every day. What you're going to do for Hannah is worth far more than dog walking. And trust me, Kitty can afford it."

"Thank you so—" Steph frowned. "Hildie. Is that a Yorkshire Terrier?"

"Yeah." Chip slung his bookbag over his shoulder. "Yaps constantly."

Goodness. That was the dog Steph nearly choked to death at the groomer's. Good thing dogs couldn't talk.

"Yes, you were wise to schedule to tutor Hannah here, away from the constant barking." Mrs. James grinned and put her arm on Chip's back to encourage him to go. "We'll see you back here Wednesday."

The landing of that second tutoring job nearly brought the spring back to Steph's step by the time she returned to the tea shop. She still carried concern about Kendall, despite the fact he hadn't complained about her to his family, but she wanted very much to celebrate her new student with Milly. Milly could always be counted on for a hip-hip-hooray.

So Steph neared the shop aware of the smile she wore. And she felt it drop—along with her shoulders, brows, and mood—a moment later, when she saw who awaited her outside the tea shop's door.

TWENTY-NINE

Steph didn't have time to pray—Rick stood right there. The best she could get out was, *Please, God.* She had to trust Him to figure out the rest. In the meantime she would have to make her best effort at behaving like a decent Christian girl. So she said nothing and walked past him as if he didn't exist.

"Hi, Steph." He spoke in a gentle, humble-sounding voice, probably as close as possible to the right approach—if the right approach actually existed. But it didn't, so she turned on him as angrily as if he had boldly insulted her.

" 'Hi,' Rick? Really? *Hi?*"

He hadn't shaved, apparently, in the two weeks he'd been gone. With his thin, fine-haired growth, he looked like a catfish. A jilting, spoiled, rich, mama's-boy catfish. At least that was the opinion of this particularly decent Christian girl.

"I'm sorry," he said. "I'm not sure how else to—"

"You've had two weeks to get your opening statement together, buddy, so don't give me your weak little excuses." She planted her hand on her hip. "As a matter of fact, don't give me anything.

Just stay away from me and let me get back to work."

He took a step forward and lightly lifted his hand in an effort to slow her departure. "Milly said she was fine with your taking the afternoon off to talk with me."

"You talked to Milly about this?"

"Well, I introduced myself and told her I wanted to talk with you—"

"Yeah, well, this isn't between you and Milly, so don't try to drag her into it."

"I wasn't trying to drag her into it. I just heard you were working here and came to find you."

"Who told you I worked here?"

"The Fox and Hounds. I went there because I figured you probably stayed there right after—"

Her pulse quickened. "Who did you talk to at the Fox and Hounds?"

"The guy at the front desk."

"Which one?"

"Man, I don't know. What does it matter—"

"Which one!"

"Skinny guy, okay? Red hair."

Ah. Jimmy, not Kendall. As if it mattered. At this point Kendall probably would have paid Rick's cab fare to come whisk her out of his life.

"What do you want, Rick? What are you doing here?"

He ran his hand through his hair. She knew that gesture. It was his nervous, let-me-get-my-argument-together move. "Steph, I made a horrible mistake. I want to ask you to give me another chance."

She shook her head. "No. You didn't make a horrible mistake. You made a decision. A horrible mistake would have been if I had actually married a man who encouraged me to leave my family, my friends, my job, and my home only to desert me in a place I didn't know."

He looked at his shoes, and she continued.

"With *no* explanation, Rick! No word at all, other than your cowardly leave-of-absence message with the receptionist at your daddy's law firm."

"You're right. It was cowardly. I've never been so ashamed of myself in my life. For two weeks I've struggled with how wrong it was to run."

She squinted at him. "Where did you get the suntan?"

"What?"

"Where did you do your 'struggling'? Where did Daddy and Mommy send you?"

She saw the pain cross his face. He obviously didn't want to tell her. "The Bahamas."

She knew her face looked like a crazy woman's, but she couldn't help it. "You . . . you went on our honeymoon, didn't you? The one you said you couldn't *possibly* take and still keep your job with the law firm. Your parents sent you on a honeymoon as a reward for dumping the unacceptable bride!"

"Look, it wasn't a honeymoon, and I wasn't there having a good time without you. I spent the entire time trying to man up. And I came to the realization that I wanted you more than my parents' approval. More than my career at my father's firm. I might have done my soul-searching while sitting on the beach, but it was soul-searching, nonetheless."

That was the first comment he made that stopped her.

Her silence seemed to encourage him, so he sallied forth. "How did you figure out what the problem was, anyway? How did you know my parents insisted that I leave?"

Oops. "Huh?" She wanted to think this one through before saying anything about it.

"You said my parents thought you were an unacceptable bride. They were wrong, but you're right. That's what they thought. How did you know that?"

Well, this told her quite a lot. Apparently his mother hadn't figured out the crazy serving girl yesterday was her son's ex-fiancée reacting to the evil things said about her to the froggy-eyed lady. Or maybe she had figured it out, but Rick hadn't talked with her yet. His mother was such a blatherer that she surely would have told him his ex-fiancée was an aggressive lunatic if she had the slightest knowledge and chance.

"You don't get to ask the questions here, all

right? You gave up that privilege when you flew off to the sunny Bahamas to 'man up.' "

He sighed and then nodded. "Fair enough."

Fair enough? She didn't want him to be reasonable. She wanted him to be the wimpy jilter she had comfortably come to loathe. This deferential Rick was difficult to hate. He didn't even look quite as catfishy as when she first saw him. This was not good.

"Steph, will you at least talk with me about what happened?"

She sniffed. "I think that's what we're doing, isn't it?"

He shook his head. "No, I mean in a better environment. Not out here on the sidewalk. Let me take you to dinner or something."

"No."

He didn't even argue. He looked as if he was about to, but then his face sank before he managed to look down, away from her view. He spoke quietly. "Please." He sounded so desperate. She'd never heard him like this. Is this how he sounded when he faced his parents? Were they actually able to make demands of him when he sounded like a five-year-old boy?

"I can't talk with you right now, Rick. I'm sorry. I'm too angry."

He looked up, plaintive. "When, then?"

"I don't know." She sighed.

"Can I call you tomorrow?"

She couldn't help one more dig. "Oh, you do have my cell phone number, do you?"

His shoulders drooped, but he didn't give up. She'd never seen him so contrite. "Tomorrow? Please?"

She didn't know what to do. She sighed again and opened the tea shop door. "I don't know. Fine." And she turned her back on him, walked into the shop, and closed the door.

Two tables in the shop were occupied, although one group made motions to leave. Milly walked out of the kitchen, a solicitous smile on her face for the customers. She saw Steph at the door and tilted her head as if Steph were a little girl who had just taken a fall.

Steph gave Milly a little wave, walked back to the kitchen, and donned an apron. By the time she walked back out, the one table of customers had left, so she set about clearing their dishes.

Milly approached her and spoke softly. "Everything all right, dear?"

Steph sighed. "I'm sorry he came here, Milly. He shouldn't have bothered you."

"No bother. He seemed rather distraught."

"Yeah, well, it's his turn, I guess."

She couldn't read Milly's expression. She suddenly realized she wanted to know what Milly thought about Rick. "Did he try to charm you?"

"Charm me?" Milly pushed her lips out as she considered. "I couldn't say. I don't know him, and we didn't talk long. I don't know if I met a charming version of the man who let you down a few weeks ago or the chastened version of a man who realizes his mistake."

Steph frowned. "Well, so what if he realizes his mistake? Does that mean I should take him back?"

"Certainly not. I would think these last two weeks have shown you that you don't have to make rash decisions. Especially not with regard to romantic relationships."

Relationships. Plural. That was right. Milly didn't know what a mess Steph had made of her friendship—or whatever it was—with Kendall. Milly loved Kendall. She would clearly root for him in a relationship competition, if that's how she saw the current circumstances. Maybe she should let Milly know Kendall was unlikely to want his horse in this race.

"Excuse me for a moment, Steph."

Milly tended to the last customers, who were ready to leave. Nearly closing time. A fat lot of good Steph had contributed this afternoon, standing around sulking. She marched back to the kitchen and started washing dishes.

Every time she thought she was making headway here in Middleburg, something seemed to tangle everything up.

First, she had been encouraged by Kendall's willingness to share his business contacts with her, but none of that had panned out well so far. Here it was, Monday evening, three days from Jane's return to the shop, and Steph was no closer to finding an employer than before she and Kendall started their "tours." Of course, her incompetence had been the main reason for entanglement in that area.

Second, she had allowed her employment hopes to rise because of Kendall's idea that she might work at the Fox and Hounds. Her impulsive anger had been the reason for entanglement there.

Third, her friendship with Kendall had been one of her favorite developments since Rick ditched her here. And the infatuation part of it was great fun. Maybe even promising. His mother didn't yet consider her horrible, as Rick's mother did. Still, Steph's temper yesterday had poured cold water on all of that too.

Fourth, despite the consequences of her incompetence and anger, she had been hopeful about the fact that she was moving on. She had been determined to land on her own two feet, prove her capability to her parents, and get over the hurt Rick had inflicted, even if she might have lost Kendall's support and friendship. She was getting beyond the recent past. And then who should choose to show up?

She sighed. Maybe God allowed her to destroy her relationship with Kendall so she could make a clear decision about Rick when he returned to town. So her behavior toward Rick would stand on its own, not on whatever development she might have envisioned with Kendall.

Oh! God. Finally she thought of God. Why did it always take her so long to turn to Him when confusion set in?

She picked up a towel and dried teapots while she prayed.

Lord, I need so much guidance from You, I don't even know how to word my prayer. Were You, by any chance, listening in just now while my mind tried to catalog my failings? All that, Lord. All that stuff is where I need help. And I need help in noticing when You're helping, so that would also be much appreciated. Amen.

She heard animated voices in the dining area, so she pushed the kitchen door open with her foot, a teapot still in hand.

Christie and Liz were the vocal ones—Christie in particular. The last customers were walking out the front door, obviously laughing with Christie over whatever she had said.

"What's all the racket about?" Steph walked out, eager for something laughable. She could count on that with Liz and Christie. The last thing she wanted to think about at the moment was love and romantic relations.

"Congratulate me," Christie said. She looked more girlie than Steph had ever seen her. "I'm engaged!"

THIRTY

O kay, this could work as a distraction too. As Christie, Liz, and Steph drove west of Middleburg to the Hunter's Head Tavern to have a celebratory dinner, all the talk centered on Christie and her new fiancé, Brant. Yes, the conversation was about romance and marriage, but at least it wasn't about Steph's lack of either one. Distraction was still possible.

They had tried to get Milly to join them for dinner.

"Come on, Milly." Christie hugged her. "The pub grub will be a happy reminder of England for you."

Milly hugged Christie back. "Ah, you're a dear to want to include me. But no, you girls go on. I have plans for tonight, and they include a good novel and a warm tub. Been looking forward to them all day." Still, before they left, Milly took Christie's face in her hands and got tears in her eyes. "I am *so* happy for you and Brant. You're a lovely couple. You have a dear man, there."

Christie nodded. "Yep."

And then the three young women were off to the tavern for beef stew and shepherd's pie.

"But you can't have been completely surprised, Christie." Steph sat as far forward in the car as she could without removing her seat belt. She wasn't snapped in merely because it was the law. She had serious concern for her own safety. Liz was an insane driver.

Christie turned around from the passenger's seat, her face radiant. "Yeah, overall I suppose I expected it, eventually. But he caught me off guard, the crafty little sneak. He called me at work, and he knows not to do that unless it's an emergency. I was about to give a riding lesson to a new client—a timid, uptight woman—so I acted sort of testy about needing to get off the phone. Especially when he said he was calling because he couldn't remember what my favorite color was."

Both Steph and Liz laughed.

"Then he called me two more times during the lesson with equally stupid questions. I was so annoyed I didn't answer the third time, but even so my client dismounted and stormed off in a huff over all the interruptions."

Liz said, "What Christie didn't realize—"

"Tut-tut-tut!" Christie shut Liz right up. "Don't you dare steal my punch line, girl! And watch where you're going!"

Liz gasped. "Sorry!" As she swerved the car off the shoulder and back into her lane, Steph wiped perspiration from her forehead. One more close call like that, and Steph would go ahead and release the shriek of panic she kept suppressing out of politeness.

"What I didn't realize," Christie said, "was that my so-called client was in on the whole thing. She works with Brant. And he was calling me from the other side of the barn. So when I ran after my client to try to make amends, there he was, waiting for me. With a ring. In a blue velvet box. My favorite color."

Steph fell back against the seat. "Oh, Christie, how romantic. I love that he made the effort to surprise you."

Liz pulled into the parking lot at the tavern, an eighteenth-century stone-and-stucco building surrounded by sturdy oaks and maples. "That shows what a great guy he is. He had to know his chances were pretty good even if he proposed in a completely unimaginative way."

As Rick had done. One afternoon, out of the blue, with no preamble. *Hey, let's elope. What do you say?* It was her own doggoned fault for accepting a proposal made with all the preparation of a decision to go to the local cineplex.

Liz continued. "But Brant went the extra mile— enlisting that coworker's help and having her set up the bogus lesson just so he and Christie would have this memory forever. So it would be special for Christie." She smiled at her sister before opening the car door. "I officially approve of Brant as my new brother."

Before Christie responded she cast a sly eye in Steph's direction. Steph didn't understand her intent until they stepped out of the car and Christie spoke to Liz.

"And who knows? Maybe I'll officially approve of Andrew as *my* new brother in the future."

Andrew?

Liz laughed. "Please. Let's not jump the gun."

They walked up the redbrick walkway and past the property's thick stone wall. Liz held the pub door open for Steph.

"Who's Andrew?"

"You know," Liz said. "That guy who's been hovering for the past—"

"Wait a second, Liz." Christie grabbed the shoulder of each of the other women and spoke to Steph. "Are you telling me she hasn't mentioned him the entire time you have been living with us?"

Steph said, "It's only been a little over a week. But no." She looked at Liz. "You've never mentioned him. What's up?"

She saw a twinkle in Liz's eyes, a toned-down version of what she saw in Christie's. Was Steph the only one not striking pay dirt in the romance department today?

A young woman wearing a peasant blouse and velvet vest tucked an empty tray to her side and approached them. "Welcome to Hunter's Head. Just the three of you?"

"Right." Christie crooked her thumb toward the two blackboards on the wall beside them. "But we haven't decided what we want yet."

Steph knew what she wanted. She wanted more clarity and success with regard to the men in her life.

Her stomach growled. All right. Maybe clarity, success, and chicken pot pie.

The server pointed to a rectangular table at one corner of the room. "There you go, by the fireplace. You can sit over there. Whenever you know what you want, just let them know up there at the window, and we'll bring it to you."

"Mmm." Liz eyed the desserts displayed on the table below the blackboards. "I'm saving room for the chocolate-chocolate cake."

Steph said, "You know, for a health store owner, you sure do have a sweet tooth!" After she said it, she thought she might have sounded a bit snarky. Maybe jealousy was casting a shadow over her behavior tonight.

But Liz didn't seem to think so. She laughed easily. "It's my curse, all right. One of the reasons I learned so much about health food was because of battling sugar cravings. But I don't really indulge them all that often. I guess your presence brings out the sweet in me."

Christie shook her head and looked at Steph, still acting as if she and Steph were teasing Liz together. "Naw. It's Andrew."

"Who is Andrew?" Okay, that time she definitely sounded more irritated than she meant to. She frowned and spoke before either Liz or Christie could. "I'm sorry. That sounded so rude."

"You know what?" Liz said. "I hate it when people carry on inside-info conversations without filling me in. I'm sorry, Steph. Andrew's just a guy I've had my eye on for some time. Nothing serious. He does medical missions trips and hasn't been around for a while. Today he stopped by the store and asked me to have coffee with him tomorrow."

For a brief moment Steph worried that Andrew was actually Rick, masquerading as a missionary to win Liz's heart. "He didn't look like a catfish, did he?"

That brought the chat to an abrupt halt. Liz and Christie stared at Steph, and then she saw both of them mentally leave her while they searched their memories for some kind of connection to the current conversation.

She shook her head and her hands in a quick effort to erase what she had just thrown out there. "Ignore me. I'm not thinking straight. I'm hungry and thinking like a nutcase."

"Then this should be an entertaining dinner," Christie said. "Come on, let's place our orders and sit."

Still, Liz smiled at Steph with such confused amusement in her eyes, Steph knew she'd have to explain herself eventually. She was glad their conversation turned to food while they studied the menus.

After they had ordered, Steph slid into their booth seat against the rustic log cabin wall. Liz joined her and left the other side of the table for Christie.

"I love the atmosphere of this place." Steph ran her hand along the log wall. "All the wood and stone and stucco. I've never been to England, but this is how I picture country pubs. How old do you think this building is?"

"Mid to late seventeen hundreds," Liz said. "At least this part of it. Lots of the buildings in Middleburg are this old. Cool, huh?"

"Wow. Very cool." Steph sighed. She experienced a quickening of her pulse—a moment's elation over the idea of making her home here. It was followed by a twinge of sadness and unease about the idea of crossing paths with either Kendall or Rick.

"Whoa." Christie waved her hand before Steph's eyes. "Where did you just go? Are you all right?"

"Are you still upset about what happened yesterday at Kendall's inn?" Liz turned to give Steph her full attention.

"No. Well, yes, but there's something else. Something happened today."

Christie said, "Did you go after Rick's mom with the garden hose?"

"Rick's back in town."

Both Christie and Liz raised their eyebrows.

Still wide eyed, Liz said, "Did you run into him?"

A playful malevolence colored Christie's addition. "With your car?"

Liz smacked at her. "Stop. What happened, Steph?"

"He found out I worked at Milly's, and he came to apologize."

"Oh." Liz shrugged. "Well, good. He should have. He should grovel for forgiveness. But it was probably hard for you to see him again, right?"

"Hang on." Christie watched Steph for a moment.

Steph didn't want to think about why she was starting to perspire. The server brought water to their table, which was the perfect reason for Steph to look away, but Christie wasn't deterred.

"Steph? He didn't just apologize and leave, did he?"

For goodness' sakes, she was like a bloodhound.

Liz looked from Christie to Steph, and then she gasped. "Oh no, Steph! You didn't take him back, did you?"

"No!" She pressed both of her hands on the table. "I definitely did not."

Now Christie tilted her head, and Steph cringed at the soft flash of pity in her eyes. "But you didn't definitely send him on his way, did you."

Steph ran her hand through her hair before realizing she had probably picked up that mannerism from Rick. She also wanted to get her argument together, even though she knew she didn't really have to argue about this.

"Yes, actually, I did send him on his way. But . . . he was so contrite, and he wants to explain himself more fully."

She saw Christie roll her eyes.

"I'm not saying he isn't still a mess." Steph straightened her silverware, napkin, and water glass. "But he seems to think he's learned a lot. He wants to stand up to his parents. I feel that I should at least—"

"So let him stand up to his parents," Christie said. "He shouldn't need your help for that. You have your own parents to stand up to."

"Respectfully, of course," Liz said.

"Yeah, I know." Steph felt a touch of déjà vu, sitting here getting defensive with girlfriends who felt she should stay away from Rick. But this was different. She wasn't considering running off with him. She wanted to stay put here in Middleburg and would just as soon he moved away. And she wasn't going to elope with him. But she didn't have to be—

"I don't have to be completely cruel to him, though, do I? I mean, I'm a Christian. I have to be able to live with my actions. To be able to sleep at night. He just wants me to understand and forgive him." She knew Rick wanted more than that, but he wasn't going to get it, so why bother mentioning it now?

Liz sighed. "He'll probably ask for more than understanding and forgiveness."

Steph said nothing. These two were formidable.

The server brought bread and their drinks to the table.

"So what's the plan?" Christie took a drink of soda and sat back. "How did you leave the conversation?"

Steph shrugged. "I told him I needed to get to work, he asked if he could call to talk with me tomorrow, and I said fine." She broke off a piece of bread. "Believe me, I'm not interested in renewing my romance with Rick Manfred."

Liz nodded. "Good to hear."

"Yeah. It would be good for Rick Manfred to hear that from you too." Christie also broke off a piece of bread. Steph caught sight of her beautiful engagement ring. Christie had done everything right with Brant. In addition to the friendship and love she built with him, she had clearly set some healthy boundaries. And she seemed so wonderfully honest with him about them. So Steph gave serious merit to Christie's next comment.

"Just keep telling yourself that 'Christian' doesn't mean 'doormat.' You don't owe that boy a thing."

THIRTY-ONE

The next day Steph used a lull at the shop to flip through the help wanted ads in the local newspaper. She sat at the table closest to the kitchen so she could hop up undetected if the front door opened.

"Any interesting news in there?" Milly walked out of the kitchen with a teapot and cups for Steph and herself.

"I'm afraid not." Steph pinched the bridge of her nose. "Milly, what am I going to do? Only two more days before Jane arrives."

"What happened to your efforts with Kendall?"

Steph sat up straight. "My efforts?"

"To find employment with one of his business acquaintances." Milly glanced at the front door as if expecting Kendall to appear. "Now that I think of it, what's become of him? You haven't mentioned him at all since Saturday. How did the banquet go? I hoped there was a chance you might find something permanent at the Fox and Hounds."

Steph knew Milly meant permanent employment, as opposed to a permanent personal relationship, but either intent stung in its improbability.

She sighed. "I'm not proud of how I handled

the banquet, Milly, so I've deliberately avoided discussing it with you."

Milly sipped her tea and smiled. "I'm flattered that my opinion means that much to you, dear, but it will take some fairly shocking details for you to fall out of grace with me."

Another sigh. "All right then. Prepare to be shocked." Then Steph told Milly everything—from recognizing the voice of Rick's mother from her day at the florist's shop to eavesdropping enough to get clobbered by Mrs. Manfred's insults and then drowning her indignation, job chances, and relationship with Kendall with two liters of ice water.

Milly's voice was gentle as a sigh. "Oh, I see." Then she raised her eyebrows and cocked her head. "I can't honestly say I wouldn't have made the same decision you did, to tell you the truth."

"No, you wouldn't have, Milly. You and I both know that. Everyone knows how classy and dignified you are. I feel so immature next to you. You never lose your cool."

"There are a few people from my past who would tell you otherwise, were they here."

Steph could tell she wasn't just making chitchat. "Really? What do you mean?"

Milly topped off their cups with warm tea before she spoke. "Do you remember my mentioning my first husband's death?"

"In England, yeah."

"Yes. In Surrey. Well, Paul and I had quite a tumultuous marriage. Neither of us was seeking God—"

"You weren't a Christian back then?"

"No. That happened after I returned to the States." She smiled at Steph. "And let me assure you, some of our arguments were quite vocal and quite public. And the Lord was kind enough to keep most people from trying to interfere. Neither of us was particularly dignified when anyone tried to help."

Steph stared, her mouth open. "Unbelievable. I can't picture you angry."

"Ah, yes." Milly sipped her tea. "My anger is what brought me back to the States, actually. When Paul died—"

"How did he die?"

"A car accident. He'd been drinking with some friends at the pub. Thank God no one else was hurt." She paused. "Not physically, anyway. I did love him, you see. I hurt so much I stayed in bed for weeks after the funeral. I can barely remember the funeral, really."

"That's so sad."

"Yes. It was. Finally a relative convinced me to get up and go to church with her."

"Oh, good."

Milly laughed softly. "You would think so, wouldn't you? But I had heard enough at the funeral about Paul's death being God's will. That

281

much I did remember, especially once I heard it from several of the women at church. I flew off the handle at them as well. Never went back. I left for good."

"The church?"

"And England." She smiled. "That truly was God's will, because I found Him here."

"Your second husband?"

Milly laughed. "Well, yes, him too. But I meant I found God—"

The shop door opened. Both Milly and Steph stood and assumed work-ready stances.

Two women entered, carrying on a lighthearted conversation. They both laughed like privileged schoolgirls.

Steph looked twice at the first one. She was movie star gorgeous. Long, thick, absolutely straight blond hair; a model figure with added curves, and every facial feature in perfect symmetry. Steph actually wondered if she might be a Hollywood type, especially when she thought she knew the companion.

But no. That companion was no celebrity. Instantly Steph recognized the tall redhead who drove a black Porsche, packed a mean punch, and could toss sticky pink mixed drinks when least expected. She was Kendall's ex-fiancée's cousin.

So Steph already knew the answer to the question that popped into her mind. Did that mean the striking blonde was—

"Amy!" Milly sounded surprised and friendly.

Amy and her cousin strolled toward Milly, smiles still ruling the moment.

The redhead glanced at Steph, but there wasn't a hint of recognition in her eyes. Steph experienced a moment of relief before she decided she was affronted. Was she really that forgettable? The girl had crossed her path twice in rather dramatic fashion. Apparently her focus had been so squarely on Kendall that he could have been with a chimp and the girl wouldn't have noticed.

Amy opened her arms and gave Milly a hug. Steph saw she almost did an air kiss but stopped herself. Either the girl wanted to quit an obnoxious mannerism or she was savvy enough to know Milly wouldn't be the type to appreciate such phony fluff.

Steph swallowed. She needed to draw in the claws a bit there. The girl might be perfectly nice. It was the cousin who was dangerous.

"Milly, this is my cousin Jessica," Amy said. "I've been living with her in McLean for a while."

McLean. So Amy moved about an hour away after she broke off her engagement. Wow, her cousin had made a couple of significant treks to come assault Kendall. Steph was both impressed and creeped out. Mostly creeped out.

"Did you girls come for tea, then?" Milly pulled a chair away from one of the tables.

"Yes, we'd love some tea, wouldn't we, Jessica?

The last time I was here you had a Chinese tea that was so good. Kind of amber colored and delicate?"

"Oolong, maybe?"

Amy pointed a well-manicured finger at Milly. "That's it! And some of those fantastic little sandwiches of yours, if you have them. Thanks! Oh, and do you have any macaroons?"

"Absolutely." Milly turned away, but Amy stopped her.

"Wait!" She laughed. "I almost forgot the reason I came in the first place." She opened her beautiful mistletoe green purse. Steph recognized the little gold Kate Spade logo plate on the front. Of course. Probably cost a mere four hundred dollars or so.

"Kendall asked me to bring you this completed order form for his event Thursday. He said you two discussed it a few days ago, and he didn't want to leave it too long to get it back to you."

"Ah." Milly glanced at Steph so briefly even Steph barely noticed. "Thank you. And we'll have your tea and sandwiches to you shortly." Now Milly looked directly at Steph and motioned toward the kitchen with her head.

Steph felt as if she weighed a ton, as if her every footstep would shake the floor. Yet she tried as hard as she could to be invisible as she trudged toward the kitchen behind Milly.

They spoke in whispers, both readying tea and sandwiches on trays.

"Milly, you never told me she was gorgeous."

"You and I never discussed Amy at all, dear. And you know beauty is only skin deep."

"Are you kidding? You could remove twenty layers and still hit beautiful on that girl."

"So it might seem, but Kendall wasn't blinded by that. He didn't choose to marry her."

"Yes, he did! *She* split up with *him*."

Milly frowned. "Ah. I believe you're right." She poured hot water into the teapot. "Well, regardless, they're not together now."

"That doesn't sound quite as definite this minute as it did half an hour ago. She's delivering his order form for him."

Milly set the pot down and waved off Steph's comment. "That means nothing. She may have stopped by to say hello and mentioned she planned to come here. He may have been trying to save himself the trip over."

"Yeah, so he could avoid me."

"Kendall has never been one to let a little conflict intimidate him. And you shouldn't jump to conclusions about your relationship with him simply because of what happened at the banquet."

Steph arranged doilies and sandwiches on a three-tiered server. "I'll bet Amy never did anything as uncivilized as pouring ice water on a woman's lap in the middle of—"

"Remember what I told you about my angry behavior when I was younger, Steph. We all are human. We all wake with morning breath. We all have failings. Amy's no different."

"But—"

"You really must stop idealizing people. You will forever pale in comparison, and you're very hard on yourself."

This was definitely a bad time to tear up, but words like that always touched Steph. She was, unfortunately, a sucker for opportunities to indulge in self-pity. She frowned and nodded. If she thanked Milly for her support right now, she would cry.

Milly surveyed the trays and gave a swift nod. "Looks good. Let's go."

The conversation between Amy and Jessica was distinct because there were no other customers at the moment. Only the soft classical CD on Milly's player accompanied them, so Steph heard them the moment she and Milly emerged from the kitchen.

Amy laughed. "It's all your fault I'm in this quandary. If you hadn't been such a vigilante, he wouldn't have called and got me thinking about him again."

"I wouldn't have been a vigilante if you had told the truth in the first place." Jessica crossed her arms and shot a superior look at her cousin. "And I think you should just leave things as they are. You aren't meant for each other. You figured that out the first—"

She stopped talking when Milly and Steph reached the table. Amy took over the chat.

"Oh, thanks. That looks wonderful." She smiled at Steph when she placed the tiered server of sandwiches on the table and then looked back at Milly. "So, Milly. How do you think Kendall has been these past few months?"

Both Milly and Steph paused for a fraction of a moment before continuing their work.

Milly gave Amy a gracious smile. "Goodness, Amy. I wouldn't know how to answer that question." She poured the tea. "Now, this is a nice Formosa oolong—"

"But you two do business with each other pretty regularly, don't you? Has he . . . does he seem content?"

Milly set the teapot on the table and flattened the empty tray against her front. "Didn't you say you just came from seeing him? Wasn't that why you brought the order form for him?"

Amy tilted her head and sighed. "Yes. But he can be so cryptic when he wants to. And I didn't want to embarrass him by asking him personal questions right there at the inn."

"I don't think I can help you, Amy. Although I suppose I would say yes, he has seemed content when we've crossed paths."

"Hmm. I wonder." Amy took a couple of sandwiches from the tray, and accepted a napkin from Steph. "Thanks." She turned back to Milly.

"Jessica says she saw him with someone a couple of times."

Steph turned away as casually as possible and padded quietly toward the kitchen. Yet she still heard Amy's next question.

"Do you know if he's seeing someone?"

Milly chuckled, polite as ever. "That's really something you'd have to ask him about, dear. Excuse me. I see we forgot your cream."

Steph was on the other side of the kitchen door, awaiting Milly's return. So, when Milly swung the door open, she heard Jessica reprimand Amy.

"I still think you're crazy to consider moving back here. There's no reason to think he's any different than he was when you broke things off. I know he's hot, but Kendall James is not for you."

THIRTY-TWO

Steph walked into the house that evening determined to improve her attitude, despite not having heard from Kendall and despite having witnessed the gorgeous elegance that was his ex-fiancée.

She had to do this from time to time, especially when she caught herself wallowing in the doldrums. Her occasional sadness was almost always based on worry about her future. When she focused on her own personal fears, she knew she needed to remind herself that God was in control, He loved her, and He wanted what was best for her.

Of course, what was best for her was often different from what she wanted—thus her need to stop and make a concerted effort to be less emotional and more practical. If she and Kendall couldn't get past what she had done on Sunday, they certainly couldn't build a comfortable relationship with one another. And if that perfect rich girl was able to get him back again, what was the point in Steph's wasting a moment's worry over it?

She wouldn't think about the way he kissed her that night after he ripped his shirt off. She wouldn't. Practical. Practical.

Still, it would have been nice to find Christie and Liz home when she walked in. To have a nice, bemoaning girlie rant before getting practical. When she walked in and set down her purse and keys on the little table up front, she saw Christie's note to Liz and her:

Hey, girls,
Getting dinner with Brant. Maybe a movie
after. Don't wait up for me.
                              Love,
                              Christie

Ah, well. She and Liz would fix some dinner together and chat. Steph wanted to hear about how the coffee date went with the missionary. And Liz was a bit less forceful than Christie was. Whatever they discussed—whether it was how she should deal with Rick, whether she should contact Kendall, or what she should do about her employment situation—Steph would likely get less pressure from Liz than she sometimes got from Christie.

Amy's image popped back in her mind. She looked at herself in the hall mirror.

"Wow." And that was wow with a small *w.* The underwhelmed wow.

She knew she wasn't unattractive. She had kind eyes and decent lips, and her teeth were pretty straight. But what had Kendall seen in her—even as far as a simple kiss—after nearly marrying someone with Amy's looks and style? And Amy didn't seem mean or snooty at all, at least not from the minor exposure Steph had to her this afternoon.

Her cell rang. Liz.

"Hi, Liz."

"Hey, Steph. Are you home yet? You haven't started anything for dinner, have you?"

"No. I mean, yes, I'm home, but I just got here." She walked toward the kitchen. "I haven't started anything." Maybe they would go out for dinner instead.

"Good, good. Listen. My coffee date with Andrew—"

"Oh yeah! How did that go?"

Liz laughed. Steph smiled at the joy she heard. *Must have gone well.*

"We're going to continue the date in a few minutes. That's how it went. Steph, he's so great. It was hard to go back to work this afternoon. But I did, and he asked if he could pick me up and take me out to dinner after I closed the store."

Despite her disappointment, Steph refused to rain on Liz's picnic. "That's fantastic! So I take it you won't be home till later."

"Right. You guys go on ahead and do whatever for dinner. I'll catch up with you tonight."

There was no point in telling her Christie was out for the evening too. Liz might feel obligated to come home to keep Steph company. "Sounds good. See you when you get home. Have a great time."

She closed her phone and heaved a sigh.

No, she wasn't going to sink. Practical, not emotional. By the time she slipped into some sloppy, comfy clothes, she had decided she would fix herself a little dinner, listen to some music, and get some novel reading in or watch something funny on TV. No need to think about . . . nope. Not going to do it.

She returned her phone to her purse and switched on Liz's CD player. She smiled at the upbeat rhythm of the first song playing. She could even do a little dancing if she wanted. At this stage she could dance in her underwear, if she wanted. But she wouldn't go that far. She had lived with roommates often enough to know the folly in assuming no one would change plans and walk in unannounced. With guests.

She chuckled at one such memory and remembered how embarrassing that had been. At least as embarrassing at what she did at Kendall's the other night. And she had overcome that embarrassment quickly enough. So maybe she and Kendall could still—

How did she get onto thoughts of Kendall so quickly?

Dinner. She would make dinner. She shimmied into the kitchen in time to the music. She was able to see herself in the mirrorlike surface of the black refrigerator, so she danced with her reflection for a while.

She remembered there had been some leftover lasagna in the fridge the last few times she looked. Christie's ultraspecial lasagna, to be exact. There was only enough for one person, so she hadn't wanted to take it. Mmm, cheesy, meaty, delicious lasagna sounded good right now.

Yes! It was still there. Surely Liz and Christie couldn't care less if she ate it for dinner. They had men—they didn't need no stinkin' lasagna. She didn't have a man, and she wasn't sure she ever would at the rate she was going. She wondered if Kendall was with Amy right now. Would they—

Unbelievable. She had done it again.

Lasagna. Liz and Christie would be thrilled she ate the lasagna. Good thing too. It didn't look as though there was much else to choose from.

She removed the plastic wrap and was just about to place the container in the microwave when she saw it. Fur. Christie's ultraspecial lasagna had sprouted fur.

"Nooooo!"

She had waited too long. She should have eaten it days ago, before she went to work for Kendall and destroyed their friendship. If only—

She paused. Was there no road that didn't lead to Kendall?

"That does it. I'm ordering Chinese delivery."

And she planned to order a lot. She would overwhelm herself with choices so she would be busy deciding which to eat first. That would distract her.

She walked back to the foyer and retrieved her purse to get her credit card. But when she opened her wallet she saw the slip of paper she had kept from her first night at Kendall's inn.

Stay? Yes X No __

Kendall had written that when she couldn't decide whether or not to stay in Middleburg. She had tucked the page into her wallet because it reminded her of him. That had been one of the most charming nights of her life. Would she ever have another charming night in her life?

At that moment the next disc on the CD player began to play. Wagner. Something funereal.

Perfect.

Her cell phone rang, and she leaped at it. Any human voice would be better than death music and furry lasagna.

"Hi, it's me."

Was that Kendall? Her heart jumped. "How . . . how are you?" she said, trying to keep her enthusiasm down to a relatively cool level.

"Well, I'm better now that I know you're at least willing to take my call."

She almost laughed, but then she stopped. This

wasn't Kendall. This was Rick. She actually almost swore.

"What do you want, Rick?" No problem keeping her enthusiasm in check now.

"Steph, I waited as long as I could. I know you don't think I'm worth a second chance, and I'm more than willing to accept that if it's really your decision. But I hope you'll give me an opportunity to explain myself better."

"Fine. Explain away."

"I mean in person."

"Forget it."

"Please? Even if you never want to hear from me again, I think we should at least try to resolve our differences before we part. I'll admit I would love it if you decided to take me back, but if that can't happen, let's part as friends."

She sighed. She could only be just so strong against a request like that. If she couldn't forgive him, how could she expect others to forgive her? *As we forgive others,* and all that.

"Fine."

"Tonight? Should I pick you up somewhere?"

Ugh. Had this been Kendall calling, she knew she would jump at the chance. But she wasn't about to drop everything—her very busy evening—for Rick. "No. Tomorrow."

"Great! Where should I pick you up?"

She didn't want him to know where she lived. Not yet, anyway, when she couldn't be sure he wouldn't get all boo-hoo stalkerlike on her if she broke off all contact. She would never have thought such a thing about Rick before, but now she was less certain of his character. "Why don't you pick me up at the tea shop at seven? I'll change clothes there after work."

"It's a date."

"Look, I'd rather you not call it that, okay?" She hated the idea of anyone hearing she was dating her jilter. "We're just having a conversation. It's not a date."

His enthusiasm diminished. She heard it in his voice. "Sure. Sorry. I'll see you tomorrow."

The moment the call ended, Steph felt acid in her stomach over the argument she would get from Liz and Christie when they found out she was going on a date with Rick. Because she had to face it—meeting Rick for dinner and an in-depth discussion about eloping, promises, and whether or not there was a romance to salvage? That was no conversation. That was a date.

Her stomach rumbled, and she realized her discomfort was more than nerves. Tonight's dinner was still pending. She would eat nearly anything at this point. She went into the kitchen and thumbed through the menus Liz and Christie kept in the mail holder. She zeroed in on one in particular.

"Chinese and Thai in one place! And sushi! Better and better!"

"No delivery your address," the owner said after

Steph placed her order. "Too far. You pick up. Ready in ten minutes."

She could handle another drive tonight if that's what was necessary for her pity buffet. She shouldn't have dressed in her sloppy clothes yet, but she wasn't about to change for a simple drive down the road. "Okay, I'll come pick it up. Where are you located?"

She hadn't realized the place was twenty minutes away. But the drive did her good. She blasted upbeat worship music all the way, singing at the top of her lungs. It was like praying without sinking into whining.

The noise level of the place hit her the moment she walked in. Chatty diners packed the place— always a good sign, especially on a Tuesday evening. The food must be as good as it smelled. And her order already awaited her, which was a plus considering how grungy she looked. She wanted to get in and out as quickly as possible. The bar served as the carryout spot, so Steph took a seat on a bar stool while they rang up her order. Something tickled at the back of her hair. She glanced over her shoulder. It was only a support pillar. She sat up to keep her hair from brushing up against it again.

She scanned the restaurant. Families, groups of women, a few single diners, and plenty of couples.

Her stomach seized when her eyes landed on Kendall. *Was* that Kendall? She jumped off the bar stool and was behind the pillar before she knew what she was doing. There really was no other cover available. One big room, the restaurant lacked nooks and crannies. And the last thing she wanted was to run into Kendall looking this slovenly. Anyway, she assumed he hoped to avoid her too because he hadn't called or stopped by the shop in the last two days.

She chanced a look at the guy. Yep, it was Kendall, all right. He sat at such an angle that he nearly had his back to her. She could see just a bit of his profile. She sighed. He was so doggoned handsome. That perfectly tousled blond hair. That strong, athletic neck. How could the back of someone's head get her so worked up?

She heard a giggle to her left. A little girl sat with her family, all of whom were ignoring her, which seemed fine by her. She obviously enjoyed watching the crazy lady hiding behind the pillar. Steph smiled at her and tried to look nonchalant.

But she wanted to see Kendall's dinner companion. She had barely peeked around the pillar when the woman at the register called out.

"Vandergrift? Vandergrift? Where did she—"

"Shhhhh!" Steph ran out from behind the pillar to try to stop the woman from yelling her name all over the place. "I'm here!"

The woman yelped before she realized Steph wasn't on the attack.

Between announcing Steph's name and punctuating it with her frightened bark, the woman might just as well have run to Kendall's table and shaken him into awareness. *Look! There's the insane water girl! She's all alone! No boyfriend. No friends. And get a load of how much food she's picking up. Can we say "Eating your feelings?"*

Steph quickly paid and kept her head down. She had broken into a cold sweat and just wanted to get out of there without Kendall seeing her. She didn't want to put him in a position where he might feel obligated to say something to her.

She needn't have worried, though. She risked a quick glance in his direction as she passed. He clearly hadn't been distracted by Steph's presence or the calling of her name. He was engrossed in his conversation.

With Amy.

THIRTY-THREE

Mercy, what happened to you?" Christie set her coffee cup on the counter when Steph walked into the kitchen the next morning, dressed but less than fresh faced. "Did you have trouble sleeping last night?"

Steph shook her head on the way to the coffee-pot. "Chinese-Thai pity fest."

"Pardon?"

Steph pulled her shoulders back in a stretch. "I had Chinese and Thai food last night. Lots of it. Must have been full of MSG. Or maybe just salt, I don't know." She poured coffee into a travel mug and pointed to the refrigerator. "There are leftovers. It was tasty last night, but I feel like the Pillsbury Doughboy this morning."

"What prompted the pity fest?"

Liz walked in. "Whose pity fest?"

Steph raised her hand and then pressed it against her temple, frowning. "Headache. Too much food. Grease. Salt. Whining."

"You should eat a healthy breakfast." Liz removed a container of steel-cut oats from the pantry.

"I need to get going. I'll eat something at the tea shop."

"No, you should stay away from sugar until you feel better, Steph." Liz measured water into a saucepan. "And drink a lot of water. Does Milly have anything without processed sugar—"

"Berries?" Steph asked. "That okay?"

"Wait." Christie grabbed two bananas from the fruit bowl and handed one to Steph before sitting in one of the sunroom chairs. "There. Potassium, right, Liz?"

"And vitamins and minerals, yeah." She grabbed a bottle of water from the refrigerator and set it on the counter in front of Steph. "And take that with you."

Christie peeled her banana. "So why the pity fest?"

Steph set her travel mug down on the counter and pulled back the banana peel. "I saw Kendall last night."

Both of the sisters perked up despite Steph's lack of enthusiasm.

"But that's good! I knew he'd come around!" Christie took a big bite of her banana, her eyes twinkling.

"No, no." Steph swallowed the small bite she had taken. "I saw him. He didn't see me. He was at the restaurant. With Amy."

Liz and Christie groaned simultaneously. They almost made Steph laugh, but it would take more than that to break through the disappointment. And the bloating.

"How do you know it was Amy?" Christie asked.

"I met her yesterday. I mean, I didn't meet her. She came to Milly's shop, and she and Milly know each other. She was with her crazy cousin."

Liz gasped. "The redhead?"

"Yeah. And I heard them talking about Kendall a little. It sounded like Amy is considering going after him again."

"And then he took her to dinner last night?" Christie softly whistled. "Girlfriend doesn't mess around."

Steph sighed. "Apparently not. I'll bet it didn't take much persuading to get Kendall back again. She was the one who broke off the engagement. And she could front the *Sports Illustrated*'s swimsuit issue without breaking a sweat. Gorgeous."

"But what about you two?" Christie frowned. "What about that romantic evening? That kiss?"

Steph rested her forehead in her hand. "Don't remind me. I'm trying not to think about that anymore."

Liz turned the heat on under the saucepan and approached Steph. "Okay, look." She put an arm across Steph's shoulders. "I'm free tonight. How about going out for a girls' night? Christie? You free too?"

"Yep. I love the idea."

Steph set her banana next to her coffee mug. "Um, I don't think I can do that tonight. How about—"

"Come on, Steph," Christie said. "It's only going to make you depressed and whiney if you spend another night eating like an MSG-bloated pig and thinking about Kendall being lured back by that Amy vixen."

Steph arched an eyebrow. "Thank you for that horribly detailed advice." She sighed. "Anyway, that's not it. I kind of already have plans tonight."

Neither Liz nor Christie said anything. They just waited for her to elaborate.

She didn't want to.

Liz said, "Well? Okay, I give up. What are you doing tonight?"

Steph picked up her travel mug and took a long drink before speaking. "I'm—"

Christie gasped. "No!"

Liz looked from Christie to Steph. "What? What am I missing?"

"Tell me you're not going out with Rick." Christie stood and placed both hands on her hips.

Steph frowned. "It doesn't mean anything. It's just that—"

"Really?" Liz seemed genuinely surprised. "I thought you were leaning toward Kendall."

Steph said, "Hello? Liz, what are you talking about? I think any leaning in that direction might have me bumping into Amy, don't you?"

"You mean you're going to give up on him?" Liz asked. "Don't you want to make sure there's no chance he's still free?"

Steph hesitated. Actually, she definitely wanted to make sure.

"Even if he's not free," Christie said, "why would you want to date Rick again?"

"I'm not dating Rick. I'm just closing out the relationship as friends." She glanced at her watch. "I really have to get to work."

"Will we at least meet Rick when he comes to get you?" Christie asked.

Steph shook her head. "I have two tutoring sessions this afternoon—Chip and his classmate Hannah—and then I'm back at the tea shop till almost seven to help Milly with a special order and clean up. He's going to pick me up there. Gotta go, girls."

She scurried out before they could detain her any further.

But she didn't get far. She walked back into the house moments later. "I left my lights on last night before my MSG-bloated pig fest. Can one of you please give me a ride?"

So much for keeping Rick in the dark about where she lived. He'd have to drive her home tonight, rather than back to the tea shop.

For now, Liz drove her to the shop. Steph appreciated the fact that Liz was willing to give up eating a comfy breakfast at home and grab a banana instead. Steph also appreciated that Liz dropped the subject of Rick and talked instead about Andrew. As nice as he sounded, Steph listened with a cynic's ear. Rick had seemed nice too. And so had Kendall. Maybe love was just too much trouble to bother with.

And now with Christie engaged and Liz developing what would probably lead to romance, Steph questioned the wisdom of staying in Middleburg. No friends, no man, no job. Not even a home, really, because Christie and Liz would probably sell the house and run off to live their wonderful lives with their wonderful new husbands soon.

What was the point? Her job with Milly ended tomorrow. Maybe the Lord wanted to guide her back to Maryland. As sad as she was, that thought made her sadder still.

Is that the point, Lord? Has my time here run its course?

When Steph entered the kitchen at the shop, Milly acted as excited as a month-old puppy. "I have wonderful news for you, Steph! At least, I think you'll agree it's wonderful." She stopped and put a hand on Steph's shoulder, pulling back to view her clearly. "Are you all right, dear?"

Steph remembered Milly asking her that the first time she spoke to her, back when Steph was ready to fall apart on the front steps of Rick's law firm. She had tried to hold backs tears then too. She did a bit better this time.

"I'm fine, Milly. What's the good news?"

Maybe Amy has decided to move to Tibet.

Maybe Kendall has confessed to Milly his complete forgiveness and undying love for me.

"Jane isn't returning until next week! Or, rather, she's still coming back to town tomorrow, but she asked if she could wait until Monday to come back to work. She wants to get everything back to normal before she starts back, and apparently that involves helping her grandmother move into a retirement community. I told her that worked out well for us. For you! Right? That gives you more time to find other employment."

In the dim fog of Steph's mood, a faint glimmer flashed.

Was that for me, Lord? A quick response to my request for guidance? How about that Amy in Tibet idea?

"Hmm. Yeah. If I bother to keep looking, that will definitely make it easier."

Milly had started to stir something in a bowl, but she stopped again. "If you bother?" She set down her spoon and again gave Steph her complete attention. "What's changed, Steph? Is this still about you and Kendall?"

Steph put on an apron and stepped over to the sink to wash her hands. "No. Or yes. It's about that and about my inability to find employment here. There's absolutely nothing in the want ads, Milly. And it's also about Christie and Liz—"

"You're not getting along?" Milly removed a few

colanders of berries from the fridge and set them on the counter for Steph.

"Thanks." Steph got a bowl and knife and worked as she talked. "No, we get along great. I love both of them. But Christie and Brant will get married at some point, and she will probably move into a place with him. And Liz—did you know she went out with Andrew?"

"That missionary fellow? He's back in town?" Milly's grin was infectious, and Steph liked the feel of smiling again.

"Yes, he's back, and I think they really like each other."

"Marvelous." Milly rolled a dense ball of dough from a bowl to the counter.

"Yeah, so that could lead to marriage for Liz soon and—"

Milly laughed. "I suppose it could, but they'll probably want to go on a second date beforehand, don't you think?"

Steph couldn't help smiling at her own thought processes. "Okay. Maybe I'm looking at the worst-case scenario." She gasped. "I mean, the best-case scenario. You know what I mean, right? I wish nothing but happiness for Liz. I just meant my social life—"

"I knew what you meant, dear. You're just saying your social life might undergo a change. Eventually. At some point you'll have to move out from the girls' place. Is that it?"

"Right. I don't do very well with change. And . . . now what are you smiling about?"

Milly said, "I get tickled about how you view yourself. Just take a look at yourself right now."

Steph stopped working and looked down at herself. She saw nothing noteworthy. "What?"

"You've been chatting with me since you walked in, but you've been working as if I had been instructing you all along. Look at you, holding that fruit masher as if you've been making that berry mixture for ages. You walked in here, put on your apron, washed your hands, started right off to work, and you haven't even noticed."

She actually hadn't noticed—didn't even remember slicing up the fruit and then picking up the masher—but she didn't get the point. "Not that your work here isn't amazing, Milly, but I'm not exactly building the ancient pyramids."

"Tell that to the girl who scraped two quarts of strawberries and me off the kitchen floor two weeks ago. You're a bit more comfortable now than you were then, wouldn't you say?"

"Well, yes—"

"Yes, indeed. People would think you'd been here for years. Steph, you're one of the most adaptable people I've ever met. You move in with a couple of young women you barely know, and you adapt to them so quickly you're already mourning the idea of either of them moving on."

True. She was a bit worried about where she

would live, but her real concern was in losing touch with Christie and Liz because of their romantic relationships.

Milly wasn't finished. "You have a few chats with a young innkeeper and adopt such an easy way with him the two of you seem to have known each other far longer. You sweep him off his feet, and you don't even realize it."

Steph pointed the fruit masher at Milly. "Now, that's where you're wrong."

"I don't think so."

"Then why was he out to dinner with Amy last night if he's so swept off his feet by me?"

Milly frowned. "With Amy?"

"Yeah. I saw them out to dinner together. And if he's so swept, why hasn't he called me? It's been three days, Milly. If I swept him off his feet, I think I poured him right back onto them at that banquet. Amy couldn't have set her sights on him at a better time. I heard her talking with that lunatic cousin of hers yesterday. She has set her sights on him again."

She watched Milly's conviction waver.

"Hmm." Milly frowned as she processed what Steph said. Then she raised her eyebrows and gave a quick shake of her head. "Well. I'll reserve judgment on that, if you don't mind. There may be more going on than what you see. Or less, I should say. Don't be too quick to come to any of these conclusions. Liz and Christie love

Middleburg. Neither of them would sell their home or leave without seeking a good deal of advice from family and friends, which includes you. And I'm confident some kind of job awaits you when you leave the tea shop. I am."

"I wish I had that kind of confidence."

"So do I, dear." Milly resumed her work, breaking the dough into smaller pieces to make her little shortcakes. "I know you think you're not the impulsive type, but when a person's confidence waivers, impulse often rules as a motivator. That's when bad decisions are made."

Milly wasn't looking at Steph, and she said nothing more specific, but somehow Steph felt this last comment had something to do with Rick.

THIRTY-FOUR

That evening Steph slipped into her purple knit dress in the restroom in Milly's shop. She had ten minutes before Rick was due to pick her up, and she wanted to freshen up her hair and makeup, if possible. She knew she was being small, but she couldn't help herself. Despite having no intention of taking him back, Steph let her pride rule her actions. She couldn't stand the idea of this loss being easier for Rick than it had been for her two weeks ago. She wanted to look *good*.

Her tutoring sessions had kept her at the library later than she expected. The time with Chip went like clockwork. So did her session with Hannah, up to a point. She was a sweet young girl, and Steph could tell she would catch on quickly in their algebra lessons. They had fun together.

But Kitty, Hannah's mother, chattered more than a teen jacked up on soda and Heath bars. Steph nearly had to interrupt her to get away. Hannah was the saving grace there.

"Mom! Please! Paula's going to be at the house before we even get there. We have a biology project to finish."

By the time Steph got back to the tea shop, Milly was ready to close.

"I'm so sorry, Milly. I thought I'd get back in time to help clean up, at least."

"Not to worry, dear. The last hour was very slow. I finished everything I planned to do today. I'm sure you worked harder with your young charges than I did here. How was the new student?"

"Hannah's a total sweetheart. She's Kitty Henderson's daughter. Do you know Kitty?"

She watched an amusing play of facial expressions before Milly settled on a soft, crooked smile.

"Ah, yes. Kitty comes into the shop with her book club on occasion. She seems to have quite a lot of energy."

"Mm-hmm. I'm not sure I'm up to it, to tell you the truth. I have a hard time cutting people off when they talk that much. Feels rude, especially when she's employing me."

"Do you think you might end up with a third student eventually? You might want to schedule someone immediately after your time with Hannah. That could do the interrupting for you."

Steph considered the idea. "But if I had three in a row after school hours like that, I'd never get back here in time to—"

She caught herself and saw a touch of sadness in Milly's eyes.

"What am I saying?" Steph forced a short laugh. "I guess I really do feel at home here. It's hard to think I won't work at the shop much longer."

"For me too." Milly rested her hand on Steph's arm for a moment. "But you'll be somewhere nearby. I'm sure of it." She dropped a key into Steph's hand. "Anyway, I know you wanted to change in the restroom. This is an extra key to the front door. Just be sure to lock up when you go."

Steph appreciated Milly's withholding any comments about her getting together with Rick. She wasn't sure if she merited it, but she knew Milly had enough respect for Steph's judgment to keep her opinions about this "date" to herself unless they were solicited.

By the time Steph was tidied up, Rick waited out in front of the shop. He rested against his baby, a midnight blue BMW M3 convertible—his parents' gift when he passed the bar. But tonight he seemed more impressed with Steph than with his ridiculously pricey ride.

"Man, you look awesome, Steph."

Because she was being honest with herself about her pride, she recognized she would have been bothered had he not complimented her. But she couldn't bring herself to graciously respond. Her voice was less than warm. "Thanks."

She refused to return the compliment, even though Rick looked awfully good too. Maybe he was up to the same shallow tricks she was. No more catfish face. He had shaved. That Bahamas tan, although a constant reminder of his betrayal, made his dark eyes more dramatic and his sandy hair sun kissed. And he wore a dark, well-tailored suit. She didn't want to study it too closely, but it looked like one of the DKNY suits she had sold him when they first met. Those had been romantic days. Maybe that's why he wore it. He was clever enough to play the nostalgia card.

The moment they started to drive, she figured she might as well get one question answered. "So, have you spoken to your parents since you got back to Middleburg?"

"Oh yes. I'll tell you all about it at dinner."

She had to admit he seemed more confident than normal. He had always *acted* confident, but because of his admission Monday about needing to "man up," she realized what an act that confidence had been. Maybe she had seen a kindred spirit in Rick when she was initially attracted to him. She certainly struggled with similar intimidation regarding her parents.

When he pulled up in front of the Fox and Hounds, Steph suddenly came to attention.

"What, here?"

He flashed her a proud grin and jumped out of the car to come to her side. One valet opened Steph's door, and she saw another take Rick's keys. She didn't get out, even though Rick extended his hand to her.

"Why here, Rick?" Suspicion flooded over her. What was he up to? What did he know? And how in the world could she show her face in there?

He squatted down so that their faces were level. If he had any cruel motive for wanting to take her in there, he masked it beautifully. But that wasn't his style. Yes, he had been cowardly, but he hadn't set out to hurt her deliberately.

"This is one of the nicest restaurants in town, Steph. I want tonight to be special." Then his eyes twinkled with mischief. "Besides, coming here tonight is all part of my . . . well, let's just say I think you'll be proud of my reasons."

What in the world did that mean?

She had taken too long to seriously protest. Another car pulled up behind Rick's, and the valets looked eager to clear the drop-off spot. She couldn't possibly launch into an admission to Rick about her behavior toward his mother here. Neither could she explain to him about her interest in Kendall and the way she had disrupted their budding romance.

"Steph?" Rick tilted his head, his eyes concerned and solicitous. "Is something wrong?"

She faced too many bad decisions. No good ones.

She took his hand and stepped out of the car. Her ears pounded as Rick escorted her through the front door. Her pulse nearly drowned out the melodic orchestral suite filtering into the restaurant from hidden speakers. Maybe she would have a heart attack and be carried out on a stretcher. With a sheet over her. Then she wouldn't have to face anyone.

Marnie, the manager who sacked her three days ago, approached them, smiling. Then Steph saw recognition dawn in her eyes.

Steph made pleading doe eyes at Marnie, silently willing her discretion. The gesture seemed to go unnoticed, but Marnie immediately acted as if Steph were a stranger. She talked instead with Rick.

"Right this way, Mr. Manfred."

Steph watched the wheels turn behind Marnie's polite mask before they all headed to a table. Did she recognize the surname as the same one belonging to the woman Steph had assaulted here on Sunday? Steph didn't know what repercussions had followed the incident. The Fox and Hounds could be embroiled in a small claims case with Rick's mother for all she knew.

She deliberately averted her eyes from all of the waitstaff. Of course, to be gentlemanly, Rick insisted she take the seat facing out toward everyone. The opposite seat would have afforded her a small degree of anonymity, which was exactly why they both made it an issue.

"No, I don't need to sit here, Rick. You know I'm not the diva type."

He smiled at her, confused. "What's the matter with you? I know that. This is just common courtesy. Please." He pulled her seat out for her, and she surrendered with a sigh.

The menu arrived just in time—a shield,

courtesy of their server. He didn't appear to recognize Steph before walking away. Small mercy there. She recognized him, the fellow who taught her how to fold napkins. She tried to think of how she might hang on to the menu after ordering. And while eating. And while walking out of the restaurant after an interminably long amount of time here.

Rick suddenly reverted to the humble guy Steph found waiting for her outside Milly's shop two days ago. "Are you embarrassed to be seen with me, Steph? You look so uncomfortable."

Uncomfortable didn't half cover it. She wished he'd stop saying her name so loudly.

She turned the menu slightly so she could talk to him without exposing her face to the staff so blatantly. "No, I'm not embarrassed to be seen with you, but of course I'm uncomfortable with you. Did you think desertion would endear us to each other?"

She felt a little mean unloading all of her behavior on his skipping out on her, but desperate times called for desperate measures tonight.

A young girl brought a basket of bread to their table. Steph was relieved to see a face she didn't recognize.

"You're right," Rick said. "It's my own fault if you're uncomfortable with me." He smiled. "But I'm going to change that. I promise."

Steph's napkin mentor returned and began to

recite the specials for the night. He announced the first two dishes to Rick and recited half of the third when he turned his gaze on Steph.

". . . seasoned and seared, and then served with rémoulade and—"

He wasn't quick enough to avoid the lift in his eyebrows. He recognized her.

Steph eyed Rick, but he studied his menu. She shot a rapid-fire glare at the server, which jump-started his monologue back into gear.

"And fresh sautéed asparagus and wild mushrooms. Just let me know if you have any questions."

The moment he left, Rick gave in to his enthusiasm. She remembered his being excited like this in the past about a number of topics. She had always appreciated that enthusiasm, but right now she refused to see anything good in it.

"Okay, I have to tell you what happened, Steph. I think you'll like this. Or at least you'll like how I handled it. See, my mother came here for a banquet last weekend."

Good night, he planned to tell her her own story! He spoke for a while before relating the climax, and he related it far too loudly for her liking. "And then for some reason this nut job poured gallons of water right into her lap!"

Gallons? Nut job? Steph grabbed a roll from the basket and stuffed a sizable portion of bread into her mouth to keep herself from responding. And she still didn't understand why he seemed so delighted by the whole story. After all, his mother might be a harridan to Steph, but she was his mother.

She labored to swallow the bread. "Why are you so happy about such a terrible thing happening to her? And try not to speak so loudly, okay?" She checked around them. Maybe some patrons' ears had perked up, but none of the staff—or Kendall—seemed within earshot. As a matter of fact, she hadn't seen Kendall at all yet.

Thank You, God, for that.

"I'm not happy that it happened to her. That's not it." Rick shrugged. "But it's not as though she was hurt or anything. Her dress was a little messed up, temporarily, but—" He cocked his head toward the kitchen, as if the kitchen represented Fox and Hounds. "They have already paid for it to be cleaned, and then some."

Ah, a tiny bit of relief amid her discomfort, knowing she hadn't cost Kendall too dearly. He wasn't forced to buy Mrs. Manfred a new dress.

Rick continued. "The thing is, my mother never forgets a slight, an insult, or even a simple mistake." He finally lowered his voice. "She's still furious with this place. She announced one of her edicts while telling me about all of this. No more patronizing the Fox and Hounds. She'll try to talk her friends out of coming here too."

"Oh no." Steph's relief abated.

Rick waved off the concern. "They'll never agree to that. They might stay away for a couple of weeks, but this place is awesome. And while we have excellent restaurants in town, we don't have a lot of them."

He put both hands on the table and leaned in. "But here's the thing, Steph. I'm her son. The standard-bearer of the Manfred name. Her one and only baby boy. Her pride and joy. Her—"

"I get the picture." Steph knew she sounded sardonic, but she had heard enough of Mrs. Manfred's adoration of the Manfred line to last a lifetime.

He smiled. "Right. You know. I've told you about her before. But the difference this time is—" He leaned back in his seat, opened his arms, and presented the entire setting, a proud grin blazing. "Here we are. Smack-dab in the middle of the forbidden zone." He leaned back in and tapped his finger on the table. "And she *knows* we're here."

"She does? She knows you're here? With *me?*"

He nodded. "Yep." He laughed. "She's furious with me! They both are."

"But why are you so happy about that, Rick? That's awful, isn't it?"

He shrugged. "In a way, yeah. I don't like having anyone angry with me, especially not my parents. I love them. But this is liberating. I'm twenty-six, and it's about time I stood up to both of them about my personal life."

He sounded similar to how she sounded the last time she talked with her parents, only more confident. He tapped his chest. "I decide where I go. What I do. Whom I see." He peered into her eyes. "Whom I marry."

"Are you ready to order, or would you like me to come back?" The napkin man had returned.

Thrilled with the interruption, Steph actually smiled up at him. "No! Don't go. We know what we want." She looked at Rick. "Don't we?"

We know what we want, don't we? What kind of moron was she to put it that way?

Rick lifted his eyebrows in response. Steph would have given anything had his expression been suggestive. Obnoxious. But it wasn't. It was hopeful. Optimistic. And most difficult of all, painfully vulnerable.

THIRTY-FIVE

For the remainder of the meal, Steph found her energy diverted. Rather than trying to avoid exposure by the staff, she tried to avoid Rick's obvious efforts at mending their relationship.

"Remember how easily we clicked, Steph? Right from that first day in the men's suits department. You were the only female working there. What were the chances you would be the one to help me? And it wasn't just a physical attraction. Right? It was more than that for me, anyway."

Steph sighed. She didn't want to remind him that he had later admitted to deliberately approaching her for assistance when he saw her. It wasn't as if their meeting was God ordained. Not necessarily, anyway. Yet he was right about the attraction going beyond the surface. Aside from the faith issue, they seemed to have everything in common. That was why their romance had progressed so quickly. And once Rick embraced Christianity, they seemed—

"We're the perfect blend, Steph."

There. Right there. That was the type of interchange that made her heart flutter when they were a couple. Their thought processes often paralleled each other. But now she wasn't sure the things they had in common were enough. Surely successful marriages were built on more than common interests and mutual attraction.

"I don't know, Rick. I'm sorry. I can't honestly encourage you right now. I can't."

"Just promise me you'll think about it." Rick stood from the table. "No pressure. Just think about it. Excuse me for a minute." He headed in the direction of the restrooms.

He had been perfectly charming all through their meal. If this were her first date with him, she would be more than eager to see him again. But their history was damaging. It wasn't even so much a matter of forgiveness anymore—

Her thoughts hit a wall when she saw Amy walk into the restaurant. She must have entered through the door between the inn and the restaurant, because she was back where Rick walked, over by the restrooms.

And she was as stunning as ever, a vision in an emerald green spaghetti-strapped dress. Everyone seemed to look at her a second time.

Including Rick.

As a matter of fact, it looked as if Rick actually said something to her. Steph saw Amy turn and respond. Was that Rick's flirtatious face? Steph had certainly seen it often enough, but would he really do something like that while they were here, discussing a future together? Or, more precisely, while *he* was discussing their future together?

He continued on his way, and Amy continued on

323

hers, but there was no mistaking the roll of her eyes as she walked away. Steph had made the same expression plenty of times when some icky customer or guy at a coffee shop—wherever—had muttered some come-on line at her.

Unbelievable.

Thank You, Lord, for letting me see that.

Relief washed over Steph. Rick could be as kind as he wanted tonight, and he could be totally sincere about wanting her back. He had told her not to feel pressured, but now she knew that's exactly what she had felt. Not anymore.

A moment later Kendall walked into the restaurant through that same door. The one connecting the inn to the restaurant—the one she and Kendall had walked through that first evening she stayed here. When they had their wonderful, cozy little chat in the middle of the night. He must have arrived with Amy to be walking in right after she did. He looked impeccable. Steph recognized the slim, clean lines of a Hugo Boss designer suit. The man could dress.

And tonight he had dressed for Amy.

If Steph's heart dropped much lower, it would be sitting in her stomach. She dabbed her napkin at the beads of perspiration along her upper lip and forehead.

Please don't let him see me here, Lord.

She was surprised he didn't head in the same direction as Amy. Rather, he walked into the kitchen after greeting a few diners in the back part of the room.

Steph didn't give much thought to her next move. He was out of sight at the moment. She simply felt this was the time for her to cross the room and hide. In the restroom. She was already up and walking by the time she considered the fact that she couldn't stay in there all night, but maybe Kendall and Amy were just passing through. Maybe by the time she came out, the coast would be clear. She had to give it a try. It was better than sitting at the table, waiting for him to spot her. What would he think of her, showing up in his territory after what she did? And with a date in tow? It would look as if she were trying to make him jealous. Or using Rick as a date so she could stalk him.

As she scooted into the small restroom, Amy's crazy redheaded cousin walked out. She must have arrived with Amy. So were Kendall and Amy together tonight or not?

Jessica's perfume just about knocked Steph down—a nearly visual wall of hyacinth. She didn't even look twice at Steph.

Steph shook her head. Clearly she had made a most lasting impression on the girl.

The hyacinth scent permeated the restroom. Jessica must have applied it while in there, and it was only a one-stall restroom. Steph actually felt nauseated by the heaviness in the air. On the vanity counter she spied a can of air freshener. She hoped it was the kind that replaced odors rather than masking them. As she picked it up, the restroom door opened. She heard someone call out to whomever was about to enter.

"Marnie, they're asking for you up front."

Marnie? Oh no.

Marnie called out to the person. "I'll be there in a second."

Steph didn't even notice the tension with which she held the spray can. Without thought she let loose with the air freshener, but the nozzle sprayed up instead of out. Marnie walked in just as Steph sprayed herself directly in the eyes.

"Aaaagh!" Steph grabbed at her eyes with her free hand and blindly sought somewhere to set the can.

She heard Marnie gasp. "What in the world? Are you okay? Here, give me that." She took the can from Steph. "Why did you spray yourself in the eyes?"

Steph groaned. "I didn't plan to do it. The stupid nozzle shoots upward. What kind of air freshener sprays upward? I'll bet this happens to everyone." She couldn't open her eyes. Marnie took hold of her and guided her to the door.

"I'm going to get you out of here and into a more private bathroom. We can help you wash that stuff out of your eyes."

"No, I'll be okay."

Marnie ignored her, and there wasn't much Steph could do under the circumstances. She allowed herself to be led a short distance through the dining area, where she could hear the diners chattering away, and into the lobby of the inn.

"Don't worry." Marnie's voice was kind and close to Steph's ear. "No one even notices."

Steph kept her head down, and Marnie spoke again.

"It's Steph, right? That is you, isn't it?"

Steph sighed. "Yes, it's me."

Almost to herself, Marnie muttered, "You are the strangest girl."

Before Steph could defend herself, Marnie maneuvered her into what seemed a more spacious bathroom and parked her at the sink. "You need to flush your eyes with warm water."

"Oh my goodness, I'm going to be such a wreck." But she knew Marnie was right. Her eyes stung too much to assume her tears would wash everything away.

"Hang on just a moment," Marnie said.

The door opened and closed. Steph didn't want to open her eyes. "Marnie?"

No answer. But within moments the door opened again. This time the voice was masculine. Gentle.

"Here. Use this, Steph."

It was Kendall. She wanted to scream, and it wasn't just because of her stinging eyes.

He handed her a little plastic something.

"What's this?"

"It's an eyecup. Don't worry, it's from a brand-new kit. I have a mild saline solution for you to use. I think regular tap water might sting a little. Just hold it there—"

He held her hand steady as he poured.

"Okay, now hold it to your eye and tilt your head to let it wash that stuff out."

She pictured what he must see—she was bent over a sink, sticking a plastic cup to her face, and craning her neck like a carp-eating heron. "Gosh, Kendall, could you wait outside while I do this?"

"Sure. Can you get the cup refilled okay without me?"

No, she probably couldn't, not without opening her eyes. But—

He seemed to understand her hesitation. "Let me just rinse the cup out and get it refilled for you, and then I'll leave you alone."

Well, by the time he did that, all semblance of glamour on her part would be pretty well shot, as far as she saw it.

She sighed. What was she thinking? Glamour on her part had been shot days ago. For some reason this entire situation made her angry with him. Or maybe she was already angry with him, and her continued humiliation just brought it to the fore.

"Oh, never mind." She rinsed her other eye. "What are you doing with an eyecup kit in the first place? Kind of an old-man thing, don't you think?"

She thought she heard him laugh softly.

Shoot. She liked that he found her verbal attack amusing. As if he was not only confident but understanding, as well.

He handed her a face towel. "I try to keep a steady supply of eyecups around for customers who are confused by aerosol sprays."

She gasped as she straightened halfway up, like Quasimodo, and smacked at him with the towel. Water was dripping from her face, and she still couldn't look at him fully. "Am I hitting you?" She wanted to snap that towel at him enough to make it smart.

He was laughing. "Not really."

"That stupid spray shot straight up in the air! It wasn't me." She started laughing despite herself. But just being around him again brought her close to tears too, so the whole eyewash thing was a godsend.

He gently took the towel and set his hand on her shoulder. "Here, hold on." Then he steadied her by cupping her face with one hand as he lightly wiped her face dry. "I didn't even know you were here until Marnie started running around looking for help."

She couldn't speak. She was mesmerized by what he was doing. By his tender touch and warm hands. His amused eyes and full lips—

He continued. "I'm just glad you're not angry with me anymore."

Angry? "What?"

"At least I assume you're not angry if you came here tonight." He had stopped wiping her face, but his hand remained where it was.

"No, Kendall, I—"

She lost track of what she planned to say the moment his eyes glanced at her lips. She suddenly realized she didn't want to say a word. Not one word that might stop him from leaning closer, which he did.

A knock on the doorjamb caused him to swiftly drop his hands and stand upright. Both he and Steph took a quick step away from each other.

"There you are!" Rick pulled the door farther open and smiled at Steph before he saw Kendall. His smile faltered at that, and he looked from Kendall to Steph, a question in his eyes.

Already warm, Steph blazed with guilt over having so thoroughly forgotten about Rick. She started speaking and barely stopped to breathe. "Gosh, you're not going to believe what a boneheaded thing I just did, Rick. Oh, my manners! Rick Manfred, this is Kendall James, the owner of the Fox and Hounds. Kendall, Rick. See, Kendall helped me after I sprayed air freshener— air freshener!—in my eyes in the ladies' room, can you believe that? I mean, look at my eyes, will you? It's a good thing we're done with dinner, that's all I can say. Right, so . . . so we . . . we really ought to get going." She faced Kendall and acted as if they had just closed a real estate deal. She thrust her hand out. "Thanks so much, Kendall, for the eyewash."

Kendall hesitated and then shook her hand. "Not at all." His eyes searched hers as subtly as possible. She detected disappointment. Kendall turned to Rick, smiled, and shook his hand. "I hope you enjoyed your dinner, Rick. Nice meeting you."

Rick's expression wary, he shook hands with Kendall. "Yeah. Nice meeting you."

Kendall frowned. "Manfred. Are you related to Evelyn Manfred, by any chance?"

That loosened Rick right up. "Yeah. My mother had an interesting evening last weekend. Is that why you ask?"

Kendall's eyes darted at Steph and quickly back to Rick. "I hope there are no hard feelings about that."

"Not as far as I'm concerned, no." Rick actually puffed up his chest. "Did you ever find out why that oddball attacked her?"

Kendall didn't so much as glance at Steph now. "Unfortunately, no. My manager saw fit to let her go on my behalf before I could—"

"Well, I guess so. Not the type of employee to hang on to, was she?"

Before Kendall could respond, Amy came into view at the doorway. She looked dismissively at Rick, and then at Steph before focusing her attention on Kendall.

"Finally! I thought I'd never find you. Come on, sweetie. Jessica and I want to go. We'll be in the car."

Steph didn't know if she had ever seen Kendall so uncomfortable. She was grateful Rick spoke into the seconds of silence left in Amy's wake.

"Yeah, we should go too, babe." He put his arm around her to steer her away.

Babe? She was not grateful for that. Or the arm. But she couldn't exactly make an issue of it here.

Kendall spoke to her as she left. "I hope your eyes feel better."

She looked over her shoulder as she walked out. "Thanks for . . . everything." She felt as if they had just said goodbye. The spray may have been washed from her eyes, but now they smarted all over again.

THIRTY-SIX

So that was that. Amy and Kendall, back together. Or more accurately, Amy and *sweetie*. Steph had suspected it wouldn't take long for Amy to get him back, yet it still shook her to see how quickly it happened.

She frowned in the dark of Rick's car. Had she imagined that moment back there, when Kendall gazed into her damp, air-freshened eyes? When he definitely seemed about to kiss her again? How could he have looked at her like that and even considered a kiss if he truly wanted to take Amy back? It didn't match up with the man she knew.

Yes, she and Kendall had never actually said anything to each other that meant they would be a couple. And she had cautioned herself for weeks not to impulsively swoon over him but to focus on friendship and nothing more.

But what about those kisses? Or near kisses? Friends didn't do that.

She struggled to pay attention to Rick as he drove away from the restaurant.

"Are you sure you don't want to stay in town and walk around for a while?" He stopped at the corner and waited for a small group of people to cross the street. "It's such a nice evening."

"No, thanks. I just feel like going home. Turn right here."

"You're not still mad at me, are you?"

She shook off her attitude. She was just being rude now. "No, I'm sorry I'm acting like such a dud. I'm not mad at you."

"For anything?"

"No, not for—" She looked at him. "What are you asking? You mean, have I forgiven you for skipping out on me when we were eloping?"

He winced. "Uh, yeah, I guess I was going for the big time since you seem to feel okay toward me at the moment."

She had to laugh softly while she shook her head.

"Hey," he said. "It never hurts to ask. I figure the worst you can say is no."

"That is so you." Steph smiled crookedly. "Just like your trying to haggle with me about the cost of your suits that first time you came into the store."

They delicately reminisced while Steph directed him to Liz and Christie's home. In their discussion neither went too close to the more romantic facets of their early days. Rick clearly didn't want her to feel any more pressure than she already did. And, despite her resolving to dismiss that pressured feeling, Steph never enjoyed hurting anyone's feelings. She hated playing the bad guy.

He drove up the driveway and parked. "Nice place."

Steph opened her door before he had a chance to

try to touch her or kiss her. He followed her lead, stepped out, and met her halfway, but only to escort her to the door. This time he didn't put his arm around her as he had done at the restaurant. She felt herself relax just slightly, but the few steps to that dark front step passed all too quickly.

"So, Steph."

"Yes?" She fished her keys from her purse and stopped at the door, hoping he wouldn't ask to come in. Or expect a good night kiss.

"How long do you think it will be before . . . I mean, do you think you'll ever be able to forgive me for letting you down?"

She had to think, but he kept talking.

"Do you see us ever having a chance together?"

She sighed. "I think I might have already forgiven you, Rick."

He smiled, and she raised her hand to stop him from further reaction. "But I'm not sure. There are a lot of things going on in my head—in my heart—right now. And I've learned I don't do well when I make impulsive decisions. There isn't much I can say to you right now because I'm not sure what I want." She tilted her head and looked him in the eyes. "That's just the way things are now."

He lowered his eyes and nodded. He looked like a kid. "I understand. I know I blew it." He met her eyes and almost looked as if he were negotiating again. "The ball is in your court. I get that."

"Okay."

He took both of her hands in his before she could do anything about it. He held them gently and gave them a soft shake, emphasizing what he said next. "But I'm not going to go away from you again unless you tell me to. Okay?" He smiled. "I mean, I'll go away from this doorstep tonight, but I'll stay in the picture until I know for sure you don't want me there."

She didn't know if she thought that was okay or not. Should she be this confused? Did she truly want the ball in her court? "Um, okay."

Before she knew what was happening, he leaned in. Goodness, she didn't want him to kiss her, did she?

Lord? Help?

Was he headed for her cheek or her lips? Were his intentions friendly or romantic? What—

The porch light went on, and both of them jumped. The front door opened, and Rick dropped her hands as if he feared he would spread a lethal disease.

Christie took a step out the door and then halted. "Gosh! Sorry. Did I interrupt something?" She held up a kitchen trash bag and gave Rick a steady once-over. "Tidying up for the evening. Don't mind me."

She walked past them without meeting Steph's eyes and headed for the garage. The sound of the television streamed out the front door, which Christie had left open, and Steph heard Liz laugh out loud at something. The bright porch light washed out all hints of romance and intimacy. Steph heard Christie clanging around in the garage, making far more noise and taking far longer than one should to empty a simple bag into a can.

Steph found she really didn't mind the interruption.

"Okay, then, Rick. Thanks for dinner."

"Uh, yeah. Okay. I'll talk with you later."

She smiled and closed the door behind herself. She felt a moment's pang of guilt but decided to ignore it. The last thing she needed to do was nurture a romantic relationship out of a sense of guilt.

Liz glanced over from the sunroom. "Hey! How did it go?" She muted the television.

"Ugh. Not so good." Steph set her purse on the kitchen counter and joined Liz on the couch.

Christie didn't walk back into the house until after the powerful ignition of Rick's car sounded outside. Steph arched her brow at her when she came into the sunroom.

The picture of false innocence, Christie batted her eyes once. "What?"

Steph laughed. "You're worse than a meddling parent."

"That's what I told her," Liz said.

Christie studied Steph for a moment before breaking into a smile and pointing at her, relief all over her face. "And you're pleased! I saved you from having to deal with a good night kiss, I'll bet."

Steph opened her mouth, but rather than responding, she looked at her lap. She gave a nearly imperceptible nod.

Liz chuckled. "So why the long face? You don't want to take Rick back, do you?"

Christie sat opposite Steph. "And now that I get a good look at your eyes, have you been crying?"

Steph rested against the couch back. "No, that's air freshener. And it's not Rick. It's Kendall."

The sisters both frowned. Christie pointed to the door. "But that was Rick. I know I didn't look closely, but I definitely would have recognized Mr. Cutie—"

"I think there's going to be a Mrs. Cutie Pants in the near future. And it isn't going to be me."

No one spoke for a moment. Then Liz scratched her head. "Air freshener?"

"Amy?" Christie wasn't as easily distracted as Liz. "It's definite? They're back together?"

"It certainly appears so. She calls him sweetie."

Liz frowned. "Now, how do you know that?"

"Rick took me to the Fox and Hounds, Amy and Kendall walked in, I sprayed air freshener into my eyes, Kendall gave me an eyecup, Amy told Kendall, 'Come on, sweetie, let's go,' and Rick drove me home and tried to give me a kiss I don't think I wanted."

Christie sat back and crossed her arms over her chest. "Old Rick really knows how to show a girl a good time, doesn't he?"

"None of it was his fault, really—"

"And what's with spraying air freshener into your eyes after seeing them together?" Christie asked. "That sounds like something out of a Greek tragedy."

"Stupid restroom accident." Suddenly animated, Steph sat up. "And that's another thing. Have either of you ever seen air freshener that sprays up? Not forward. Up."

Neither answered, but she watched them envision what had happened to her earlier. They both struggled not to smile.

Finally Liz reached over and gave Steph a gentle squeeze on her knee. "You had a rough night. Tomorrow will be better."

Steph sighed. "I'm not even going to joke that it couldn't get worse. At least tomorrow won't be my last day working for Milly."

"No Jane?" Christie smiled.

"Not until next week. That gives me a little more time to find another employer."

"Good! So you're not going to let the Kendall thing keep you from staying in Middleburg?" Liz asked. "Or the Rick thing, for that matter. Or—"

Christie slapped at her sister. "Are you trying to run the girl out of town?"

"No, it's all right. I might have come here for a

man, but I don't need one to stay. Maybe God wants to keep my thoughts clear of men right now."

"That's the spirit." Christie gave her a quick wink.

Steph loved these two women, despite Christie's occasional pushiness and Liz's emerging ditziness. There was much to love in Middleburg. Plenty besides Kendall James.

Not that she loved Kendall. That wasn't what she meant at all.

THIRTY-SEVEN

S teph removed the baking sheet from the oven and inhaled. "Mmm, wonderful!" The delicious scent of toasted pecans was almost enough to make her forget more serious matters.

Milly's upbeat mood this morning helped Steph immeasurably. Yes, praying for gratitude and a healthy perspective immediately upon waking had been the main impetus for looking at her current situation in a more positive light, but Milly's mood and behavior often fell in line with Steph's answered prayers. Today was no exception.

"Yes, everything about this particular recipe smells decadent," Milly said. "Chocolate-pecan scones. I haven't made them for a while. I had a customer ask about them yesterday and realized it was about time I featured them again." She handed a food chopper to Steph. "Those pecans will cool quickly. You can chop them coarsely for me on the cutting board."

Another thing Steph appreciated was Milly's discretion. She had yet to ask about last night's date with Rick. Maybe if the date had been with Kendall she would have asked, but Steph wasn't even sure of that. Milly always seemed ready to lend a sympathetic ear but was never hungry for the juicy stuff.

Steph's phone rang, and both she and Milly looked in the direction of Steph's purse.

"You mind if I check on that, Milly?"

"Not at all, dear."

Steph still had the food chopper in her hand when she read the phone display. Her mother.

"Hi, Mom. I can't really talk long, okay? I'm at work."

"I wouldn't have called, honey, but I feel that I'm not going to hear from you unless I do. You don't call often enough. Is everything all right? We're worried about you."

She sighed. "I'm sorry. I should have called you. I just had so many things going on this week—"

"Like what?"

Steph glanced at Milly, who bustled about, intent on her own business. Still, these were tight quarters and this was the workplace. "Can I call you later today, Mom?"

"Have you been seeing that handsome Kendall fellow?"

"Uh, no. Not since this past Sunday. Mom, can I just—"

"So you've been seeing Rick since Sunday?"

Steph halted her efforts to get off the phone. "What do you mean? Why do you ask that?"

"Nothing. We just got a letter from him, that's all."

Rick wrote to her parents? What was he up to?

"A letter? What did it say?"

"It was touching. He wrote to apologize."

"To apologize? To you and Dad?" Steph walked back to the counter, knowing she needed to get back to work, but she couldn't exactly pound the food chopper on the pecans while on the phone. And now her curiosity was piqued.

"Yes. He said he was responsible for persuading you to uproot and move to Middleburg against our wishes. And for hurting you so much when you arrived."

"So why did you think I was seeing him now?"

"Because he said he wanted to try to find you and apologize to you too. I thought maybe he found you, and that was why you weren't seeing that handsome Kendall fellow."

It was as if her mother thought Kendall's name was That Handsome Kendall Fellow.

"No. I mean, yes, Rick found me, but no, that's not why I'm not seeing Kendall. I messed that up all by myself." She looked at Milly just as Milly looked over at her. Milly didn't look annoyed that she was still on the phone. She simply gave her a sympathetic smile and went back to work, not a flustered cell in her body. Steph wanted to be Milly when she grew up.

The front bell jingled, and Milly removed her apron and walked out.

"Look, Mom, I really have to get to work. I'll call you tonight, okay?"

343

The moment she closed her phone she dropped it into her purse and got to chopping pecans. But her thoughts were on that letter. It didn't sound as if Rick wrote to her parents with any intention of soliciting their help in getting her back. From the way her mother took it, the letter was purely a gesture of graciousness. Rick had done nothing but admit responsibility ever since he came back to Middleburg. And he sent that letter to her parents before he even knew whether or not he'd find her. She found herself agreeing with her mother—his effort seemed touching.

She wondered if she had truly forgiven him. Was she allowing bitterness to cloud her view of him? But something niggled at the back of her mind. Something beyond the big elopement letdown.

Milly walked in, sporting a smile. "Interesting development out there."

Steph pointed toward the dining area. "Out there?"

"Mmm. Three women. I can't say I recognize any of them. They placed their order and then asked if you were here today."

Steph straightened. "Me?"

"I told them I'd see if you could leave what you were working on and come out. Any idea as to who they might be?"

"Shoot, Milly, I wish you had a little window in your kitchen door. I don't have a clue who would be after me."

"They seem harmless." Milly chuckled. "Go on out. I'm curious to know how you've brought fame to the tea shop."

Steph gasped. "What if they're friends of Rick's mean old mother?"

Now Milly laughed outright. "I didn't see any weapons. Not even water balloons. I think you'll be all right. And I'll be out with a pot of tea in a moment anyway. Don't worry. I won't allow anyone to speak harshly to my dear employee."

Steph eyed the kitchen door. Then she removed her apron and walked out.

Another group entered the shop at the same time. The weekly visit by the women's counseling group. Well, good. Now Steph felt less vulnerable, with all of them and a licensed therapist witnessing whatever these ladies had in mind.

The three women who asked for her didn't even see her approach. They chatted and laughed with each other, not a care in the world. They couldn't possibly be friends with Rick's mean old mother.

"Excuse me." Steph stopped at their table. "I'm Steph Vandergrift. Were you ladies asking for me?"

They broke off from their conversation and gave her their attention. One of them, a pixie-haired brunette of about forty, smiled at her. "You're Steph?"

"That's me."

Another of the women, blond, heavyset, and

expensively dressed for so casual an outing, also gave her a smile. "You're the Steph who tutors math students?"

Math students?

Ahhhhh. Relief enveloped Steph. They were mothers! Mothers of prospective students. Three of them!

Now Steph was able to return their smiles. Her heartbeat picked up its pace. "Yes. I love tutoring. Do your children need a little help?"

The third woman laughed softly and ran her manicured fingers through her rich black hair. "My Antonio needs much more than a little help. Kitty Henderson—"

"Kitty can't shut up about you," the heavier woman said. "She raves about what you've done for Hannah."

"But we only—" She'd just had one session with Hannah. Still, they had made good progress. Anyway, what was she about to do—talk these women out of hiring her? "That's very nice of Mrs. Henderson. Hannah and I enjoy working together."

Pixie-Hair extended her hand. "I'm Fiona Middy." She and Steph shook hands. "We wanted to come get on your calendar before anyone else had the chance."

"Anyone else?" There were more? Goose bumps erupted on her skin.

Milly approached with a tray and set a teapot,

cups, and saucers on the table. She spoke to Steph while she placed the cream and sugar before the women. "Steph, did you want to bring some cakes and tea sandwiches out for the ladies? I've set up a tier of trays in the kitchen. I'll see to the other table."

As she spoke, Milly seemed to take measure of the situation. Steph smiled, hoping to signal that all was well. "Sure." She addressed the three mothers. "I'll be right back, and then we can chat a little more."

Milly returned to the kitchen shortly after Steph did. Steph grabbed her shoulders and laughed. Then she felt tears smart her eyes as she spoke.

"Milly! They *all* want me to tutor their kids in math! And they came here to snatch me up before 'anyone else' does. There are others! Kitty Henderson and her chatty nature are a blessing in disguise."

The two of them gave each other a quick hug.

"You see?" Milly pulled free, her eyes sparkling. "Could anyone but God have timed this better? You may very well find enough clients to tutor full-time."

Steph gasped. "Can you imagine? I swear I can't think of anything I'd enjoy more."

Milly turned Steph toward the counter and the loaded tray she had prepared. "Then get out there and negotiate with those women. And remember, you're obviously a hot commodity. Don't you charge one penny less than you're getting from Kitty."

Steph chuckled. "You know me well, don't you?"

"I know you sell yourself short too readily. You have what they want. Don't forget that."

Before Steph even finished serving the food to the women, the heavyset lady broached the topic at hand.

"Now, I understand you tutor Hannah Henderson at the library."

"Yes, ma'am."

"That's not going to work for my schedule. So I wondered if you could come directly to my home. I'm a few miles west of the library."

Steph hesitated. Certainly she could drive to the woman's house, but she thought about what Milly said. She had what they wanted. So she figured she'd better know just how flexible she wanted to be with her time and where she would work.

Her hesitation apparently communicated something.

"Of course," the woman said, "I'd pay a premium on top of what you charge to tutor Hannah there at the library. Say ten dollars more per hour?"

Steph nearly dropped the small pot of clotted cream she held, but no one seemed to notice.

"Yes!" Fiona pointed at her friend and then looked at Steph. "I'd be willing to do that as well.

I'm not too far from Gina here." She ran her finger in a circle to include all three of the women. "We're all just outside of town, but we understand your gas, time, and convenience would certainly warrant that additional amount."

Steph couldn't believe what was happening. These women weren't just wealthy and in need of help for their children. They were far more considerate than some of the people she had faced while working in retail. She decided she loved Middleburg and its people.

Thank You, God, for bringing me here!

She couldn't believe she had considered running back to Maryland just a few days ago.

In a rush of joy and confidence she put on her most businesslike manner. "I think we can work that out, ladies. Let me go get my phone, and we'll schedule your children right now. I'm only working here with Milly for another couple of days, so you've come at a good time. I'll have a much more flexible schedule next week. And for each new student any of you sends my way, I'll throw in a free tutoring session."

She allowed a briskness to emanate from her as she swished away. The only slip in her step happened when she heard what the large blond woman said to her two friends.

"This has really been my week. First my Amy comes home, and now some calculus help for J.B."

THIRTY-EIGHT

Steph went to sleep that night before either Christie or Liz arrived home from dates with their respective men, but both of her roomies tried to downplay Steph's situation the next morning when they all discussed her new connection with Amy.

"So what?" Christie said. "So you're going to tutor her teenage brother. Minor coincidence."

"Yeah, I guess," Steph said. "I shouldn't be imagining too far into the future. I just picture Amy and Kendall getting married and my having to come into contact with them because of her brother. You know, because his mom wants me tutoring him at her home."

Christie said, "You've already married them off, have you?"

"Hey, it's not completely out of the realm of possibility." Steph topped off her coffee. "They almost married before, and they're obviously back together."

"Well, if she marries Kendall, she's not going to be living at her mother's house," Liz said. "She'll live with him. That's one good thing to keep in mind."

Steph stared at her for a moment. "Why doesn't that cheer me up, I wonder?"

Liz grimaced. "Sorry. But it's kind of interesting that Amy keeps crossing your path, both directly and indirectly."

"That kind of interesting I can live without." Steph sighed and decided to at least try to let it go. "But you're right. I should just let this happen and stop worrying about it. God totally blessed me with the whole job situation, and that came about simply from running into Chip at the tea shop that first time, not from any of my efforts."

"You think you'll be able to tutor full-time?" Christie asked.

"I won't need that many more students to earn enough to get by. And if I keep acquiring clients, yes, I could definitely do this full-time." Her grin felt great in the middle of her worry over Amy. "I'm so excited about this."

"I thought you didn't like the idea of being a teacher." Liz took her dishes to the kitchen.

"Not in a classroom full of kids, no. But one-on-one tutoring? It's a blast." Steph stood and rubbed her hands together. "Okay, you guys got me happy again, Amy or no Amy."

"Right! Kendall or no Kendall. Wedding or no wedding," Liz said, as if she were adding something positive to the conversation.

Both Christie and Steph frowned at her, and Christie shook her head. "I think dating that missionary boy has addled your head, girl."

Liz's grin was almost cartoonlike in its silliness.

351

"No argument here." She glanced at Steph and rolled her eyes. "Sorry, Steph. I'm a little too self-absorbed right now to think straight."

As Steph drove to work, she reflected on Liz's romance-fueled addle-headedness. Surely the infatuation would calm down eventually, but she hoped Liz and Andrew were headed for a happy future. She hoped the same for Christie and Brant. Then she tried to hope that for Amy and Kendall.

She spoke out loud as she drove. "Sorry, Lord. I'm just too human for that right now. I don't wish them ill, but I wish they would get out of my head altogether."

As if in answer to her drive-time prayer, the shop hummed with business all morning. Steph and Milly barely spoke in passing while tending to everyone and replenishing tea sandwiches and pastries.

For a brief moment they both prepared trays at the same time in the kitchen.

"It's a very good thing you helped me prepare food after closing yesterday, dear," Milly said as she picked up a container of smoky salmon and cream to assemble more sandwiches. "I believe we'll go through everything we have by the time the lunch crowd has their fill of us."

They were so rushed Steph thought of nothing but customers, tea, and food for hours. It wasn't until the lunch crowd dispersed and she and Milly had a few free moments that Steph thought again of romance. She would have lasted longer, had not a huge vase of flowers been delivered for her.

Her stomach flipped. Two days after her "moment" with Kendall. But also two days after her date with Rick.

Please, Lord?

She opened the card, Milly at her side, and read it out loud. "Still here. Love, Rick." She sighed and turned to Milly. "Maybe I should have been more specific in my prayer just now."

"Oh, Steph." Milly put an arm around her. "I'm sure God knew what you wanted. Just remember not to make any rash decisions. All right?"

"All right. But I wonder if God's trying to tell me to pay attention to who accepts me rather than who's chosen not to."

Milly opened her mouth to respond, but they both turned when the door flew open and Steph's mother and father walked in, both with purpose in their every movement.

"Mom! Dad!" For reasons she couldn't quite fathom, she stood in front of the vase of flowers as if hiding a secret. "What are you doing here?"

Her father strode closer, her mother not far behind. He seemed to only then notice Milly. "Oh yes." He put out his hand. "Mrs . . . ."

Milly shook his hand. "Jewell. But please call

me Milly. Would you and Mrs. Vandergrift like to have a seat and—"

"No, no, that's not necessary. Thank you. We've come to talk with Stephanie, and we shouldn't take long."

"Ah." Milly hesitated and then smiled at Steph. "I'll be in the kitchen for a moment, Steph. I'll be back out shortly."

Milly had barely turned around before Steph's mother spoke.

"You never called me back yesterday, honey."

"I'm sorry, Mom. I got caught up with some wonderful new developments and I forgot."

Her mother glanced at her father. "You should have called, honey. I—"

"We've come to talk some sense into you, Stephanie." Her father's frown seemed to spread all the way down to his chin. "You said you would be coming home Thursday, and that was yesterday. Yet here you still are."

"Dad! I never said I'd be home Thursday. I said this job only lasted that long. But it ended up lasting a few days longer. And I already have another job set up."

"Rick?" Her mother smiled.

Steph widened her eyes. "No, not Rick, Mom! Rick's a person, not a job. And I don't have him lined up, anyway."

"That handsome—"

"No, not Kendall, either, Mom. I'm going to

tutor students in math. I've actually started tutoring already, and I have more students scheduled for next week."

Her father's frown grew deeper. "Tutoring? How do you expect to support yourself tutoring? That doesn't sound terribly secure."

Steph stiffened. Goodness. Her mention of tutoring and her father's reproof had been mere seconds apart. Could he have given any consideration to the idea before shooting it down?

"Well, Dad, I'm already slated to earn hundreds of dollars for only a few hours of work next week. And I'm only getting started. I haven't had to dip into my savings yet while I've been here, and I have a feeling I'll not only leave that money intact, but I'll be adding to it shortly."

The three of them stood in silence for several seconds. Finally, her father shook his head.

"No."

Steph jerked her chin in. "No?"

"Stephanie, this isn't going to do. I can't see you supporting yourself on something so unstructured. I think it's time you called this little experiment off and came on home. Get yourself something safe. None of this would have happened if you had listened to your mother and me and kept your retail job while waiting for a better opportunity. Better than that Rick fellow."

Before she opened her mouth, Steph scrambled for clarity of thought. Had her father always managed to put so much discouragement into so few words? Perhaps, but she was just now able to see it.

She took a deep breath and released it, hoping to discharge some of her anger too. She drew her hands together as if she were about to break into song.

"Mom. Dad. I appreciate your driving all the way out here to show me your concern—"

Her father opened his mouth, but she gently put her palm up to stop him.

"Hang on, please, Dad. Let me just get this out. I love you both very much, and I know you love me, but I'm twenty-five years old. I've made a decision to live here in this lovely little town. If you visited for longer than an hour, I think you'd understand why. God has blessed me with an amazing opportunity—yes, better than Rick, and *not* that handsome Kendall fellow—and I intend to take God up on His offer. I would hope you would be thrilled that I want to be self-supporting, but even if you aren't, even if you completely disapprove, this is what I'm going to do."

Her mother's gasp was barely audible, but she heard her father loud and clear.

"We paid for your college education, young lady!"

"And I *so* appreciate that, Dad! I do! But you didn't buy me. I don't mean to sound disrespectful because I have so much respect for you. That is why I wish you had—" She willed herself not to cry. She took a deep breath and then said, "More respect for me."

Her mother put her hand on Steph's arm. "Oh, honey, we do respect you."

Steph placed her hand over her mother's, but she looked at her father. "I'm more capable than you think, Dad. Just relax and watch. I think you'll be proud of me someday."

She watched her father's face nearly crumble from its hard, angry knot to a sad awareness of how he came across.

"Stephanie, I'm proud of you already. It's . . . it's very hard for a father to let go. To trust that his child will survive on her own. It's difficult to believe your little girl doesn't need—" His voice caught and he coughed roughly into his hand.

Steph could tell he wanted to say more but didn't want his voice to waver again. She stepped up to him and wrapped her arms around his neck. If he was going to get all choked up, she figured she might as well join him. It was easier to allow her broken voice to spill into his ear when neither of them could see the other. She breathed in his familiar, woodsy scent and exhaled the words, her voice shaky and small.

"I love you too, Dad."

THIRTY-NINE

A small measure of resolution settled over Steph as she walked into the library that afternoon to meet Chip for their tutoring session. She didn't expect her parents to turn into completely different people as a result of their exchange back at the tea shop, but she knew the three of them had taken a definitive step toward the break she needed in order to feel like a real, live grown-up.

She hadn't noticed before how strongly she still craved her parents' acceptance. Maybe standing up to her father was long overdue. He obviously didn't like her deciding against his wishes, but he hadn't withdrawn his love as a result.

She spotted Chip at one of the tables on the periphery of the library. Two young girls sat with him, and he was clearly the center of the conversation. He said something that made both girls break into giggles, which they energetically suppressed as if they expected a lecture from the librarian.

With a grin Steph reflected on how happy Chip's confidence made her. She loved the fact that she no longer felt pangs of pity for him because of his leg. Her default reaction to someone who faced a physical challenge was exactly that: pity. Chip broke through that default. As someone who had just struggled to establish a position of independence, she marveled at his self-assurance at so young an age.

Chip spotted her and waved. He said something to his companions, who watched Steph approach.

"This is her." Chip held out his hand, presenting Steph as if she were a wonder. "Steph, both Jilly and Samantha are interested in getting help from you." He looked back at the girls. "She's awesome. Really."

Unbelievable. More business! Steph worked to keep her voice calm and steady.

"Terrific!" She gave them each a smile. "Just have your parents give me a call." She grabbed a scrap of paper from her purse and jotted her number down. Maybe she should get business cards.

A thrill ran through her as she considered again this entirely new career. Four days ago she had no idea that God would bless her like this. "I'd be happy to talk with your mom or dad about working you into the schedule," she told the girls.

One of the girls stood. "Cool. My mom will call you." She smiled at Chip. "See you tonight, Chip. Come on, Jilly."

They left and Steph saw Chip watch them for a moment before he pulled his textbook from his bookbag.

"Is one of them your girlfriend?"

He looked up and then glanced toward the girls again. "Nope. I'm not going to date anyone while I'm in high school. Doesn't make sense."

"Really? Wow, I can't imagine what my high school experience would have been like if I hadn't dated." She smiled. "I probably would have gotten better grades. I was a little boy crazy."

Chip opened his book and laid out his binder and other materials. "Yeah, lots of kids are like that, but I'd rather just have fun and not get all serious. I'd probably have to break things off when I went to college, anyway."

She loved that this was a choice he made. He clearly had the opportunity to date if he wanted. She raised her eyebrows at him. "I don't know. That Samantha girl seems pretty taken with you."

He grinned. "You've got a good eye. But Samantha has goals, same as me. She just thinks she wants to start something with me. I think she's looking for acceptance, that's all." He scratched his head. "Who isn't, right?"

Steph nodded and found herself stunned by this kid's insight. Wasn't that what drove her to consider keeping Rick in her life? Her search for acceptance? When she honestly considered an entire life with him, she knew immediately she didn't want it. What she wanted—what she had found attractive—was that he had returned and tried to win her back. If that wasn't acceptance, what was?

And that was why she hesitated for so long in standing up to her parents. She feared losing their acceptance. Their love.

Chip pointed to a problem in his textbook. "Here's what's making me nuts today. I just can't get past this part."

Steph turned her focus to Chip's calculus, and he explained his confusion.

"See, the problem restricts the bounded area to the first and second quadrants, so I'm kind of stuck here."

She read over what he had done so far and then tapped her finger on one of the details. "Here you go. The graph is y-symmetric. You can calculate the volume by doubling the value of the integral on the half-sized interval."

Chip studied it for a moment. "Oh. I make x equal two, right?"

Steph grinned. "You're my easiest student. I'm afraid I'm not going to have you under my wing for long."

"Don't push me away yet." He laughed. "It's always easier when I have you sitting right there, filling in the blanks." He erased a few figures and corrected his work. Without looking up, he said, "My brother was right about you."

A flush ran all over Steph at an amazing rate. Talk about acceptance! There was no way she could let that comment slide.

"Your brother? Kendall? What do you mean?"

Chip brushed eraser crumbs away and glanced her way. "Why are you blushing?"

"I-I'm not blushing." She patted at her forehead with the back of her hand. "It's just stuffy in here."

"I guess. Anyway, Kendall said you were quick-witted. That you think fast on your feet or something like that."

"Me?" This sounded like the very opposite of how she had performed in front of him. They even discussed her inability to act well on impulse. And his inability as well. Amy had even complained about that way about him, he said. "Are you sure he meant me? Not Amy?"

As soon as she asked, she regretted having said too much. Chip was her student, not her connection to Kendall's personal business. "I mean—"

"Amy?" Chip chuckled. "No offense to Amy, but there was no way he meant her. The only thing Amy is quick at is changing her mind."

Steph steeled herself. Mercy, mercy, mercy, how would she focus on calculus if this boy kept talking like this? Could she care about integrals and derivatives when ex-fiancées and their actions were flitting about the conversation?

She took a deep breath and shot up a quick prayer for a sense of discretion.

"Let's focus on your calculus. Your mother is paying me good money, and we need to keep making progress here."

"Gotcha." He worked on the problem before him, and Steph helped him understand every time he stumbled. She managed to dismiss thoughts of Kendall's impression of her and Chip's apparent lack of fond feelings for Amy. Still, in the back of her mind she wondered if Chip's impression was his own or something he heard from his brother.

They finished Chip's work with a few minutes to spare before Hannah was due to arrive for her session with Steph.

"Awesome," Chip said. He packed his books away and pushed himself away from the table. "You make it so much simpler than my teacher does, Steph."

"It's always easier when it's one-on-one like this." Steph leaned forward and handed Chip a pencil he had forgotten to pack. "But I appreciate the compliment."

He took the pencil. "The acceptance, right? Like I said. We all want it."

Steph sat back and crossed her arms. "So, you don't feel driven to get acceptance from Samantha or other girls, huh? I guess that's good at your age."

"Good at any age, don'tcha think?" Chip stood and slung his bookbag over his shoulder. "You're a Christian, right? Kendall said you were."

She sat in surprise at how often Kendall seemed to have mentioned her to his brother. "That's right."

"So you know where we find acceptance."

She nodded. But it wasn't until he gave her a subtle wave and walked away that his words truly sank in. Steph watched Hannah approach the table while she sorted through what this clever, unusual boy had given her today.

Whose acceptance was she really after? Whose acceptance did she already have?

FORTY

The moment Steph and Hannah completed their tutoring session, Steph dashed to her car. Not only was she eager to escape Kitty, who arrived with the ever-yapping Hildie in her arms, but she was also a woman on a mission. There was a good chance Rick was still at his office, and she wanted to act while she was inspired.

Middleburg had only one traffic light, and she caught it red. She pulled her phone from her purse. She always made a point of turning it off for tutoring sessions. Maybe she should call Rick to make sure he waited for her. But before she even turned the phone on, the light turned green, the person behind her tapped his horn, and she sped away.

She managed to find a parking spot in the firm's small lot. She rushed to the front of the building, a sense of drama in her steps. She knew she was embracing important decisions right now. Yes, this was impulsive, but there was a wonderful rightness about it.

The thought of impulsiveness caused her to stop still. The one thing missing in her hasty decisions in the past had been guidance. God's guidance. And yes, she had felt a nudge from the Lord while she sat in the library considering Chip's words, but she hadn't actually sought connection with Him. She subtly lowered her head, right there in front of everyone and prayed a silent plea.

Lord, You have blessed me in so many ways since I came here. Could You bless me with discernment about Your will right now, please? I'm pretty sure I've figured this out, but if I'm heading away from Your will, I don't mind a clarifying slap. Sometimes that's all I seem to understand. Thanks. Amen.

When she raised her head, it dawned on her that she stood exactly where she had huddled in despair the day she had arrived in Middleburg. She glanced across the street at Milly's tea shop and smiled. When she had felt completely rejected, Milly had crossed that street and given her total acceptance. Right after Steph's desperate prayer. Coincidence?

Certainty washed over her. This conversation she was about to have with Rick was the right thing to do. She turned and quickly took the steps into the building and headed for the elevator.

On Rick's floor she stepped off the elevator and entered through the firm's glass doors. She wasn't sure, but she thought the receptionist was different from the young woman she encountered the day she and Rick were slated to wed. Steph glanced at the clock on the wall. "I'm surprised they still have someone at the front desk this late."

The girl gave her a manufactured smile from

behind the raised desk front. "We take turns as the overtime receptionist. May I help you?"

Steph returned the smile. "Yes, thanks. I'm here to see Rick Manfred. I'm Steph Vandergrift."

The girl's smile held while she studied something under the desk front—something out of Steph's sight. She quietly parroted Steph as she read. "Steph Vandergrift." A slight twitch in the smile was the only hint that something was amiss. She looked back at Steph and tilted her head. "I'm sorry. It appears he's taken a sudden leave of absence."

Steph straightened, and her mouth fell slightly open. "A sudden—" What? Was he running from her again?

And then it became clear to her. She laughed out loud and peered over the edge of the desk. "How old is that list?"

Again, the smile twitched, and the girl placed her hand farther under the desk's countertop. "I'm sorry?"

"No need to be sorry. Just do me a favor, please. Ring Rick's office and let him know I'm here."

"But he's away. A sudden leave of absence."

"I understand that. But please tell him anyway. I'll wait over there." She sat in a comfortable, leather chair in the waiting area and pretended not to hear the receptionist when she finally called Rick and spoke between nearly closed lips.

The poor girl hesitated to look in Steph's

direction when she hung up the phone. Steph was relieved for her when Rick came around the corner and strode into the reception area.

"Steph! What a wonderful surprise!" He enveloped her in an embrace before she was fully upright. She turned her head to the side as she grasped his arms to gain her balance and managed to deflect a kiss to her cheek.

"I'm sorry to barge in like this. I hope I haven't interrupted something impor—"

"No, not important at all. It'll wait."

Steph wanted more privacy than the reception area afforded. She cocked her head toward the elevator. "Could I speak with you in private for a minute?"

"Sure." He glanced over his shoulder as he opened the office's glass door. "Dee Dee, could you—"

"Mimi. It's Mimi."

"Right. I'll be back in a few minutes."

"A few minutes. Got it." Steph saw the girl strike a line through something on her desk and thought she heard her mutter what sounded like *leave of absence, my foot.*

Rick barely waited for the door to close before he spoke. "Did you get the flowers?"

"The flowers? Yes, the flowers. They were gorgeous, Rick. Thanks."

"No need to thank me. Just tell me they did the trick. Am I forgiven?"

She sighed. "I already told you I forgave you, Rick. This isn't about forgiveness anymore."

"This isn't about forgiveness?" His smile began to resemble the receptionist's, just shy of genuine. "What do you mean, this?"

Steph drew an imaginary line connecting herself to Rick. "Us. Don't you think it's possible, in a romantic relationship, to forgive someone for something they have done to you but still realize they aren't the person you thought they were?"

He hesitated. She saw the lawyer in him as he formed his answer. "Well, yeah. But I am the same guy I always was. Better, even, because I'm defying my parents. You know what I'm talking about. You've said yourself that you felt kind of pushed around by your parents, right?"

Hmm. He had her there. But something about their two situations was different. She needed to figure it out quickly. Was it the word "defiance"?

He continued his case. "Listen, Steph, I'm not the only one who needs to man up. I mean, you might have shaken things up by coming out here to Middleburg when they didn't want you to, but our getting married will show our parents we're serious about resisting their control."

And bingo. She suddenly saw the difference.

"Rick, no. You're hoping to build a marriage on a foundation of defying your parents. I wanted to get married *despite* my parents' disapproval. Not because of it."

Rick waved off her comment. " 'Despite.' 'Because.' That's just semantics. Either way, we're both getting what we want." He held her by the shoulders and looked intensely into her eyes. "We both need this."

"No." She shook her head. "I don't need this. I've taken a stand with my parents because I think they need it as much as I do. It breaks my heart to see them struggle with letting me go, but none of that has anything to do with building a lasting marriage. That's what I came to tell you, Rick. I appreciate your coming back and apologizing. I considered what you offered this second time because I liked feeling that you finally accepted me despite your parents' disapproval. But you weren't accepting me. You were just embracing me because your parents didn't." She stepped back from his grip. "It's not going to happen for us, okay?"

She was amazed at the flash of anger that drew his features down.

"There's someone else, isn't there?"

For some reason his comment brought back the image of his ogling Amy in the restaurant the other night, even while trying to woo Steph. That had been what niggled at the back of Steph's mind about Rick. He hadn't just deserted her. He showed hints of unfaithfulness.

Steph's eye grew wide. "After all that, you think this is about someone else?"

The elevator doors opened. When Steph turned and saw who walked out, she half expected dramatic horror movie music to creep out of the elevator. Rather, a treacly Muzak version of Led Zeppelin's *Stairway to Heaven* accompanied Mrs. Manfred. It took Rick's mother just a moment before her polite smile morphed into an angry mask of shock.

She pointed at Steph. "You!"

Rick looked from his mother to Steph. "You know her, Mother?"

The way he said "her" made Steph's skin shiver. As if she were naked and scarred amid expensively adorned, beautiful people.

"She's the one, Rick! The horrible . . . *thing* who poured water all over me at that ghastly restaurant. I'd remember that face anywhere."

Steph felt as if she were in a nightmare. Yet she had the wherewithal to step forward and push the down button on the elevator. Three times.

"Steph? She's the one who doused you?"

While Steph hadn't thought Rick's mother could register more alarm than she already had, she watched Mrs. Manfred's mouth drop, her eyes bulge, and her breath draw in like light to a black hole. "Steph? This is the woman you considered bringing into our family?"

Rick turned his back on Steph and put his hands on his mother's shoulders, just as he had done to Steph only moments before.

"Don't worry about a thing, Mother. I was just showing her the door. You have nothing to worry about. You were absolutely right about her. She's not remotely worthy of the Manfred name."

Now Steph's mouth dropped open, and she had to fight that black hole kind of gasping herself. Could Rick actually be that shallow? That much of a turncoat? Where was the so-called Christian man he once claimed to be?

She didn't know what to say. Her need to defend herself reared up so strongly, she wanted to scream. Or hit. If a pitcher of water were available, she would even consider a repeat performance.

But something wonderful happened. The tableau before her suddenly seemed hilarious. She didn't know if it was relief or nerves or simply a blessing from God, but she found herself laughing, honestly tickled.

The elevator's timing couldn't have been better. The doors opened and she stepped in. She said nothing, but she saluted Rick and his mother right before the doors closed on their indignant, sour faces.

The ride down was slow, but that was all right. Steph needed a few moments to process. She had one more stop to make.

FORTY-ONE

Steph's mind buzzed as she headed for her car. That confrontation with Rick and his mother would have destroyed her two weeks ago. Now it almost felt as if it happened to someone else.

Thanks to Chip's comments, she realized acceptance had been her only remaining attraction to Rick. After that scene at the elevator, she embraced the freedom of not needing him at all. The Manfreds hadn't made the tiniest dent in how she felt about herself.

Now for Kendall. This one might not be as easy, but she looked forward to it just the same.

When she approached her car, she found it blocked by an unattended delivery truck. A lone man leaned against another blocked car.

Steph called out to him. "Excuse me? Do you happen to know where the driver of this truck is?"

The man shook his head. "Sorry. If I did, I'd wring his neck."

A quick search around the area didn't turn up the driver. Steph glanced at her watch. She didn't know if Kendall was working tonight or not, but it was Friday evening. If he was at the Fox and Hounds, he would soon be busy with the early dinner crowd. She didn't have a minute to spare if she wanted to talk with him today.

And she did.

She walked the first few steps, but something spurred her into running. Her heart was light. She was light.

After one block of running, the shoes had to go. She barely slowed down, pulling them off and nearly tripping over herself. She knew she must look a little crazy, especially when she laughed at her own antics, but she loved the rush toward the inn.

She had rid herself of the conflict with Rick. She had established healthy boundaries with her parents. She would start fresh with her tutoring business next week, with more terrific kids like Chip and Hannah. She loved her awesome new friends—Liz, Christie, and Milly. Now all she needed to do was to clear up the situation with Kendall, and her life would be the perfect blend of God's loving acceptance of her and her trusting acceptance of His will, whatever it turned out to be.

When she reached the front of the Fox and Hounds, she stopped just short of slamming directly into Kendall. He had stepped out of the restaurant's front door and turned in her direction. He broke into a grin and opened his arms to stop her. The two of them gasped together and broke into surprised laughter.

Steph considered the contrast between this and the tense atmosphere of their last parting, when she realized he and Amy were together. She suddenly teared up.

Kendall said, "I was just coming to find you! You're not answering your phone. What are you doing here?"

She tried to tilt her head so her tears would fall back into their ducts, but that didn't work. She swiftly wiped at her cheeks as she spoke. "You were coming to find me? Where were you going to look?"

But he didn't answer. He did what he had in the past, gently cupping her chin and wiping her tears away. He spoke softly. "Hey. Hey, what's the matter? You okay?"

She wasn't about to let inhibition set in. Not this time.

"I just really like you, Kendall. I do."

And doggone if she didn't tear up again. This was not the plan. She had to persevere with what she planned to say.

"I mean, I don't care if you're engaged again and if I never see you, even as friends. I only want things to be all right between us."

Kendall looked about to speak.

She took another breath and held up her hand to stop him. "I just met with Rick. My ex? You saw him the other night?"

Kendall nodded and let her continue.

"I told him to forget about my taking him back, and it was partly because of what Chip said to me today."

Kendall frowned but smiled at the same time. "Go Chip."

"No, really. I realized I just wanted to feel accepted. It clouded my judgment. And it kept me from listening to God's guidance."

"Uh-huh. I get that. I *do* that."

"Yeah, but *His* acceptance, you know? God's? I stopped paying attention to it. So I looked for it elsewhere. And I was almost lured by Rick's saying I was good enough. But he wasn't right for me."

Kendall shook his head but said nothing.

She continued. "He's really not a very nice person. And then there's you."

"Me?"

"I think you're a good guy, Kendall. And if you and Amy are back together, that's fine. I'm not looking for anything from you. I just hope we can be comfortable around each other."

He hadn't stopped holding her face. In fact, he reached up with his free hand and cupped the other side. "Steph, are you at all interested in our being more than just comfortable around each other?"

His thumb brushed a lingering tear away.

"But, what about Amy? I heard her say things that made it sound—"

"Like she wanted to get back together with me?"

"Mm-hmm."

He barely shook his head. "Not an option. I told her that as soon as she hinted at it."

"But I . . ." She lowered her eyes as if she had done something wrong. "I saw you with her at the Asian restaurant last week."

He gave her a crooked smile. "I love that you seem to be everywhere at once. You're like a superhero."

They both laughed. She suddenly wanted to kiss him.

But she didn't.

He said, "No, I was there with Amy and her cousin. Maybe Jessica was in the bathroom when you saw us? Amy was already over the whole idea of our getting back together by then."

"She wasn't upset?"

"She couldn't have cared less. I told you Amy thought I wasn't impulsive enough. The converse of that was true too. I always thought she was too impulsive. It took no effort on my part to change her mind. She decided I wasn't for her within five minutes of talking with me."

"But I heard her mother say Amy came home—"

"Only for a visit, superhero."

"But she called you sweetie that night at the restaurant."

He shrugged. "She calls everyone sweetie. Even her dog. And that is *not* a sweet dog."

The twinkle in his eyes drew her in. She spoke,

an amazed whisper, "I can't believe she was turned off to you within five minutes."

He straightened in mock indignation. "Who said she was turned off to me?"

"But you said—"

"I said she changed her mind. Easily, yes." He grinned. "But that was because I told her about you."

The pounding in her heart became embarrassingly loud. At least it seemed that way.

"About me?"

"I told her I'd met a girl I felt I'd known forever, even though I never knew what to expect from you. I told her I hoped she'd find someone as well suited to her as you are to me."

"Oh my goodness, Kendall." She drew a relieved breath in and let it go. "That's so great."

He chuckled.

"Because I was honestly okay with your choosing to get back together with Amy. And I meant it when I said I liked you. I like you so much. And I wanted to be friends with you, regardless of how you felt or didn't feel about me." She gulped. "But mercy, am I ever attracted to you."

He threw back his head and laughed. A couple of passersby turned their heads in his direction.

Steph felt as if she were in the middle of her own personal romantic movie.

Kendall finally removed his hands from her face, but only so he could wrap his arms around her and lift her up. With one arm he pulled her close, and with the other he gently drew her head toward his.

And right there on the corner, in front of God and all of Middleburg, he gave Steph a kiss that was gentle, passionate, and absolutely perfect.

FORTY-TWO

I can't get used to the idea that I won't be coming back after today, Milly." Steph peered into the oven and watched the sugar on the scones broil to a golden sheen.

Milly handed her a couple of pot holders. "I certainly hope you'll be back, dear. You're not leaving town are you?"

"No! Although I do plan to visit Maryland soon and try to make amends with my friends back there. I owe them all apologies." She pulled the scones from underneath the broiler. "I did it! Not a burnt top in the bunch!"

"Didn't I say you were a natural?" Milly sighed. "It's not going to be the same without you here."

"Right. No slipping and sliding on the kitchen floor. No exploding strawberries. No melodramatic scenes with my parents in the dining area."

"I've enjoyed every minute of it." Milly smiled. "Well, maybe not the slipping and sliding."

The bell up front rang. Milly left the kitchen briefly and returned with Liz and Christie in tow. "Some visitors for you, Steph." Steph looked up from her work and arched an eyebrow at them.

"We don't want any trouble from you two," she said.

Christie put her hand on her hip. "Milly, did this one tell you how brazenly she threw herself at Mr. Cutie Pants yesterday?"

"That's right," Liz said. "She was a space cadet— even worse than me—by the time she got home. We were worried she wouldn't find her way to work this morning."

"We thought we'd better check before minding our own business." Christie crossed her arms and faced Steph.

Steph pointed a spatula at her. "I like the last part of that idea." She winked at Milly. "Anyway, I've already fallen all over myself telling Milly about what happened with Kendall. She was duly pleased, as she is the brilliant woman who introduced us in the first place."

Christie and Liz faced Milly, who shrugged and raised her hands. "What can I say? I'm a regular matchmaker."

Liz sniffed. "It smells great in here."

"It sure does. Chocolate something." Christie eyed the scones Steph was transferring to cooling trays. "Milly, maybe you'd like us to have a little celebratory toast to your matchmaking talents. Or, should I say a celebratory scone?" She wiggled her eyebrows. "Hmm?"

Milly shook her head. "You're shameless, Christie." She took two of the chocolate-pecan scones from the tray and wrapped them in paper. "Now off with you both. Steph and I have work to do."

"Thanks, Milly." Christie took the pastries and gave Milly a quick peck on the cheek. "Thanks also for looking out for our girl Steph. Want to come with the three of us tonight? We're having a girls' night. Dinner and then a movie back at our place."

Milly turned to Steph. "I thought you said Kendall was coming by for you at five."

"He is, but we're just going for a drive before dinner. You know, to spend a little time together. Please join us girls, Milly! That would be great fun."

"I think I might just take you up on that," Milly said. "Dinner, at least. I'll skip the movie."

The younger women all beamed.

"Awesome!" Liz said. "We'll meet you both at the Fox and Hounds at six?"

Milly and Steph spent their last workday together amid the typically busy Saturday crowd. Just as the lunch numbers thinned, a slight, pretty strawberry blonde came into the shop, full of energy. Milly was in the kitchen, so the young woman walked up to Steph and put out her hand.

"You must be Steph. I'm Jane." Her British accent distracted Steph for a moment.

"Jane who works here?" Steph shook her hand. "Welcome home!"

"Thanks. I thought I'd just pop in on my way to Gran's. I'm helping her move this weekend, you know."

"Yes. Milly mentioned that. You saved my life, actually, allowing me to work a few extra days here."

"I think we both needed this arrangement, then." Jane's smile was genuine, and Steph could see why she and Milly would work well together.

"Milly's just in the kitchen if you want to—"

But the kitchen door swung open, and Milly broke into a wide smile at the sight of her returning employee. "My girl! You look lovely!"

They hugged, and Steph envisioned a similar experience for herself if she stayed away for a while before seeing Milly again.

As it turned out, she didn't have to go away and come back again for a similar experience. When the day's work was done, and Steph assumed she would simply say goodbye and leave, Milly sat her down at one of the tables.

"I have a little something for you."

Steph gasped. "Oh, Milly, no. I have nothing for you. I feel—"

"Don't you worry." Milly stepped toward the kitchen and spoke over her shoulder. "You're going to give me exactly what I want in a moment."

Steph wasn't sure what that meant, but before she could give the comment too much thought,

Milly walked back out carrying a teapot Steph had never noticed at the shop before. The fine bone china pot was lovely and feminine, with scalloped edges, detailed shaping on the handle, and delicate roses on either side.

"Every woman should have her own teapot." Milly set the pot on the table. "I thought of you when I saw these roses in full bloom. You've completely blossomed since you came here, Steph. It's been a privilege to watch."

Steph couldn't talk past the lump forming in her throat. She stood and wrapped her arms around Milly.

"There, see?" Milly spoke gently. "I told you you'd give me exactly what I wanted." She hugged her back before pulling away and looking her in the eye. "Remember now. Always a clean kettle. Always a clean pot. Cold water that tastes good. Filtered is best. Warm water in the pot while you wait for your kettle to boil."

Steph nodded, a few tears in her eyes. "I'll remember. I'll remember everything you taught me, Milly."

The door to the shop opened, and the most stunning man Steph had ever seen walked in.

"Ah, Kendall," Milly said. "Your timing couldn't have been better. I think this young lady is ready to go." She looked at Steph. "Let me just get the shipping box so you can take that teapot home."

"But you're meeting the girls and me for dinner, right?" Steph checked her watch. "In one hour?"

Steph and Kendall left the shop, hand in hand, and silently walked to his car. He had driven the 1961 Corvette his late father gave him. He carried the box from Milly and placed it gently on the car floor. When he turned and looked at her, she actually shivered at the openly passionate expression in his eyes. She loved that he was so frank, even while steadfastly being the perfect gentleman.

"That was sweet of Milly to give you that gift. Typically Milly."

Steph nodded. "I'm going to miss working with her." She opened her purse to retrieve a tissue, her eyes still moist. It wasn't until she closed her purse that she remembered something. She opened her purse again and rooted around. "Shoot."

"Shoot?" He opened her car door for her, but she didn't get in right away.

She gave him a shy smile. "I kept the note you wrote my first night here. I must have . . . oh yeah. I used it to give my number to those tutoring students yesterday. I was in a rush, so I didn't—"

"I wrote you a note?"

She laughed softly. "I'm being stupid. It wasn't an actual note you wrote to me. It was when you got a pad of paper and decided to solve all of my concerns my first night here."

He smiled. "Oh yeah. I remember that. You were so cute. All sleepy and smart mouthed."

"I wasn't sure whether to go back to Maryland or stay here. You wrote a one-word question, 'Stay?' And then you wrote 'Yes' and 'No' and marked a big X next to the 'Yes.' You acted as if it were that simple."

"No, I acted as if that's what *I* wanted you to do."

She sighed. "See? That's why I kept it. And now it's gone forever."

He gently took hold of her by the shoulders and let her rest against his car. "Now, there's where I can help you."

She could tell he was teasing her, and it made her smile. "You can?"

"Yep. Because I intend to remind you daily that this is exactly where you belong." He leaned in until his smile was an inch from hers.

"You do?"

He nodded, and seconds before he kissed her, he whispered, "Sometimes I'll even use words."

DISCUSSION QUESTIONS

1. Steph comes to the realization that she has allowed her desire for acceptance to cloud her judgment. What mistakes, or near mistakes, does she make as a result of that desire?

2. The desire for acceptance colors all of our lives: in matters of love, in how we relate to our peers, and in whether we live according to God's will. Under what circumstance would you say you have allowed your desire for acceptance to influence your decisions and behavior? Share a specific incident if you like.

3. Not all women would choose, as Steph does, to stay in Middleburg after her fiancé jilts her. Why do you think she chooses to do that? What would you have chosen to do, were you in her position? Why?

4. Kendall, Christie, Liz, and Steph all seem to consider a stamp of approval from Milly to be worthy of merit. Why do you think they all put such great store in Milly's ability to judge character in people?

5. Does anyone come to mind in your life whose judgment you especially value, as Steph and her friends do Milly's? Who and why?

6. Christie tends to be blunt and assertive with her opinions and advice. What did you think of her personality? How do you tend to interact with such people in your own life?

7. What was your impression of Steph's parents? How do you think they influenced Steph's life, in good ways and in bad?

8. Kendall's brother, Chip, suffers no lack of confidence, despite a physical challenge which might have held others back. Why do you think that is?

9. Do you know anyone who has overcome physical or cognitive challenges? How has that person's attitude affected you?

10. Although Steph isn't looking for a rebound relationship, she and Kendall certainly click quickly. Their relationship gels as a result of more than physical attraction. What draws her to Kendall, and him to her?

11. Have you ever experienced a quick "click" like that with a member of the opposite sex?

Was it romantic (immediately or otherwise), or was it strictly platonic?

12. How does Steph grow between the first time she stands on the steps in front of Rick's office and the last?

Milly's Individual Berry Shortcakes

Ingredients
  3 cups unbleached flour
  3½ tablespoons sugar
  1 teaspoon salt
  3 teaspoons baking powder
  10 tablespoons butter
  1 cup heavy cream (for dough)
  1½ pounds strawberries (or an equivalent of
    strawberries and other berries)
  Sugar to taste
  1 cup heavy cream, whipped (for topping)

Directions
  Preheat oven to 425 degrees.
  Butter muffin tins for 24 muffins.
  Sift the flour, sugar, salt, and baking powder into
large bowl.
  Using knives or a handheld pastry blender, cut
the butter into the dry ingredients, as you would
pie dough.
  Whip 1 cup heavy cream until soft peaks form.
Use a spatula or palette knife to stir cream into
flour mixture until you form dough.
  Knead just briefly—the less the dough is
handled, the better.

Divide the dough into the 24 muffin slots, pressing down just enough to slightly even the top.

Bake 20 to 25 minutes, until a toothpick comes out clean.

While they bake, mash half the strawberries with a potato/fruit masher. Fold remaining berries in and add sugar to sweeten.

Turn baked shortcakes out of tins. Serve two per person, with berry mixture between and on top of the cakes.

Serve with a bowl of whipped cream for topping.

Serves 12 (or 24, if serving only one shortcake per person).

Egg and Watercress Tea Sandwiches

Ingredients
5 hard-boiled eggs, shelled
5 tablespoons mayonnaise (Milly won't mind if you use mayo from a jar)
2 tablespoons Dijon mustard
Salt and pepper to taste
½ cup clean, chopped watercress
Softened butter (for bread)
10 slices thin white sandwich bread (Pepperidge Farm White Sandwich Bread works well for tea sandwiches)

Directions

Roughly chop the eggs in a medium-sized bowl. Stir in mayonnaise and mustard. Add salt and pepper to taste. Use a potato masher to smooth egg mixture. Add chopped watercress and gently stir in.

Lightly butter five slices of bread. Spread the egg mixture onto bread. Lightly butter the remaining five slices of bread and add to sandwiches (buttered side down, of course).

Gently (and I do mean gently—eggs are gushy) slice crusts from the sandwiches. Then slice each sandwich into fours. Can be sliced diagonally to make four little triangles or sliced straight to make three rectangular "fingers."

Makes 15-20 tea sandwiches.

Steph's Cream Cheese Cucumber Tea Sandwiches

Ingredients

1 medium-sized cucumber
8 ounces softened cream cheese
Salt and white pepper to taste
20 slices thin white sandwich bread (Pepperidge Farm White Sandwich Bread works well for tea sandwiches)

Directions

Peel the cucumber. Slice lengthwise. Remove seeds. Chop cucumber into very small chunks.

Combine chopped cucumber with softened cream cheese.

Add salt and white pepper to taste.

Spread mixture on 10 slices of bread and top with remaining slices.

Gently cut crusts away and slice each sandwich into three "fingers."

Makes 30 finger sandwiches.

Cucumber Tea Sandwiches for Sticklers

Ingredients

1 medium-sized cucumber
Butter
Salt and white pepper
20 slices thin white sandwich bread

Directions

Peel the cucumber. Slice very thinly. Lay out slices on a paper towel, lightly salt and pepper, and let sit for a minute or two to remove excess moisture.

Butter bread slices.

Lay cucumber slices atop 10 slices of bread and top with remaining bread slices.

Gently cut crusts away and slice each sandwich into three "fingers."
Makes 30 finger sandwiches.

Smokey Salmon Tea Sandwiches

Ingredients
¼ pound Nova smoked salmon
1⅓ cups heavy cream
½ teaspoon white pepper
¼ teaspoon nutmeg
2 ounces Nova smoked salmon (flaked)
12 slices thin sandwich bread

Directions
Chop (by hand or with food chopper) ¼ pound salmon until fine.

Put into a bowl, add ⅔ cup cream, and stir.

Further refine mixture by squeezing it through a ricer (easier) or by pressing it through a sieve with a spoon (messier). Even a garlic mincer works, if you can stand mincing so little at a time.

Blend in pepper and nutmeg, and store in refrigerator until needed.

Whip remaining ⅔ cup cream and then fold into the chilled salmon mixture. Mix well.

Spread the mixture on 6 slices of bread.

Distribute the 2 ounces flaked salmon over the 6 sandwich halves and top with other slices of bread.
Cut off crusts and slice each sandwich, butterfly-style.
Serve immediately.
Makes 24 tea sandwiches.

Milly's Chocolate-Pecan Scones

Ingredients
½ cup pecans
2 cups flour
¼ teaspoon baking soda
¼ cup sugar
¼ teaspoon salt
1¼ teaspoons baking powder
½ cup cold butter
⅓ cup chocolate chips
⅔ cup heavy cream
2 tablespoons maple syrup
1 egg, beaten and combined with 1 tablespoon milk
Confectioners' sugar

Directions
Preheat oven to 350 degrees. Toast pecans on baking sheet for 9 minutes. Cool and coarsely chop.

Increase heat to 400 degrees.

To prevent burning, stack two baking sheets atop one another and line the top baking sheet with parchment paper.

Stir together the flour, baking soda, sugar, salt, and baking powder.

Cut butter into pieces. Use a pastry blender to cut it into the flour mixture until it reaches a crumblike consistency.

Stir in pecans and chocolate chips.

In a separate cup, mix cream and maple syrup, then stir into flour mixture. Try not to overstir.

Lightly flour counter and transfer dough—it will still be crumbly.

Lightly knead dough to bring crumbs together, about fives times. The less you handle the dough, the lighter the scone.

Pat the dough into a 1½-inch high circle (about 7 inches wide).

Cut circle in half, and then cut each half into 4 wedges.

Brush egg/milk mixture over scone tops.

Bake 20 minutes. Inserted toothpick should come out clean.

Remove baking sheet and turn broiler to high.

Liberally sift confectioners' sugar on scone tops.

Place scones under broiler and move sheet around to allow sugar to uniformly turn golden brown. Don't leave the oven at this time—scones will burn quickly!

Cool on wire rack, at least enough so chocolate won't burn your mouth. (I speak from experience.) *Makes 8 scones.*

ABOUT THE AUTHOR

Trish Perry is the author of numerous novels, including *The Guy I'm Not Dating*, *Beach Dreams*, and *Sunset Beach*. She is also an award-winning writer and former editor of *Ink and the Spirit*, a quarterly newsletter of the Capital Christian Writers organization in the Washington DC area. In addition to writing novels, Trish has published numerous short stories, essays, devotionals, and poetry in Christian and general market media, and she is a member of the American Christian Fiction Writers group.

Center Point Publishing
600 Brooks Road ● PO Box 1
Thorndike ME 04986-0001 USA

(207) 568-3717

US & Canada:
1 800 929-9108
www.centerpointlargeprint.com